I0585894

THE TRUE HISTORY
OF JUDE

STUART CAMPBELL

This is a work of fiction. Names, characters, businesses, places, events, locales, and incidents are either the products of the author's imagination or used in a fictitious manner. Any resemblance to actual persons, living or dead, or actual events is purely coincidental.

Stuart Campbell

First paperback edition, 2022 v2(i)

Published by Stuart Campbell
Copyright © 2022 by Stuart Campbell

All rights reserved. This book or any portion thereof
may not be reproduced or used in any manner
whatsoever without the express written permission of
the publisher except for the use of brief quotations in a
book review.

www.stuartcampbellauthor.com

ISBN: 978-0-6457198-3-3

Public domain material:

Quotes from *Jude the Obscure* are from the Project Gutenberg edition at https://www.gutenberg.org/files/153/153-h/153-h.htm

Quotes from *Onward Christian Soldiers* are from Public Domain Hymns at https://pdhymns.com/SheetMusic/B_Normal/I-Q_Normal/O_Normal/Onward%20Christian%20Soldiers_3vs_N.pdf

Quotes from *Scouting for Boys* are from http://thedump.scoutscan.com/yarns00-28.pdf

The New Testament extract is from the King James Version.

Cover illustration: Image used under license from Shutterstock.com

The author acknowledges the traditional custodians of the land where this book was written and of the Australian locations mentioned in the book.

TABLE OF CONTENTS

PROLOGUE

By the age of seventy, Professor Susan Bridehead had learned that writing the introduction to a book was best left till last. *The History of the Principality of Australia: The First Century* was no exception.

The portrait of Princess Maureen, a standard fitout item in offices at the Oxford campus of The University of Sydney, dominated the room. The exiled monarch of Australia stared at Susan with amused condescension.

A pang of arthritis in her hip made Susan shift in her office chair. The low English summer sun blazed outside the window. It was too early to hobble across the campus to her apartment. Perhaps she should use the hours before sunset to make some last amendments to the introduction.

No, dammit! If they didn't like it, they would send it back, just as they sent back chapter after chapter until they achieved 'optimum alignment between the historical record and Her Royal Highness's knowledge of events'. Susan could have declined the commission, let someone else take on the job of chief hagiographer. But no, when the exiled monarch of Australia said 'jump', you played kangaroo.

She hit SEND.

Stuart Campbell

The History of the Principality of Australia:

The First Century

Introduction

New Year's Eve. Billions of viewers around the world watch the Sydney Harbour fireworks. The Lord Mayor hosts the traditional VIP party on the Opera House waterfront. The cream of Sydney society toss back champagne and canapés behind the new two-metre sea wall built to hold back the tidal surges that cut the Opera House off from the mainland the previous year. Two million tourists and locals cram the public areas of the foreshore.

At ten minutes to midnight, Police Airwing pilot Kirsty Makarios swings her helicopter south from Manly Beach past the great cliffs that guard the outer harbour. In minutes, she is heading west at low altitude and can see the white shell of the Opera House. "Best seats in the house," her co-pilot Jimmy Q says. Kirsty's husband and parents are down there somewhere.

Fifty kilometres out to sea, the continental shelf slumbers, its subterranean cliffs washed for millennia by the tepid currents of the South Pacific Ocean.

The reverberation of a distant earthquake nudges the shelf, but the immense mass of compacted sediment sleeps on. The earthquake nudges again, harder this time. In answer, an ancient fissure opens three kilometres in from the cliff face, slowly at first, and then more rapidly. A network of cracks races across the shelf, separating a piece six kilometres long. It breaks into sky-scraper sized chunks that slide onto the seabed. Three cubic kilometres of sea water are displaced from the ocean floor. There is only one place it can go.

At midnight the skies over Sydney explode in reds and greens. As every year, the Harbour Bridge turns into a waterfall of flame. Two million voices cry out in joy.

The leading edge of the tsunami is halfway to Sydney in two and a half minutes. The wave rises and slows as the water becomes shallower. In another five minutes it is within ten kilometres of land.

Kirsty Makarios is slammed sideways in her seat. Jimmy Q fights the controls as a wall of air shoves the helicopter forward. They wrangle back control and watch as the Harbour Bridge buckles. A diabolical carpet unrolls, snuffing out the lights of the city and the suburbs until all is roaring blackness.

***

In Canberra, Prime Minister Barbara Macfarlane drank her tenth espresso since midnight. For this veteran warrior of Australia's corporate, legal and political battlefields, this was a crisis like none other. She ordered the Cabinet room cleared except for Foreign Minister Dave Davey and her defence chief, General Angie Smith. Dave Davey hit a button to activate a secure military conference network. The six most powerful figures in the world came on line: The US, Russian and Chinese presidents, and the chairmen of multinational corporate giants SLUZHBA, CareMundo and Sino-French. They greeted each other curtly.

"Gentlemen. This catastrophe meets the threshold to trigger the execution of the Grand Bargain. Please indicate your agreement or otherwise."

The three Australians waited a full minute while the scenes of disaster in the dawn light played on the monitor. The camera operator in the helicopter switched from right to left, catching a glimpse of the pilot with a blonde ponytail protruding from her helmet. She was gulping back tears.

The ragged breathing of the six leaders could be clearly heard over the conference call network. One of the remote group muttered, "God save us". There was a stifled sob.

"Ladies and gentlemen. Execute or otherwise. Please."

A heavy Slavic voice intoned: "Execute." The other five voices echoed the Russian President. At exactly 5.45 am, the Prime Minister of Australia said, "Carried unanimously. This is the beginning of a new world order".

Prime Minister Macfarlane had been preparing for this day all her life. Nicknamed 'Bubbles' for her deceptively innocent blonde curls, she could crutch sheep and shoot wild pigs on the family farm by the time she was twelve. She represented Australia in fencing before a stellar university education that took her from Melbourne to the Sorbonne and Harvard. In her corporate law career, Macfarlane formed lasting bonds with the giants of international commerce. She was drafted into SLUZHBA as Chairman at just thirty-five. She described her entry into politics five years later as 'my sacred duty to humanity'.

The day after the Flood of Sydney, the Australian Governor-General, under Section 57 of the Constitution, dissolved both Houses of Parliament. Using a broad interpretation of Section 21, he asked Barbara Macfarlane to form an Australian Government in Exile in England, issued an executive order to excise Australia's territory from itself, and signed a one-thousand-year uranium mining lease with the SLUZHBA corporation.

The Grand Bargain was closed. Patria Nullius— 'nobody's homeland'—became the world's sole legal source of uranium and the dedicated location for the safe disposal of depleted nuclear fuel for the next millennium.

In the Paris headquarters of the International Bureau of Weights and Measures (acquired the previous year by a consortium of SLUZHBA, CareMundo and Sino-French), a technician activated a set of instructions to reset Coordinated Universal Time.

Thus began Year Zero Zero Zero One of the New World Order and the foundation of the Principality of Australia.

PART FIRST - AT ORANGE

SUSAN TO ALEX, JUNE 0099

Dear Alex,
This letter will come as a surprise. How long has it been? Too long to think about. I do hope you are well. Life proceeds here in the Kingdom of England and Wales. I use the word 'proceeds' for want of a better one. One is immersed in social order, material sufficiency, and total apathy: Life doesn't flourish or roar or stumble or jump up and down. It just proceeds.

The second surprise, I'm sure, is that this is probably the first letter you've ever received written on a typewriter. I found the beautiful machine - a Remington portable - wrapped in a blanket in a nook behind my apartment building. People leave things there that don't have a PIP, so you never know what you might come across. My device is a veritable antique. It takes me ages to write just a sentence, and my fingers quickly get sore. The keys are so noisy that I have to type while sitting on the lavatory with towels stuffed under the door. You will know that writing offline is illegal under the Sedition Act here in the Kingdom, and probably a hanging offence when an antique typewriter is involved! But I do so admire the way Mr Remington's delicate steel keys skip up to peck the paper and then jump back into their nest. My treasure has an ink ribbon which had dried up, but I experimented with a mixture of cooking oil and hair dye to get it working. I could opt to write by hand, of course, but there's a gratifying sense of absurdity in courting death with a typewriter.

I hope this gets to you safely after the hours I spend getting sore fingertips where the nail is pushed back from the quick. Whoever would have thought that we in England would need to have letters smuggled in and out of the country? My delivery boy says they've got it down to four days to North America, with 0.15 percent chance of loss or interception.

But that's enough waffle about typewriters and delivery boys. Let me get very serious: I should report that a couple of years ago, I was commissioned by Princess Maureen to write The History of the Principality of Australia: The First Century. I was reluctant to accept the job, but as a K.E.W. citizen rather than an Australian, it was that or demotion to university cleaner (second class), and I was damned if I was going to clean the stains off the Rector's private facilities until I shuffle off to wherever Fate locates dead professors. They quietly eliminated retirement here when FreePay was brought in a few years ago, the aim being that the populace be 'appropriately employed' and 'proportionately remunerated' until death.

So the question is, what do I do after the book is published? Years more of pretending to teach students who are pretending to learn? Another tome lionising some Prince or General? And then another?

Well, I have plans, not very clear ones, but plans anyway. First of all, I want to write some real history - in fact a new book, but not for money or to keep my university job. Call it my private project, except that I could spend the rest of my life in jail for writing it. Second - and here I'll come right out with it - I'm afraid for my sanity. You see, the book I want to write is to do with my own history, and there are things in my past that are nudging into the light - dark things that aren't what you'd expect of an esteemed and upright seventy-year old lady professor. If I don't let these ghouls out into sunlight, they will - well, I don't know what will happen. The third thing is that I'm going to leave the Kingdom of England and Wales one way or another. Yes, you read that correctly.

By the way, if it's not Alex reading this but some SLUZHBA functionary whose execrable job it is to intercept letters, I'm actually past caring. But I do hope you end up in the special flaming hell reserved for people like you.

So, Alex, here's my request. I want to send you my new book in instalments so you can keep it safe until I get out. Dare I ask you to tell me what you think of it? It's very personal, but I will be blushing a continent away as you read it.

Once I'm free of the Kingdom, I'll decide what to do with my new work. Show it to a psychiatrist? Get it published in North America courtesy of the First Amendment? Let's wait and see.

For old times' sake, will you help me? There's not a soul in England I trust.

I'll be watching out for your reply each day. You know the delivery details. Please don't disappoint me.

Best, Sue

SUSAN TO ALEX, JUNE 0099

Dear Alex,

Your letter arrived very early this morning heralded by a small pebble on my window; that's the signal that the boy is waiting behind my building with mail. I almost tore the envelope open as I walked back to the entrance in sight of a camera, but had the presence of mind to poke it into my sleeve. Thanks so much for agreeing to help. It's a vast weight off my shoulders to know that I'm not alone. I'm indebted forever.

So, 'what's this new book all about?' you are no doubt wondering. Well, in those two years in Chicago you often asked me why I never told you about my early life. All I ever said was that I had some connection with Australia. In fact, it was more than just a connection. I was born in Patria Nullius in 0030 and I spent my early adult years in a tropical hill town called Kuranda in the north-east. I was married twice, the first time to an old man, and the second time to a boy called Jude, a wild, lost soul who was born in an isolated community called Orange, a long way to the south. Jude and I escaped from Patria Nullius in 0052 and came to England. This is what the book's about - his life in Patria Nullius. Or perhaps my life in Patria Nullius as seen through his life, I'm not completely sure at this point.

You're probably reaching for a strong drink as you read this. You'll know that it's illegal here in England and Wales to refer to Patria Nullius outside of official bulletins (although I have a Royal Dispensation for the <u>History</u>), so I'm committing a crime as I type.

But back to the book. It begins in Orange in Eastern Australia about fifty years ago. Let's say 0050. The narrator is Jude, not me, but I come into it later. You'll need to get used to the way I've created Jude's speech style. I've peppered it with phrases from a copy of Thomas Hardy's <u>Jude the Obscure</u> that he owned, as well as words from the Creole language they spoke in those parts. The quotes and Creole words are underlined, and I've added some endnotes for the sake of clarity - it was too hard to write footnotes on the typewriter.

Best, Sue

JUDE THE STORYTELLER

It was mid-afternoon on the day when I finally knew those days must end.

There was red dust in the air and a dry heat, but I could feel the tingle of a coming storm in my nostrils. The highway stretched away to nothingness. The food truck had been and gone for the day. It would whoosh in from the north at first light and be gone again within an hour. The garbage truck would come in the evening and also be gone within an hour. Actually, there were no working clocks in the town but I knew what an hour was because I read in my book that there used to be twenty-four of them in a day.

Once I asked the man who rode in the food truck where he was from. But the uniforms never replied - just stared from behind the blue masks that covered their mouths and noses.

Nobody stopped us from leaving. But how would we know where to go? There was a road in and a road out. When I was a boy, a gang of us walked a day and a night across the hills, but all we found was more hills.

And if you had kept walking, where would you get food? Where could you find <u>three buns on a plate of the willow pattern</u> or <u>apples and jam</u> like the ones in the book? Or the loaves and fishes my mother told me about, that Jesus fed the five thousand with. Not in those hills with their snakes and wild pigs.

I'd never eaten buns or apples or jam, and I couldn't make the taste of them in my mouth.

We ate meat pies and tinned pineapple mostly, cheese from tins if there was any, and always beer to wash it down. Loaves - yes, we got that in slices, but not fishes, apart from the golden ones in the creek, but they were all bones.

Aboriginal traders came through the town every few weeks when there weren't any uniforms around, sometimes riding horses and sometimes motorbikes. They didn't talk our language, these traders, just English, which we used to call oldtalk. They had a few things to sell for those of us who had some bucks - jerky, tobacco, perfume, underpants. I asked one of them if he had any black-pot and sausage, but he said in oldtalk "fuck off", which meant buggeroff in our lingo of course. Nobody knew where they lived, these Aboriginals. When I asked one of them, he said, "Nunya bisnis", which I thought must be a town beyond the hills.

On the day when I knew those days must end, I was grabbing a snooze with my mates on the bench, enjoying the shade of the huge tree that grew in the middle of the main street opposite Post Office Lane. I knew what a Post Office was: It was the place where Jude - the Jude in the book, not me - went to collect the books sent from Christminster.

I got off the bench and stepped past the broken concrete around the tree roots and into the sunlight, looking up, squinting. The sky was a hard, hot blue. It would stay that way until black clouds swept in before a rainstorm, whenever that might be. And then

the hard blue would return to fill our days
with a dry, scouring heat that left us slumped
in shady corners. I often thought of Jude in
Wessex, and how the winter sleets and snows
fall and lie. I thought those sleets and snows
must be very cold, perhaps like when a big
rain cooled us down. But it must have been
colder than that because some people in Wessex
had a swallow-tailed coat, and all I had was
two pairs of shorts and two T-shirts that I
got when the food truck brought in a bale of
clothes.

One of the mates asked where I was going. I
told him to go back to sleep, and I'd be back
in nowrotu.

I don't know when the feeling came over me
that those days were to end. Perhaps I'd had
it for years. But that day it was like an itch
I couldn't ignore.

It was time for me to visit Auntie Vicky.
Her house was just a short walk from the Post
Office tree. She was lying on a lounger on the
shady side of the house, flapping her dress to
make a breeze around her thighs. The flesh
above the hem of her dress was white and
tender. Her lower legs and shoulders were dark
as nut-brown soil. She stuck a fat joint in
her mouth and sucked hard, holding the smoke
inside her. The seeds and stems crackled and
spat, and the cigarette paper flamed and
glowed reddy-black. There were little charred
spots on the front of her dress. When she
spoke, her voice was raw and dry.

"Will you tell us a story tonight, Jude?" She stretched and yawned, scratching her scalp.

"Sure," I said. I told them a story most nights. I was Jude the storyteller. It was my nobby.

"Good boy."

There was something very important I wanted to ask her, but this wasn't the time because she'd rested the smouldering joint on an aluminium pie dish and gone to sleep. Her lips fluttered loosely with a rippling farty sound when she breathed out. A sliver of burning sunlight was creeping around the corner. I laid a rag over her shoulder to stop her burning.

The smell of weed floated along the street on warm drafts. There were the sounds of children's voices in the hot gardens and under shady trees. The voices got me thinking; the children were getting bigger, and you didn't see babies anymore.

Auntie Vicky wasn't my real Auntie, but she gave me away when I got married. An old hubby called Tent made me and Arabella hold hands and repeat some English words that I now know were nonsense. Auntie Vicky said some more English words, and Tent said Arabella could kiss me. My new wife grabbed me and slobbered her lips on my face and told me not to try anything with other women.

I suppose Auntie Vicky owned me, otherwise how could she give me away? I didn't really know who she was, except that I grew up in her house. At least, I grew up there most of the

time. I always remember her smoking <u>yarndi</u> -
well that's what some people called it, but
others called it <u>ganja</u>. She had a corner of
her house where she made cigarette paper from
a mush of leaves and bark, soaking it, rolling
it flat, and then slowly drying it. It was her
<u>nobby</u>. A few people around there had a <u>nobby</u>.
But most did nothing because they thought
having a <u>nobby</u> was a <u>bigfuckup</u>.

I knew I had a mother once. She taught me
to read English. I can't remember her face
very well but I have the clearest memory of
sitting close to her while her finger traced
the <u>oldtalk</u> sentences and I said the words
aloud. "A secret," she told me. "Don't tell
them you can read."

Auntie Vicky snored on. Her face was
wrinkly. I think she must have been forty
something. Me, I was a <u>young squire</u>, about
nineteen years old, like the Jude in the book
who was <u>a stone-mason's apprentice</u>.

I looked around to see if anyone was moving
in the afternoon heat: Nobody. Even the
children had dozed off in untidy heaps of arms
and legs. I silently eased myself off the
concrete veranda and sneaked around the back
of the house. Down the side lane to the disused
shed. A look back to check no-one had followed
me. The low door to the underfloor area was
undisturbed, propped at an angle as if nobody
had opened it for years. I eased it back,
checking again that I wasn't being spied on.
Once I'd crawled inside the cobwebby basement,
I pulled the door back and fixed it in the
frame so that it was properly closed. It was

cool in there, smelling of earth and roots. The plastic box containing my book was behind a brick pillar. I took the book out and laid it carefully on a piece of old cement sheet. There was a loose brick in the wall. When I jiggled it out, a square of light shone on my treasure. I turned it over to check for wear. It had soft front cover that was coming loose. On the front was a picture of a young man who looked a bit like me. His eyes were sad and half-closed, and his hair was long. The words at the bottom of the cover said Jude the Obscure, and above that was the name of the prophet Thomas Hardy. My mother told me about the prophets, about how they told what would happen in the future days. Across the middle of the book was written Penguin Classics, with a tiny picture of a fat man in a white shirt. I never understood Classics, but I thought the fat man must be a penguin.

Inside the front cover there was handwriting: Tracy Dunmore, Class 9, 6 April 2015. I slowly turned the pages, seeing things like 'learn this speech' and 'for test after Easter' and 'revise with Milena at sleepover'.

I thought a lot about Tracy Dunmore. Sometimes I would put Tracy Dunmore into a story so that I could know about her life. My mother had told me about the three shepherds, and I made a story where Tracy Dunmore was the angel who told them a Saviour had been born. I always told this part in a crying voice, in English so the audience couldn't understand it properly and really wanted to know the meaning. Then I said it in our lingo. They all cried, but not Arabella, who knew my tricks.

The last part of the book had been ripped out, and the back cover was missing. It happened when I was about ten. A gang of boys caught me reading in a gully. They snatched the book and surrounded me, tossing it back and forth above my head. When I started to bawl, one boy caught it and tried to give it back to me, but another grabbed it, tore off the back cover and some pages, and pretended to wipe his guda with them. I ran home with the ripped book up my T-shirt. I never knew what happened to Part Sixth and the back cover.

The book was my mother's. I used to see her reading it, and I found it in her mattress the day she went out and didn't come home. When I asked Auntie Vicky where she'd gone, she just looked at me. Sometimes I wonder if my mother is just something in a story, but when I touch the book I know she was real.

After the boy damaged the book, I decided to make a copy of what was left of it. It took me two years because I was always looking for paper. Hardly anyone used it in the town, but you could find it if you looked hard enough. There were lots of empty houses and buildings on the outskirts, where you might find some brown paper bags in an old cupboard or a child's schoolbook with some blank pages. Once I found a book belonging to Alice West of Year 6 in Orange Public School in 2009. I spent hours reading stories she had written about her pony, trying to picture Alice in the classroom. She had stuck into the book a picture of an animal that was the same as a horse, so I knew that pony and horse were the same. The school was still there in Kite Street. It had arches and windows just like a church in Christminster. But by then it was just a house with different people living in the rooms.

I didn't understand a lot of the words in my book, but I had my favourite stories, and if something didn't make sense I just made up that part of the story in my mind. Sometimes I made up new stories by adding things I'd heard about Jesus.

I didn't feel like reading that day under the house. I just wanted to remember about the happy parts of the book and not think about the terrible thing that happened: Actually, I couldn't remember exactly what it was because it was in Part Sixth, but I knew it was horrible.

That day when I knew those days were over, I wanted to be in those other lives, not in my life. I wanted to be eating luncheon at a big table with Sue Bridehead and Mrs Edlin and Mr Phillotson.

When I'd woken up that morning, a fantastic idea popped into my head: I could go out of Orange and find Sue Bridehead, wherever she was. I straightaway prayed about this to Jesus. Poor ignorant Jude.

There was a noise. Somebody or something was rustling in the pile of rubbish outside the door. A crack of light. This had never happened before. I felt sick in my zazzy. I clutched the book to my chest and crept behind a brick pillar. Someone shifted the door sideways. Two crawling shapes filled the square of bright afternoon light. They merged into one and then collapsed onto the earth giggling. I recognised the voices of my cousin Mimi - well, Auntie Vicky's grown-up daughter - and her boyfriend Vijay. It was dark but I could make out Mimi astride Vijay. She was making rough grunts and telling him to grab her backside hard. Her white rump was pounding up and down, while Vijay's brown body squirmed below.

A fleck of dust tickled my throat and I coughed. Vijay saw me and pushed Mimi off. He grabbed my neck with his sticky fingers, but I shoved him away. I was shorter than him, but he was trying to protect his flopping choni. Mimi's huhus were bouncing up and down in time to her hoots of laughter. Vijay saw my book and frowned.

Mimi covered herself. She suddenly had a suspicious expression.

"What's this then, Jude?"

"Nothing," I said.

"It's a book," she said.

"It's just some rubbish," I said.

"It's a book," Vijay said. "Show me." He put out his hand, but I didn't give him the book. He snatched it, looked at it upside-down, handed it back. His fingers had left a sticky smear on the cover. I wiped it off on my shorts.

"Can you read?" Vijay asked.

"Nah, course not. How would I learn to read?"

"Well, that's alright then," Mimi said. "Reading's <u>bigfuckup</u>." She didn't look as if she completely believed me.

"Let's get out of here," Vijay said. His <u>choni</u> had shrivelled and he was pulling his shorts on. They crawled out of the underfloor.

I had to find another hiding place.

* * *

There was a full moon the night I knew those days must end. Nearly everyone was out in the street in deck chairs watching the big screen. Most were drinking beer or smoking yarndi, chuckling at the cartoons or chatting in low voices.

The garbage truck was emptying the skip. A uniform wearing a blue face mask and plastic gloves watched the clattering river of cans and pie dishes. The truck had words printed on the side in <u>oldtalk</u>. I could read AUSTRALIAN BORDER SECURITY INC, but I couldn't form a clear idea of what it all meant when you put it together. In the book, Wessex had a border. And Jude's wife Arabella - the Jude in the book, not me - went to Australia. I didn't properly understand SECURITY or INC.

The cartoon movie ended, and heads started to turn, looking for me.

"Jude, time for a story!" Storytelling was my <u>nobby</u>.

My wife Arabella called to me from the crowd. She was older than me - I think she must have been thirty-five at that time.

Arabella was strong, and smart in the way of a rat. And she was beautiful in a dangerous and frightening way: Fierce blue eyes in a freckled face, thick hair that wasn't black and not red, strong arms, swelling huhus that were glorious to fondle, if she gave you the chance. The expressions swept across her face as fast as the sun following a storm, and you never knew what would come next. The men used to ask me what she was like naked, what she did with me on her bed, what her choot was like. I made a stone face and said nothing. People talked, and all the talk went back to Arabella.

My wife stepped up onto a box and introduced me, mentioning at least ten times that I was her hubby. The younger women in the crowd shrivelled when she pinned them with her ratty glare of triumph.

Arabella stepped down and I stepped up. The tips of joints glowed in the dark. Pop and crackle. The audience took a minute to make a chorus of coughing and then freshen their throats with beer. They were ready to listen. I began the story of how Jesus and Mrs Edlin and Mr Phillotson followed the star to find baby Sue Bridehead at Christminster.

The people sat listening to my words, mouths open. They made little grins or frowns when I got to exciting parts of the story, which they knew by heart. As I went along, I repeated short bits, just changing one word at a time, and I waved my finger from left to right so they swayed with the rhythm of my words. My favourite part was when I told how Thomas

Hardy appeared with an angel, but I said it in our Orange lingo as best I could, and then I chanted in oldtalk,

Glory to Thomas Hardy in the highest tree (I swayed left)
Glory to Thomas Hardy in the highest sky (I swayed right)
Glory to Thomas Hardy in the highest heaven (I swayed left)

When I said highest heaven, I used a very high, long voice, closed my eyes, and collapsed on the ground making babbling noises.

Everybody gasped. Arabella asked the crowd if anyone had a wish.

Hands went up. Her rat eye swept the crowd. She pointed to a weeping girl, who ran forward to crouch by me.

"What's your wish?" Arabella asked her.

"I want to marry Vin," she sobbed.

Arabella babbled in my ear. I babbled back.

"Jude says you will marry Min, not Vin," she said to the girl, whose jaw dropped in puzzlement. Arabella glared at her: "Min, not Vin - that's what Jude says."

The dim girl nodded and scampered off, sobbing even more. This was one of Arabella's old tricks, using me to get her way. Sometimes I had to look for a message in the sky, or Arabella would kill a turkey and make me look in its guts. But it was deadright that after one of my stories at night, the people were even more scared of her than they were in the morning.

When everyone had gone home, I lay on the ground and searched the sky for Thomas Hardy in the highest heaven, wondering if I would see him one day.

Notes

In the Orange creole some English words were sometimes adapted wholesale with the indefinite article. Nobby meant job. It came from 'an obby' (a hobby). Nowrotu came from 'an hour or two'.

The face is from a photograph by Julia Margaret Cameron, identified by some as the Italian model and actor Angelo Colarossi (1875-1949). There is a copy of the edition Jude owned in the Palace library.

One of my linguistics colleagues thinks zazzy was based on a Vietnamese word.

The population of Orange at the time was between one thousand and fifteen hundred.

deadright meant 'certain'.

SUSAN TO ALEX, JUNE 0099

Dear Alex,

Still typing. I've rather got to like it: The purposeful clack of the keys, the jolly rhythm of my flashing fingers. And there's something immensely satisfying about outwitting whoever owns The Universe right now - with an antique writing machine. Last time I checked, CareMundo ran The Universe, but I do lose track. The order is SLUZHBA, CareMundo, Sino-French. You don't really notice any difference when the management changes each year except that the language detector makes the odd slip, so it might try to talk to you in Chinese or Russian or Spanish at first, and then corrects itself. No point in complaining about The Universe, but I do admire your government's guts in rejecting your citizens being permanently plugged into state apparatus. Oh, that's right - you don't really have any state apparatus. American exceptionalism still going strong! A country with meat, oil wells, wealth, poverty, crime, printed newspapers! My chapters in The History on America's exit from the Grand Bargain were set aside for 'further review', code for 'you risk jail for referring to this topic'.

You ask whether there is a 'plan' to my book. Well, there is and there isn't. Perhaps it's more a methodology than a plan. I'm trying to burrow into Jude's spirit, and in that way I hope I'll burrow into my own dried-up spirit - if I can locate it, if I can find myself. Oh dear, that's a jumble of thoughts. Must do better.

And that's a peculiar phrase - find myself. It infers that I'm lost, which is not entirely untrue. I can find myself just by looking up from my desk: I'm in Office E115 at the Oxford Campus of the University of Sydney in the Kingdom of England and Wales. More accurately I'm the skinny pale woman in black with no friends, the one who doesn't fit in, the one the Rector avoids speaking to because he can't think of a comment that will penetrate my icy carapace. I'm the one who wrote a book on the history of knock-knock jokes but who appears utterly humourless. I'm the one they envy because I write popular history bookoids that people actually read. I win awards but I never turn up at ceremonies to receive them. I'm the only person in the university who smokes. (I'm also the only one who speaks Orange Creole, but I keep that to myself.)

I also find my esteemed and celebrated self hobbling to the staff apartment blocks with their shrouds of vertical vegetable gardens.

I dislike vegetables. Waking up to aubergines outside my bedroom window is not appealing. I was brought up on wallaby and wild pig. I still have dreams about pink, fatty, fibrous meat. After waking from such dreams, a faint meaty aura hovers about my face until it fades in the cool piped air.

But, sorry, I was finding myself, wasn't I? You see, I find myself in the Provost's office explaining why I fail students when they haven't submitted their assignments. Poor darlings, all dressed up as medieval lords and ladies (Hold that image - I'll explain in another letter). I'm not sure why they even have assignments. Or a university even, since the technical experts who run the kingdom learn their stuff from educhunks at the Poytechnicum.

I find myself gulping in fear in the university doctor's surgery when he explains that I need an 'investigation' to eliminate any 'nasty surprises' behind my recent headaches.

But I can't find the Sue who was me fifty years ago. I know she's there somewhere. I'm looking for her essence (yes, completely unscientific term). She's a stranger to me, but I want to know her. Sometimes I think I should mourn her, but you can't mourn someone you've forgotten.

I've puzzled over why I can't find her essence (that word again). I happened on the answer when I got chatting to a psychologist in the university doctor's waiting room. She was there for anxiety medication, which is rather ironic in her line of work. Anyway, in no time my new friend was telling me about how personality can completely change over a lifetime. There were some studies on it back in the early two thousands. Those were the days when you had to enrol experimental subjects and write ethics protocols. Now of course we just ask a research question and a Social Science Mass Data Analysis Provider spits out the answer after sucking the information out of The Universe. Whichever provider your job is randomly assigned to - SLUZHBA, CareMundo, or Sino-French - you get the same answer, which is not surprising since they all run off The Universe anyway. And of course you can only ask research questions that the SSMDAP has the capacity to answer.

But that's all beside the point. And just a diversion from the fact that I feel as if I'm fading here in beige, meatless England. I catch a glimpse in a glass door of a skinny and undistinguished woman, and it's as if my ghost walks with me.

But let's get back to one of your other questions: Yes, there was a matriarchal system in Orange, but it hadn't really bedded down in Jude's time. That's natural I suppose, when a society flips from patriarchy to woman-power in just a few generations. They used the word 'hubby' for 'husband' in that strange Creole they spoke, but there was no stable term for 'wife'. It was as if the real purpose of a wife - from the man's point of view - hadn't been settled. For a woman, the value in a hubby was that he had a nobby - something socially or economically useful that elevated her status or wealth. When Jude came up to Kuranda, he told me about some of the 'nobby-nobby' the men had. There were some who mended clothes, others who could sing, some who grew flowers, some who knew how to cremate bodies (an emerging caste of priests, I suspect). The men had to accept whatever marriage offers came their way, and provide whatever was required - the fruits of their nobby if they had one, and sex when it was wanted. Jude told me he sometimes used 'missis' when he referred to Arabella, and sometimes 'kalu'. I suspect that kalu comes from a Fijian word for God.

But they're all long dead now down there in Orange, poor souls. I'm the last link, the last primary source, even if I was just a child when I left Orange with my father and went north to Kuranda. It's funny how the language is still lodged in my head; sometimes I have dreams when I speak Orange Creole, or at least I think I've been speaking it when I wake up with some phrase circling in my waking mind. At any rate, I've included a chapter 'by' Jude.

That rotten headache is back. 'The Thing', I've taken to calling it.

Damn, I just remembered Sir Bruce Withers is to pay us a visit soon. He's the Keeper of the Monarch's Bookes, and my nemesis. I'll explain in due course.

Best, Sue

JUDE'S PROMISE TO ARABELLA

After I told them the story, I watched their
faces in the moonlight. They were sated,
happy, another identical day ticked off,
another day in an endless chain of such days.
A couple more smokes and beer before bed. Some
of the older people used to talk about 'eleven
o clock' and 'ten o clock' around bedtime,
just as the prophet Thomas Hardy did. But
there were no clocks there that worked. No
church clocks or alarm-clocks like the ones
that Jude saw, the Jude in the book.

The women were stirring in their chairs.
They were sharper-eyed, keener-witted, as if
they held special secrets. A few of them, like
Auntie Vicky, could speak in English, and some
could read and write it, but oldtalk was
something they preferred to keep quiet about.

The women left with the children, and I
heard the soft murmurs as hand-in-hand groups
walked through the hot streets. I loved this
time as a child, forming up with different
friends each night, sleeping at whichever
house the group happened to choose. We were
all cousins.

The moon had disappeared behind some clouds,
and you could only see the houses by the candle
lamps at the front doors. Clouds - there was
surely a storm coming. I sniffed the air. It
was crackly, different from earlier.

The men lolled in deck chairs sniggering and
winking while they waited for the late-night
movie, which would have plenty of huhu and
choot. There were only about ten of these huhu

and <u>choot</u> movies, so they'd seen them all hundreds of times. That didn't stop them from cheering every time a stiff <u>choni</u> appeared, and leaning forward in dazed silence when a man performed on top of the woman instead of underneath. When it was over, they'd sleep wherever they ended up, some of them in pairs, but that was a secret thing.

I felt Arabella's hot presence behind me in the street. She glowed, large and sensuous and frightening.

"I don't need you tonight, <u>larka</u>." I hated it when she called me that. I was a man, not a <u>larka</u>. It was different when she wanted my <u>choni</u>. Then it'd be <u>bigfella</u> or <u>jigijig</u> Jude. Why didn't she want me that night?

I hung around to see what mischief she was up to. She linked arms with two other women — weak suckers who craved her favour — and the three ambled towards her house. I ducked over a low garden fence, and followed the line of overgrown lantana, drowning in the sweet night stink of a flowering bush close by. Once I was in Arabella's garden I squatted, invisible between two messes of hedge laced with webs bearing swollen spiders.

She dismissed the hangers-on, who blubbered their goodnights and made clumsy curtsies. Her house was a <u>doublegranny</u>, made from the same grey cement sheets as the others, but with two bedrooms. It used to belong to an old woman and her daughter, but Arabella made them move to a smaller house. I never knew why they had to move, but Arabella was always involved with who lived where.

When she went inside, I slid silently to the front window, where the curtain didn't quite reach the bottom. She was in the front room, lighting one candle, then another and another until her plump shadow flitted around the walls in a lolloping dance. She peeled off her dress and folded it across the back of a chair. I could almost feel the heat from her flesh, which strained to escape from her underwear. My choni twitched but I force myself to think of the angels of the seven churches and the first among the angels, Sue Bridehead.

There was a cough in the dark of the garden. I swivelled my eyes and they set on a dark mound that became a man approaching the front door, where I picked out his blue face mask and black uniform in the light of a candle. He slipped inside and I watched him speak words with Arabella that I couldn't hear. His shirt had AUSTRALIAN BORDER SECURITY INC. written on the back. Arabella stood unflinching and fleshy. Her face was scornful. The uniform unbuttoned his sweat-drenched shirt and peeled it off. He took off his mask. His face was fat and dumb.

Arabella rattled around in the ice box on the floor and handed him a can of beer, which he rubbed over his shoulders and chest. She pointed to a chair and a little table. He sat. She brought the timbox. Her hand slipped between her legs and there was suddenly a key. She unlocked the timbox and gave him a package. He handed her a wad of paper money, swigged the beer in a single swallow, and began to put his shirt back on. He looked as if he was anxious to leave, but Arabella motioned for him to stay. She slowly counted the notes and put them in the <u>timbox</u>. I'd never seen so much <u>bucks</u>. People might have one or two notes to buy small things, but this much? What did Arabella want it for?

She took a pencil and a little book from the <u>timbox</u>. She wrote something in the book. She could write.

Arabella could write.

I gasped in shock and stepped back into a spider web. I clawed my face, cried, "<u>bigfuckup</u>". I swallowed back the yell, but too late. The uniform dashed out of the house and was running hard down the hot, dark street towards a truck emptying a bin.

Arabella stood over me, panting and rage-faced in the crack of light from under the blind. There was the flash of a lightning bolt, then another, and the sky was laced with silver arrows and streaks. Arabella pulled me to my feet and breathed searing words in my ear. I heard "secrets," and "never tell nobody," and "I'll gut you with a blunt knife," and then, hoarsely, "a night you won't forget". She groped between my legs and I couldn't resist the squirmy stiffening feeling. I was torn between disgust and desire. A single lightning strike turned her into a white demon against the black reeking lantana. The biggest clap of thunder in the Kingdom of Thomas Hardy rattled my teeth and my soul. She dragged me inside just as the night sky dumped slabs of water on the parched garden, and under the hammering roof Arabella pinned me down and used her scalding body to turn me inside out in exchange for my poor promise never to tell about the little book and the <u>timbox.</u>

Notes

doublegranny was probably derived from 'granny flat', a separate residence built in the gardens of houses in the late 1900's and early 2000's.

Paper money was known as 'bucks' in Orange, although the banknotes in circulation were roubles.

SUSAN TO ALEX, JULY 0099

Dear Alex,

Pretty raunchy scene with Arabella, you said in your reply. I must admit I blushed a little when I wrote it. And how did I make it up, you ask? Well, I lived with Jude as his wife for three years, and his history came out in bits and pieces over that time. More accurately, it was his capacity to <u>tell</u> his history that came out in bits and pieces. You see, Orange was a place where the past and the future were pretty fuzzy concepts for most people (you try smoking weed all day and you'll see what I mean). People in Orange didn't have histories; they lived in a present in which (I gather) each day was a replay of yesterday, and there was little point in reaching back further. There were events anchored in the past - a marriage, a death, sometimes a birth, although Jude told me these were rare and that the settlement's children were mostly approaching their teenage years. When I asked him what happened to people who died, he wasn't sure. "They were there one day, then they were gone, and people said they'd died," he replied. Rather than being part of conscious recall, these events formed a vague mental scaffold of the present.

Here's a funny habit of speech in their Creole that I think was related to their 'presentness': When they gave directions, they'd say "a tree goes past you", instead of "you go past a tree" as if a person in motion was at a fixed point, and the landscape did the moving.

Of course, there has been a gap of many decades between listening to his stories and remembering them now, so I can't vouch for the accuracy of what I've made him say.

The way I've been creating the text is to go into a meditative state where I try to be him, and then make him think of me. Somehow, this state of mind gets fed with concrete memories from another part of my mind - snatches of conversation, words, deep feelings attached to events - and old Mr Remington the jolly typewriter takes over almost automatically. I call it a 'state of grace' when it's happening. Anyway, enough metaphysics! There's another chapter of Jude's story (or memoir, or biography, or whatever) attached to this letter.

I promised to tell you about my students' costumes. Just to backtrack a bit, you need Australian virtual citizenship to enrol at the fair dinkum Oxford Campus of Sydney University. Fair dinkum, by the way, used to mean 'genuine' or 'honest' in Australia. I rather like it! Most of the students are hangers-on of the Macfarlane clan. At least half have titles with stipends attached - Duchesses, Barons, Countesses, and of course assorted minor Princes. Each morning they pass the golden statue of the source of their beneficence, Barbara Macfarlane, erected in the year 0040 on her passing into the 'Golden Halls of Fate', as they refer to the old idea of paradise. The students treat the university as a cynical joke, in which they are astonishingly insightful (having few other insights worth mentioning). These precious flowers attend mainly for the social life, and lots of them enrol in the same courses decade after decade. They don't need to work, after all. From time to time there is great excitement when one of them wins a holiday in big bad North America in The Princess's Lottery. When the lucky winner returns, they adopt an air of sophistication and mystery, drip-feeding their gasping fellow students with scandalous anecdotes. I occasionally get invited for lunch in their homes, luxurious gated mansions in the Oxfordshire countryside.

But I meander. At this year's Salvatorem Mundi ball (it's held every New Year's Eve in the Bodleian Function Centre), Princess Maureen (Mother of All Australians) and her Inner Court wore medieval, which set the campus fashion trend for the year. At my first lecture this year, I had to ask all the ladies wearing tall wimples to sit at the back. Presumably there's a warehouse somewhere in the Oxford suburbs packed with top hats, tiaras and monocles from last year's Roaring Twenties fashion mode.

That was the time a student passed away when I was lecturing. She was a dear old thing - just had her 120th birthday - and a regular at my 'History of the Knock-knock Joke' course (I'm bored to death teaching it!). Such a poignant sight it was: She lay on the carpeted aisle with her head cradled by a sobbing boy in tails and patent leather shoes. One of her silver dancing pumps had come off, and for some reason the sight of delicately veined ankles through her silk stocking set me off crying too. Soon the whole lecture theatre was ringing with sobs. I stood there wondering if we were crying for the dead student, or for the damned futility of it all.

Ahem. The English royals are of course in thrall to their Australian co-monarchs. Officially, Australia is an 'Annexed Principality of the Kingdom of England and Wales', i.e. a shiny modern extension welded onto the rusty Anglo-Welsh hulk unsteadily steered by King Nigel. The Windsors are hopelessly in debt to the Macfarlanes' Australia, but then the entire world is in debt to them except for you rash Americans. I've had to be terribly careful writing about this in my History, not that I would avoid discussing fair dinkum true facts.

Not good news from my doctor. A lot of sighing and clapping of hand to brow on his part. You'd think he was the one with a Thing in the brain. Yes, he's fairly sure there's a Thing, but wants me to undergo tests to confirm it.

"Are you a person of faith?" the poor man asked me yesterday.

"Not really," I said, (me being a card-carrying Fatalist, like 99% of the population of England and Wales. Not that we actually carry cards since we are fitted with a PIP). I didn't mention that I spent a lot of time in churches in Patria Nullius when I was a girl.

"And you, Doctor, are you such a person, a person of faith?" I said, surprising myself by my boldness. He went red and wrung his hands. I leaned forward and gave him a sort of hug. "I'm sorry," I said, "for my unaccountable antipathies." Strange words, you'll agree. They just popped out of nowhere, well actually out of somewhere.

Another chapter attached.

Best, Sue

PS. (Just an odd thought: PS means postscript. It's like INSERT but you obviously can't INSERT a line on paper you've already typed on, so you INSERT at the end. It would be better called SUBSERT).

At any rate, I noticed that I casually mentioned in my last letter that I smoke, so I'd better explain. Here in K.E.W., we do unofficial business through certain street children, who are generally called boy bankers or girl bankers. Every neighbourhood has one. It happened that I met my boy banker one evening last year in the area where I found Mr Remington, to hand him some letters. He's usually in a hurry, but this time he took a cigarette and a beautiful metal cigarette lighter from his inside pocket. A tiny wheel made a spark, there was whiff of oily spirit, a flame, and then the tobacco smoke. I swayed, caught in the memory of smoking rough tobacco as a young woman in Patria Nullius. The boy crinkled his eyes. He was a wary brat, all darting eyes and legs braced to flee.

"Wassat round your neck?"

"A coin," I said.

"Wassit worth?"

"Nothing," I replied. "A lot, I suppose. Never you mind."

He filed the answer away as I covered the coin with forefinger and thumb.

"What's your name?" I asked. He looked at me and shook his head.

"How old are you?" A shrug. About ten, I thought.

"Want one?" he said. I nodded. When the lighter flicked I saw the engraving on its side: VIETNAM 71-72 - MISS YOU JEN. I drew in the smoke. My lungs burned but I held back the cough.

Dizzy clarity. The boy and me.

"I can get more," he said. "Regular." He offered me the lighter. "Give it to you for that coin around your neck. Historical, isn't it, this lighter?"

"Where did you get it from?" I turned it over in my palm and felt his warmth still on the metal casing.

"I did get it from a man. I'm like get better one if you want," he said. These boys' families speak a slang of their own called Arg, and I wondered why he had just used it with me. Perhaps I bore some resemblance to his granny.

"Thanks, just the cigarettes." I went inside, stomach fluttering and the filthy taste of death on my tongue.

Stuart Campbell

JUDE LEARNS ABOUT SUE BRIDEHEAD

I woke at first light, hot, thighs stuck
together. Arabella was breathing gently in her
dreams. Her waking face was always a play of
scheme and calculation. Asleep, she found a
state of innocence and sweetness.

Auntie Vicky arranged my marriage.
Arabella's name was Marian then. People often
changed their names there, usually when they
were ill or having bad luck. On the morning
after our marriage, I woke up in my new wife's
house instead of Auntie Vicky's. She sent me
to the trucks for food and beer. When I came
back, she was lying on the bed, stiff and
shaking with bubbles around her mouth. I held
her down but she flung us both onto the floor,
and passed out.

It took her a week to wake up. Her first
words were, "I am no longer Marian." The next
day, she said, "I am Arabella."

It was as if a terrible hidden truth had
shown itself to me. I begged her to choose
another name, but she couldn't be moved.

"Why not Annabelle or Jade or Trish or
Beulah?"

"What's wrong with Arabella?"

"Nothing," I said.

"Tell me why you don't like it, Jude." She
was holding in a cruel smile, making an ugly
dimple in her cheek. What did she know? Had
she read Jude the Obscure? Was that why she'd
chosen such a name? Or was it pure chance?

"Can't tell," I said.

"Call me by my new name, Jude."

42

"Can't."

"You will."

I spent my nights quaking at this work of fate. By day, I hid in the bush with <u>Jude the Obscure</u>, reading over and over about Jude and Arabella: Our miserable story foretold by the prophet Thomas Hardy; my life now surely to be full of cruelties and failure, except for a few bitterly sweet years of marriage to Sue Bridehead; the terrible event in the lost Part Sixth lurking lost in my memory.

With time, the fact of my wife's new name healed like a deep cut, layer by layer from the inside. Eventually there was just a scar to remind me that we were bound to a certain future.

I was hungry. The food tables at the Club would be open. I eased myself from the bed but Arabella didn't stir. I went to the water tank outside the back door to sluice myself. The water was fresh and cool from the rain. The tank might last till the next storm, or it might not, so I'd have to walk to the river to wash with the others.

The garden was beginning to steam as the first hot rays penetrated the wet earth. Often, though, the earth was dry and hard for months, and the plants turned to dry sticks.

Early risers drifted along the street towards the Club, ten minutes' walk away. It's a good day for fishing, someone said. If they made it beyond breakfast beer, some of them would walk down to Spring Creek and catch a few of the fat golden carp that teemed under the surface begging for the whack of a big stick. I sometimes told a story about Jesus feeding the people with one fat carp and a sliced loaf.

We didn't have dinner or lunch or supper or tea like the Jude in the book did, just breakfast, and then you helped yourself to food for the rest of the day.

The Club had some oldtalk writing above the locked door: ORANGE EX-SERVICES CLUB. When I didn't understand writing, I'd sometimes make up a story for myself. I knew from the book that services was a kind of work that people offered, and that when the Jude in the book was dying, Arabella went to a boat club So in my story, there was once a river next to the ORANGE EX-SERVICES CLUB and people did work around about.

We crowded around the trestle tables next to the daily truck and the masked stranger with AUSTRALIAN BORDER FORCE INC on his shirt. The uniform supervised as people took breakfast from the truck and laid it out: Rows of pies, opened tins of pineapple, cans of beer, bottles of water, and bags of ice. No weed till evening when the uniform came back with the garbage truck.

We took breakfast in the early sunshine with quiet cheer and muted chatter. There was plenty of munching and swigging but it was the company that was important; same old chums, same old food, every day, with the men sitting apart from the women. Some men went back for more beer, and soon it was clear who had been defeated by breakfast. We had a word to describe our lives: semold.

Now and then <u>semold</u> was disturbed. I remembered when a man broke his leg falling off a verandah, and they took him away in the evening with the garbage. What was his name? Ngwin? Jase? Mas? Did he come back? Maybe. No. That's <u>semold</u>, when you couldn't remember and it didn't matter.

Today was <u>semold</u>.

"Ah, fishing. It's <u>bigfuckup</u>," one woozy fellow said, looking around for the shade of a tree that wasn't already occupied with a circle of <u>hubby-hubby</u> playing cards.

"Squeeze in here, Razza," a wobbly voice said, and the circle of men jiggled so that a gap formed.

Someone got together a gang of kids, and they stuck water bottles in their pockets before heading for the Creek.

I wasn't going fishing. I was going to talk to Auntie Vicky. I took a bag of ice for her.

She was on the front porch stroking a white cat.

"What is it, Jude?" she said as if she wasn't really interested. I stretched out a hand to stroke the cat's head but it hissed and ran up a tree, to glare down at me with an arched back.

Auntie Vicky was alert now, frowning at the cat.

"What did you tell her, Jude? Did you put a <u>tang-ling</u> on her? You frighten me with your powers."

"I don't have powers, Auntie Vicky. Arabella made them all up." She looked doubtful.

My wife went around telling her enemies that her <u>hubby</u> could make spells. I wish I could. Then I would make a spell to magic away Thomas Hardy's prophecy. Or find Part Sixth. Or turn Arabella into a spider.

"I want to ask you a question. About Sue."

"There's nothing to tell, Jude." Auntie Vicky put on a possum's <u>bumhole</u> mouth. Why wouldn't she ever tell? I knew she knew something about Sue. I tried another way:

"I want to put you in a story."

Auntie Vicky looked around until she spotted a half-smoked joint. She lit it and took a few slow lungfuls. Mellower now, she gave me a wily look.

"Me in one of your stories?"

"Of course. With Jesus and the Virgin Mary. You can be Mary."

"I want to be both of them." I thought for a moment. I was sure I could find a way for Auntie Vicky to be Jesus and the Virgin Mary all at once. Like God the Father, the Son and the Holy Ghost the women talked about.

"No problem," I said.

"Will it come true?" People always wanted to be in my stories because Arabella told them they could come true. This was a bit harder, so I said something that didn't mean anything:

"Every story can come true."

Auntie Vicky thought for a minute and then nodded.

I was good at this. Sometimes I finished one of my stories like this so they all clapped, and Arabella puffed up like the penguin man in the book.

"All right, I'll tell you about Sue," she said.

I emptied the lukewarm water out of the icebox, and poured in the fresh ice, rushing it because I was excited about what she would say. I swished the beer cans around to cool them off and gave her one. She shoved the can inside her dress to cool off her huhus, then emptied it in one swig and burped.

"Sue's your cousin, well, a sort of cousin I suppose. Her dad Frank brought her here to Orange. He said his wife had died a year or two before. I don't know where they'd come from, but they weren't our sort of people - they only spoke English when they got here. The little girl learned our lingo quickly, but Frank couldn't speak it very well. He set up a place for people to meet in that shed by the river, going on about Jesus and God and all that. He caused a lot of trouble, promising things he shouldn't have, upsetting people by telling them they'd be punished after they were dead, stuff like that. Sue used to write letters on paper to make decorations for the shed. Every Sunday, Frank read aloud from ... a book."

Auntie Vicky looked up at me sharply. Had she been about to say Bible?

My heart tingled. I knew about heaven and hell. About Christminster. About churches. About the Bible.

It was a church that Sue's father had set up.

She went on: "The uniforms closed the place, and Frank and Sue disappeared. It was around the year you were born. We didn't hear anything for months, until one day a weed trader came through town with a story that he'd met a <u>tang-ling</u> man and his little girl just outside a place called Kuranda - that way." She pointed north.

I was still tingling. Perhaps there were a lot of churches in Kuranda, just like in Christminster, with arches like the Orange Public School in Kite Street.

"What was she like, this Sue?"

Auntie Vicky's voice went croaky. "She was small, but lively. A girl - just four or five when they left - but like a person who knows <u>tang-ling</u>, someone who could magic you."

Like a <u>plaster angel</u>, I thought, although I didn't know if a <u>plaster angel</u> was a girl or a boy. When I tried to make a picture of Sue in my mind, I saw a flitting <u>bird</u> with a sweep of golden hair, and then with dark hair.

"How is she my cousin?"

Auntie Vickie frowned and thought for a moment. "Can't remember. All you kids are sort of cousins, aren't you?"

"Was she pretty?"

"Pretty? Yes, I suppose so, but so delicate that a good fall of rain would wash her away. Yes, like a butterfly is pretty."

I was captivated by Auntie Vicky's words. The women seemed to speak differently from the men, whose sentences consisted mostly of <u>choot</u> and <u>bumhole</u> and <u>bigfuckup</u>.

I remembered what the Jude in the book thought when he first met his Sue, that <u>she</u>

<u>was light and slight</u>, just like Auntie Vicky
had said. Just like a butterfly.

"And is she like me?"

Auntie Vicky looked at the cat in the tree
and then back to me. She answered slowly in
English. Some women used <u>oldtalk</u>, as they
called it, when they wanted to keep the <u>tang-
ling</u> away.

"I do not know if my words are coming out
right, Jude, but she IS you, and you ARE her.
Bugger. That does not sound right at all, but
you know what I mean. Pass me another beer and
see if there are any meat pies left."

"Can I ask you another question, Auntie
Vicky?" I asked her, in our lingo, not
English.

"Was Sue called Bridehead?"

"You mean like a second name?"

"Yes," I said. Some people had a second name
like Win or Jackson in Orange, but most
didn't. Arabella was the only Arabella in the
town, so how could you confuse her with
someone else? There were three or four other
Judes but I was Jude the Storyteller.

"I suppose she might have had a second
name."

"Was it Bridehead?" I asked.

"It might have been."

"Can you try hard to remember, Auntie
Vicky?"

Auntie Vicky closed her eyes.

"Yes, Jude. Maybe it was Sue Bridehead."

My blood ran hot and fast.

Stuart Campbell

THE MOTHER OF ALL BARGAINS

TOP SECRET
FROM: SIR BRUCE WITHERS, KEEPER OF THE
MONARCH'S BOOKES
TO: HRH PRINCESS MAUREEN

Highness,

You asked me to carefully check any passages in
Professor Bridehead's draft concerning your revered
ancestor Barbara Macfarlane. The appended pages seem
to be respectfully penned, but I beg your indulgence to
read them for yourself and to inform me of any
departures from historical verisimilitude.

Humbly, Bruce

THE MOTHER OF ALL BARGAINS

The Grand Bargain jolted the world into rethinking the
very concept of nationhood. But leaders like Barbara
'Bubbles' Macfarlane had long ago glimpsed its form
through the fog of geopolitics, international commerce,
and war.

Macfarlane had cultivated an aura of trustworthiness
and candour throughout her career. Allies and
opponents alike were disarmed by this outspoken
Australian with her trademark flute of champagne
always on hand. But behind the gregarious facade was
perhaps the most incisive and determined political mind
of the era. Supported by *Cerebrum*, her private think tank
staffed from the cream of the world's universities,
Bubbles had spent her years in the legal and corporate

worlds nudging into place the pieces in a game of global chess.

If Bubbles was the queen, dominating the board with speed, versatility and surprise, husband Reggie was the king: Unobtrusive, stolid, deliberate - and lethal if directly threatened. Reggie was the man in the background, the flash of spectacles caught in the light, the tall figure in the nondescript grey suit. It was Reggie who moulded *Cerebrum* into Barbara's intellectual killing machine.

The balance of contemporary opinion holds that Barbara and Reggie had worked towards the total confluence of corporate, military and political interests for years. Under Barbara's leadership of SLUZHBA, the multinational contracting and consulting firm pushed the concept of privatised defence to the point where almost half of all aircraft carriers around the world were leased from SLUZHBA. The old adage that no two countries with a McDonalds would ever go to war was superseded by a new orthodoxy on the morning a French frigate poised to target missiles on an Iranian submarine went into total shutdown: With both frigate and submarine leased from SLUZHBA and accessing its cloud service, the company's IT department cut off data to both vessels under a business continuity contract provision. In an interview for his memoir *A Life in the Shadow of Greatness*, Reggie commented, "We could have let the frigate destroy the sub by overriding the clause in the contract, but we preferred to let the event speak for itself: The private sector now decided who went to war and who didn't."

But Barbara and Reggie had an even broader vision. Through joint ventures with CareMundo and Sino-French, SLUZHBA gained ever increasing commercial stakes in hospitals, vaccines, schools, prisons, information technology, military hardware, and the glittering prize of mineral resources. Three years before The Grand Bargain, Australians turned on their televisions to see 'Bubbles' raising a flute of Tasmanian *grand cru* to celebrate SLUZHBA's acquisition of the Olympic Dam and Ranger uranium mines. The figure of a lanky grey-suited man at the back of the room can be glimpsed in archive footage.

Having laid the foundations of a post-capitalist corporatised global economy, Barbara Macfarlane entered politics, retaining her links with SLUZHBA by moving from CEO to Chairman. Within a year she was drafted to fill the role of Australian Prime Minister after the death of Polly Kebabjian in a mysterious car accident; three months later she called a general election and won her mandate. In her victory speech, Macfarlane listed her policy priorities: The first was to resolve the North Korea question for all time.

The Pyongyang Doctrine was proclaimed jointly by the General Assembly at the opening of the new flood-proof UN headquarters in Xingjiang. Barbara and Reggie watched the speeches from their hotel room in the quiet satisfaction that they had, as Barbara Macfarlane is reported to have said, 'saved the world from itself'. The number of states under the Treaty on the Non-Proliferation of Nuclear Weapons increased to fifteen, with provision for further membership applications. Nuclear missiles were the new normal, but their use would be dictated by the discipline of the market rather than political impetuosity.

Meanwhile, energy companies around the world had dumped coal in favour of renewables and storage. At the same time, gas production was tapering down as the need for a 'transition' energy source diminished. The shale oil boom in the US was petering out in the face of compensation claims by agribusiness companies and the mountains of throwaway plastic that were poisoning China and India. The age of clean, cheap energy had truly arrived.

And when nuclear power stations in Japan,and England were devastated by tidal surges, the writing was on the wall. Nuclear power was finished.

But was it? *Cerebrum* launched a global campaign advocating a nuclear power production facility in each nuclear-armed state to serve as an essential reserve of technical expertise. Nuclear power production had massive employment spinoffs in precision engineering, electronics, information technology, construction, project management, and materials science. There would be new job opportunities for thousands of young people. University research centres would develop advanced manufacturing techniques. Any country that can produce nuclear power, Barbara Macfarlane said in speech after speech, can colonise space, cure cancer, and live in peace and prosperity.

Cerebrum flooded the media with its 'teardrop in the heart' logo - the graphic expression of the idea that good - nuclear energy, prevails over bad - nuclear war. Reggie, always active behind the bastions of power, negotiated the joint venture among SLUZHBA, Sino-French and CareMundo to operate nuclear power stations worldwide. The logic was unassailable. If nuclear weapons were the new normal, nuclear power production would walk alongside them towards a grand new vision of human endeavour.

The dismantling of Old Australia under the 'Grand Bargain' was a natural outcome of the Flood of Sydney.

Three years before, insurance companies had refused cover for properties below the 2-metre inundation line along the east coast. Elevator and fire control contracts were voided, and whole floors of Sydney's and Melbourne's corporate towers were converted to illegal rental accommodation as businesses relocated in Europe, China and the US. Brisbane's Central Business District had been abandoned. Individuals who had read the economic and environmental signs had long since exported their capital and obtained residence papers overseas. Government tax revenues were rapidly drying up. Australian stocks were at junk valuations. The Australian dollar had plunged to a level where even bottom-feeding speculators dared not touch it.

The Grand Bargain was ratified by a Resolution adopted at the 25th Emergency Session of the General Assembly of the United Nations on 14 February 0001. The key points were that the General Assembly recognised New Canberra, the one-square kilometre territory leased from Oxford University, England as the legitimate capital of Australia, and '*recalling* the Pyongyang Doctrine, *affirmed* the right of all nations to aspire to nuclear weapons status'. It '*recognised* the necessity to excise Australia's territory from itself, *recognised* the name Patria Nullius to refer to the excised territory, and *requested* the Government of Australia to make provision for the well-being of the remnant population'.

Watching the vote from the back of the chamber in a 'teardrop in the heart' cap, Barbara squeezed Reggie's arm and said, "Game on".

PART SECOND - AT THE TRUCK DUMP

The True History of Jude

Dear Alex,

You said in your last letter that you were confused about Jude's book, so I'd better explain. When he arrived in Kuranda (you'll learn the details later), Jude had a thick bundle of papers covered in scrawl from multiple smudgy pens and stubs of pencil – hundreds of sheets of different sizes and colours that he roamed the countryside to find in abandoned buildings and rubbish dumps. The first time he saw a bookshelf in Kuranda, he sank to his knees in wonder. You see, there were said to be no books in Orange. The local story down there was that all reading material had been collected up and burned by Fatalists years before, next to a big tree outside the Post Office. (Actually, when I get to North America, I'm going to write a history of Fatalism.) But people believed that some women still kept secret libraries. There must have been some Bibles around judging by Jude's admittedly misty familiarity with Christian belief when he arrived in Kuranda.

Jude's bundle contained a handwritten copy of Thomas Hardy's <u>Jude the Obscure</u> he said his mother gave him. He was completely obsessed by this book. Nobody reads fiction in England these days since the government gradually throttled the supply of novels, and the people gradually throttled their imaginations in response. But as a senior scholar I have access to the University's Proscribed Books Archive, where I found a copy. I can see how

Jude the Obscure intrigued him. It's rather
heavy-handed and over-sentimental, full of
unlikely coincidences (try the Mayor of
Casterbridge if you really want to see Hardy
defying the laws of chance), but the romance
between Jude and Sue is delicately and
tragically done. Can I ask you an enormous
favour - to read Jude the Obscure if you
haven't already. You'll have no problem
finding an old copy in one of those bookstalls
near the campus.

Ah, memories! Those afternoons I spent
leafing through gloriously grubby paperbacks
and mouldy textbooks while the students smoked
and argued and flirted in the sunshine.

Before I hand over to 'Jude', I've received
clarification about the publication of The
History. Sir Bruce Withers visited the
university last week to make a graduation
speech. As befits his post of Keeper of the
Monarch's Bookes (they love faux-archaic
spellings in their titles), he and his retinue
arrived on the Royal Shuttle to a military
band welcome. The poor old soul manfully
survived the three-hour ceremony in his robes
and ceremonial chains, with the paramedics
watching anxiously. He demanded a private
audience with me, and we had tea and Iced Vovos
in the University's Council Chamber. Iced
Vovos, by the way, were a popular brand of
cookie in antediluvian Australia. Modern
interpretations (e.g. with silver leaf) are
traditionally prepared for regal functions. To
resume the story, this misdescribed room (the
University Council hasn't met in decades) is

lined with portraits of Macfarlane ancestors going back to the matriarch Bubbles, who as we are tediously and frequently told, Saved the World from Itself.

At any rate, it turns out that people won't be able to download The History to their PIPs and bookoids any time soon. Instead, the work is to be published as a single printed volume and presented to Princess Maureen on New Australia Day next year. Sir Bruce showed me a mock-up of the cover, all emblazoned with gumtrees and kangaroos. The text may not be released to the public at all, which gives me some comfort as a supposedly professional historian.

Before he was shunted away (an ornate wheelchair was on hand for his return to the Royal Shuttle) Sir Bruce, not being exactly the best Keeper of the Monarch's Secretes, passed on a snippet of gossip: Our rector Dame Lucy Macfarlane-Macfarlane has been appointed to the board of a Sino-French subsidiary company based in Shanghai. It's one of those third-tier boards used to mop up retiring presidents and prime ministers from the remnants of countries like Iceland and Laos. She is apparently rather annoyed, having been given hints about a second-tier SLUZHBA board in Paris. Tee-hee.

I mentioned New Australia Day. We're just a month away from this year's bash. I was startled to receive an invitation to the Royal Barbecue because tickets are much coveted. The one I attended six years ago was terrifyingly enjoyable. At sunset hundreds of guests crammed into The Paddock at the Bodleian Function Centre; it's a grassy walled garden, once called The Quad, with a stand of gum trees in one corner, and a sheep pen containing real lambs. On entry we were all given wide-brimmed khaki hats with dangling corks, and a sheet with the words to Waltzing Matilda. A ring of blazing barbecues turned out groaning platters of synthetic steaks and sausages amid clouds of savoury smoke. Roving bands of waiters sloshed Grange 0082 into glasses or flipped the tops off bottles of Princess Pale Ale specially brewed for the occasion. The dignitaries soon turned into a mob of cackling red-faced drunks with collapsing paper plates, spoiled frocks and greasy chins, me included I confess.

We bellowed Waltzing Matilda six times, all remembering to rotate clockwise on the words "in me tucker bag". Next, the diminutive Dame Irma Macfarlane-Belkovskaya stepped up and led the crowd in a piping round of Nessun Dorma, which I could have sworn is normally sung by a tenor.

Princess Maureen made her closing speech from a window in the Tower of the Five Orders flanked by a bemedalled white general of the male variety and a white woman in blackface holding a boomerang, reminding us all that on that hallowed day ninety-four years ago, Australia relinquished its lands to save the world from self-destruction, and established itself as the first virtual nation on earth. I tremble in anticipation of this year's revels!

That's all for now. I had a dizzy spell yesterday, and fell. I'm rather tired and nursing a big bruise on my shoulder.

Best, Sue

Stuart Campbell

JUDE MAKES PLANS

I went to sleep in the open air last night under a net I hung from a bush to keep the insects from biting. Auntie Vicky's words hung heavy over my dream: I rode on a plaster angel across yellow hills to Kuranda. Three white bundles flew behind me, just out of my sight, and then Arabella appeared before me mixing a great pot of hot blood. I was in a church and the blood was sticky on my fingers. Sue floated down towards me, but Arabella took a great knife and stuck Sue's neck, spraying her white dress with red.

I woke with the vision of Sue's soiled dress fresh in my mind. The vision slipped away but left a swirl of sorrow and fear. I had a clear plan: I would go north to protect Sue from harm - tomorrow, early, before the breakfast trucks arrived. My heart pounded at the enormity of my decision - to leave all I knew, to strike out beyond the yellow hills. My last day in Orange lay ahead.

I had to do one important thing: Move the copy of my book to a safer place. I'd take the original book with me. If I lost it, I could try to come back to Orange for the copy.

I aimed for the swampy area an hour's walk from Auntie Vicky's house. You had to pass through a graveyard of old trucks where the copy was hidden. I went there from time to time to check for footprints or other signs of disturbance, but I wouldn't be able to do that when I was with Sue at Kuranda. I had to bury it in a special place I knew, so nobody would come across it by accident.

It was dangerous here among the trucks - sheets of rusty metal blown into sharp heaps, pools of oily water hiding broken glass, clumps of weeds, fierce wild pigs.

I looked for the truck — the one with streaks of yellow showing through the rust. You could still read SPEEDY KEV SYDNEY TO BRISBANE OVERNIGHT. I'd worked out all the English words except KEV. SYDNEY and BRISBANE weren't in the book, but I knew they were towns from what some of the older people said. Maybe KEV was another word for truck.

My copy was still there, wrapped in a plastic sack that I found in an old shed. It said 10KG POULTRY LAYER PELLETS on the side, whatever that meant. I wished I had a book that explained all the words. I found LAYER in Jude the Obscure when Jude's aunt died and the layer-out did something with her but I couldn't figure out what it was.

We played here when we were kids - my cousins and me - and although it was off limits by then, somebody might wander around out of idle curiosity. I swung the plastic sack over my shoulder. I'd bury it deep under some rocks in the special place.

The route took me through thick bush, much thicker than when I was a boy. But there was a track of sorts, weaving its way up rock ledges and around fallen trees where horrible rustling warned me of dangerous animals. Pigs, snakes, yellow dogs, they could all kill a person. The tree canopy was dense. It stank sweetly, damply cool and dark, like at dusk.

Who made this track? Maybe there were people living around there. Should I go back, find another hiding place?

I smelt smoke nearby and heard the crackle of fire. I was at a crossroad of two paths. Should I go forward, left, or right? The choices looked the same: Three tunnels of grey-green thorny bush. The noise and smell of the fire were coming from up ahead to the right. I took the left path and ran, stooping, silent, ears and nose straining for danger. But the path suddenly veered sideways and I was in a sunlit glade where a man and a woman squatted by a fire. They looked up, fixing suspicious eyes on me. I stood and stared back. They keep looking. I didn't know what to do.

"Hail, fellows," I said in oldtalk. They looked like Aboriginals, and I knew they didn't speak like us.

"Whatcha say, mate?" the woman asked. She was brown-skinned, a bit darker than me, with a wide mouth.

"I said hail."

The man spoke to the woman and I heard her mutter in oldtalk, "Just a bleed'n kid," and "won't do us no harm".

They stared at me. I was too scared to try to run. I gave them a smile. They looked at each other and shrugged. There was a rich, savoury smell I remembered from a long time ago. It was meat. I wiped dribble from my lips.

"Ungry?" The man pointed at his mouth and then at the fire, where a piece of charred animal was dripping juice into the hot embers. There was a motorbike on the other side of the clearing with a sidecar and a trailer attached to it. The traders used them all the time.

"Yeh," I said. We said bookhee in our lingo but everybody understood ungry.

They called me over to squat with them. The man looked at me and at the woman, and then closed his eyes and clasped his hands in front of his chest. He said something very fast and I heard "Jesus" and "thanks fer the grub" and other things I didn't understand. He opened his eyes and nodded to the woman, who lifted the meat off a framework made with sticks. She delicately pulled strips of flesh from the bone and laid them in a pile on a tin foil dish, then licked her fingers and said, "Help yerself".

I held back. It'd been years since I tasted real meat. There was a stingy feeling in my nose and I realised I was going to cry, but I didn't know why.

"Gwan," the woman said, passing me a dripping gobbet in her fingers. My tears stopped and I filled my cheeks with hot spongy chunks, ecstatic with the feel of chewy fibres and warm bloody fat coating my teeth and gums. I had a funny idea – I was an animal eating an animal.

"Slow down," the man said. "You'll spew the lot up."

"Dun gettit me," I say, forgetting that I had to speak in English.

The man frowned, put his finger in his throat, and made a choking noise. He meant gonna luraka yu.

I was soon full. I burped and got up to go. But the man held my ankle and told me to stay, while the woman wandered to the trailer and came back with a handful of loose seeds and flowers, half-dried. They passed a pipe around. I couldn't refuse, although weed wasn't to my taste. The stem of the pipe was shiny with animal grease, and the scorched seeds crackled and popped in my face. I felt dizzy, and the meat churned inside my zazzy. I fixed my eyes on a point in the embers until my head and guts were steady. My eyes moved around, testing my brain till the man's fat toes appeared. For some reason, they seemed funny and I began to giggle. It was the weed speaking and stupefying me. I prayed to Jesus, and my giggling turned to snivelling. I wanted to go home.

The woman put an arm around my shoulders. Her skin was wrinkled like a big goanna. She pulled me close and asked me in oldtalk, "Wassa matter?" but I pulled away. The tears had gone. Jesus had answered. I controlled my wobbling head, and sat away from the woman. She shrugged.

The man made tea. I'd heard of it but had never drunk it. In the book, Arabella made a good strong cup of tea that would set everybody right for going home. Could I go home after the tea, I wondered?

It was sour and planty, and there was something cosy and satisfying about the feeling on the back of my tongue, and the way it cleaned away the meat fat.

The woman said we had to have a proper talk. What was a proper talk? Maybe she meant like my talk with Auntie Vicky.

"Business, like," the man said. He gave his woman a wink and she nodded back. They had a secret. What could it be?

"Yep. A proper talk about business and stuff," the man said. "Now, where were you going with that bag?"

I figured that if I told them I was going north, they might tell me how to get there.

"I'm leaving Orange tomorrow."

"Where're yer headin' exactly?"

"Kuranda."

They looked at one another and made low whistles.

I waited for them to say something.

The man scratched his ear and said, "Yer can't go alone,"

"Why not?"

"Yer too pretty," the woman said, and they both laughed.

"Lotta men out there who'll take advantage of yer," the man said, serious this time. I remembered the oldtalk word advantage from my book but it had so many meanings. The Jude in the book told Sue she was a girl who had no advantages. And, Jude remembered, Mr Phillotson took advantage of Sue's inexperience. All those meanings! And yet no meaning I could pin down.

"Can I come with you, then? To keep me safe from the men's advantage?"

They didn't answer, but the man leant forward to take the sack from my shoulder. I resisted, but it was useless: He was big and muscly. I sat defeated as he unwrapped my book.

He looked at it, holding it the right way up.

"Read."

I found the sheets for the first chapter and started to read:

"The schoolmaster was leaving the village, and everybody seemed sorry. The miller at Cresscombe lent him the small white tilted cart and horse to carry his goods to the city of his destination, about twenty miles off, such a vehicle proving of quite sufficient size for the departing teacher's effects."

"Orright. Vera, get the 'Oly Bible."

The woman walked over to the sidecar and came back with a book. She handed it to me.

"Read," the man said.

The paper was very thin with gold edges. My clumsy fingers flicked through the pages until they found one with 'Jude' at the top. I read aloud, stumbling over the words, hoping - praying - they didn't notice my trembling hands.

"Jude, the servant of Jesus Christ, and brother of James, to them that are sanctified by God the Father, and preserved in Jesus Christ, and called: Mercy unto you, and peace, and love, be multiplied."

The man said, "Amen", and waved his arm for me to stop. "What about a story?"

"A story?"

"Yeah. I reckon you're the one who tells stories."

My brain whirred. I came up with the story about Sue Bridehead being married to the innkeeper where Jesus lay in the manger, and I began, trying to tell it in <u>oldtalk</u>. But I'd never told it in this English language before, and I couldn't find the best words. The man waved his arm again.

"It's 'im," he said to the woman. "I knew it."

"Are you Arabella's husband?" she asked.

I nodded.

They left me by the fire while they talked in private by the motorbike. When they came back, the man told me they'd take me to Kuranda, but it was a long journey. I had to give them something for taking me.

"Give you what? I asked."

"Arabella's tin box." I nodded again. I knew why they wanted the <u>timbox</u>.

"Be here tomorrow at sundown. Now piss off." I knew piss off from the uniforms.

SUSAN TO ALEX, SEPTEMBER 0099

Dear Alex,

Excuse the double-sided sheets and the coffee stains. You probably heard that in the blessed Kingdom of England and Wales, they made possession of writing paper an offence under the Sedition Act. These laws are forced on the Kingdom by Australia since its own legislature is too ossified to make its own these days. At any rate, I've got a secret store of this dangerous commodity but it's running low. Do you like the seal on this missive? I bought the wax from the boy banker. Seals are all the rage since envelopes became contraband, six months incarceration being the penalty for possession thereof on the first offence.

Anyway, I'm sorry I've taken a month to reply.

To answer your point about Arabella's trade with the 'uniform', you guessed right that she was a drug dealer, and you are right to ask why Orange had drug dealers when the government handed out weed for free. Arabella was actually trading in high-strength marijuana that was produced by outlaw farmers deep in the bush. The uniforms paid in roubles (although in Orange, as I've mentioned, they used the Creole word bucks to cover any kind of cash). The drugs were sent to Vladivostok on uranium carriers that were owned by a SLUZHBA subsidiary.

It's covered in a chapter in The History, although with the Macfarlanes portrayed as ignorant of the outrages perpetrated by 'rogue employees'.

But back to my excuses for being such a slow correspondent. I've been unwell in several ways: Besides The Thing in my head, I've had muscle weakness and all sorts of odd symptoms that the doctor believes could be Post-polio Syndrome (not that he's ever seen another case of it). And he wants me to give up smoking, bless him. 'It'll kill you,' he said. 'So what?' I almost said, but I'm fond of the man and wary of rebuffing his kind attentions. I made a token effort at quitting just for him, made a big fuss about how hard it was. The reality is that he thinks my smoking very exotic and medically enthralling because there are so few of us these days. Fate knows it's a struggle just to buy the cigarettes; the boy banker has an intermittent supply from North America. The doctor finds my 'struggle' to give up smoking even more fascinating. The other day, he told me how privileged he'd been to lecture a group of Polytechnicum medical students on nicotine withdrawal from FIRST-HAND experience.

I also delayed writing because I've taken a battering from some colleagues lately. One snarky Scot stood up at a virtual history conference and made some pointed remarks about my professorship being funded by Her Royal Highness's Australian Government. You know the kind of thing - how could my forthcoming History ever be taken as unbiased scholarship when my 'patron' was living off an ocean of uranium mining royalties? There were sniggers

from some of the other participants who were
beaming in from outside England. I replied
that at least my bookoids sell, and asked how
many downloads my learned Caledonian colleague
could boast of his monumentally tedious
<u>Bicycle Pump Production as an Economic
Indicator in French Indo-China 1940-1950</u>. I
was more furious because of his reference to
Princess Maureen. It's easy to commit lèse-
majesté when you're sitting in the enlightened
Republic of Haggisland, but we at the
University of Sydney live a more precarious
intellectual life, preferring to avoid
slighting the Australian Crown when its
corporeal embodiment is nibbling on Iced Vovos
a stone's throw away. It's hard enough to get
permission to join an international hook-up,
and Dr. McSnarky has probably 'scotched' my
chances of another for some time to come.

I'm rambling again.

I mentioned that the account of the drug
trade in <u>The History</u> is somewhat sanitised.
I'd <u>like</u> to say that I've agonised over how
much sanitising history can withstand, or more
exactly, how much <u>The History</u> can withstand.
But to be honest, I've hardly agonised at all
up till now because I have a good intuitive
sense of which topics need to be treated
carefully. However, last week something very
odd happened. I got two messages: One was a
card from dear old Sir Bruce Withers asking me
to review a section of <u>The History</u> to "check
the accuracy" of comments about the Macfarlane
family's involvement in Australian Border
Security Inc. With the card was a printed

proof of the blurb for <u>The History</u>. (The Palace is exempt from the ban on paper, and Sir Bruce is rather fond of legacy technologies. He has the news downloaded from his PIP each morning and printed up as an old-fashioned newspaper with <u>The New Canberra Bugle</u> on the masthead.) I've enclosed the blurb with this letter. You'll see that it has Princess Maureen's robust handwritten annotation at the top. Guard it with your life, or better still lodge it with the Library of Congress (not a joke).

The second message was a phone call from, no less, Princess Maureen's Principal Private Secretary inviting me for tea with Her Royal Highness the Tuesday 'henceforth' at three.

Well, Alex, how could I turn down an invite to pineapple scones and a cosy brew with Australia's monarch? I went, hair precariously upswept instead of my usual scholarly pudding bowl. There was a slightly nervous tingle in my stomach, not unconnected with the ominous note on Sir Bruce's blurb.

HRH hadn't changed much since the New Australia Day barbecue. Divine right to be condescending, rotten listener, foul-mouthed. It's all a cover, I think, for her ordinariness. The old adage about wealth lasting just three generations doesn't quite fit in her case - she's theoretically the wealthiest woman in the world. But she hasn't inherited her ancestor's vision and ruthlessness. When it came to understanding political power, Bubbles Macfarlane was up there with Julius Caesar, Elizabeth I,

Napoleon and Hitler. But poor Maureen is carted in her palanquin from one crass public event to another, barely aware that the six men on the Triopoly Coordinating Council actually run the globe (except your North American bit of the world of course).

At any rate, I'd hardly been there for five minutes when HRH offered me a title, accompanied by a heavy hint about 'cooperating' with the Keeper of the Monarch's Bookes. There was some muttering through the scone crumbs on the lines of "being careful about sources". We believe we have some spare Duchess spots, she opined, and if herself wasn't mistaken, a Baroness-ship might even be possible.

"One surely must be married to a Baron to be a Baroness?" I ventured. "I be not wed." (Flexing my mock-archaic muscles as required at the Palace).

"We got rid of that silly rule," quoth she.

Here's a test, Alex. Try to guess what I told her. Answer at foot of page*.

Meanwhile, I continue to entertain my costumed ninnies with a course on the history of the Windsors - the kind of old-fashioned kings and queens nonsense they love. This week they had to submit a piece of writing to demonstrate evidence of intellectual engagement, (however faint). When I downloaded their efforts from The Universe, I was surprised to find some fine writing - well, fine in the sense that sentences began and ended properly, and ideas flowed in some kind of logical progression. There were even verbs.

Further checking revealed that each piece was different, so they evidently hadn't been copying each other. A chat with our faculty manager revealed that this month, all students were given full access to Predictive Composition. You'll no doubt gather that this miracle of state-sponsored inanity is based on the old Artificial Intelligence text generators that were all the rage in the last century, and that were largely abandoned outside the domains of instruction manuals and cookery books. Predictive Composition (colloquially known as PC) works by monitoring the author as they gingerly enter a few sentences, and then takes control of the writing when it has worked out what might be in the scholar's mind. It is programmed to pause periodically to prompt the victim (ahem, 'end-user') to touch a key or make a little grunt, which releases the next sentence with a rewardicon, for example, 'good work!' or 'you're on track!' Naturally it makes sure that each student's version is unique, which is why there was no 'copying'.

When it came to assessing their essays, I gave them randomly assigned marks from 0% to 100%. I'm planning to enter them into the system later today, so there'll be tears before bedtime!

So to my biography, memoir, writing therapy, whatever you will call it: I'm beginning to feel at home in Jude's mind. As I clack away at his history, I make it my own. As I make it my own, he walks alongside me. There are moments of queer mental perturbation, when I'm reminded of those singers who perform duets with recordings of their dead mothers or fathers: The living and the dead entwined. I think it's beginning to come out in the pages I've attached.

I am yours, humbly and devotedly,
*Baroness Susan Bridehead, Guardian of the Keys of The City of Maroochydore (so it says on the bottom of the scroll they sent me).

Bruce: what the hell is this about
clandestine diaries and the role of
the Macfarlane family? You're supposed
to be keeping an eye on her. Get
that bloody woman in for a meeting
with me or you'll be wearing your
arsehole for a hat.
HRH

A NEW HISTORY TO CELEBRATE THE
FIRST HUNDRED YEARS OF THE WORLD'S
FIRST VIRTUAL NATION

The History of the Principality of Australia: The First Century
is a comprehensive account of how Australia excised
itself from its own territory and became the first
sovereign nation possessing no land. Written by
eminent historian Professor Susan Bridehead of the
University of Sydney at Oxford, this is essential reading
for an understanding of the roots of the Second Nuclear
Era.

Part One, *The Crisis Years*, deals with the events leading to Australia's offer to lease its territory to the international community for a millennium to serve as a secure source of uranium and a storage facility for spent nuclear fuel. Key topics include the environmental crisis in the South Pacific, the collapse of Australia's economy in the face of international divestment from coal and gas, and the UN Emergency Conference of 0001 at which Australia's Grand Bargain proposal was debated and accepted.

Part Two, *Patria Nullius*, discusses the social and economic conditions in the remnant population after the closing of the borders in 0001. A number of the chapters draw on primary sources comprising clandestine diaries, sketches, and oral histories by individuals who evaded Australian Border Security Inc. to escape Patria Nullius.

Part Three, *Sovereign Exile*, focusses on the political, legal, and financial challenges of establishing New Canberra, the seat of the exile government in Oxford. Newly released archive materials throw light on the contract to commercialise Australian Border Security Inc., and the role of the MacFarlane family in the multinational conglomerate SLUZHBA.

Part Four, *Union*, discusses the evolution of the Australian Government in Exile into a principality, and its annexation to the Kingdom of England and Wales.

ABOUT THE AUTHOR

Baroness Professor Dr Susan Bridehead is the author of ten books and more than five hundred scholarly articles. Arriving in the Kingdom of England and Wales in 0052 as a refugee, she attended The University of Sydney at Oxford, gaining a first-class honours degree and a PhD in History, before travelling to the North American Union for postdoctoral studies at the University of Chicago. After two years teaching and research in America, she returned to The University of Sydney at Oxford as the Macfarlane-Gillette Professor of Modern History.

JUDE IS INJURED

I didn't go straight back to town. I needed to think through what the weed traders had asked me to do. When I got to the truck graveyard, I stuffed my book copy back in the hiding place; I'd have to risk leaving it here.

A tree that had sprouted between the axles of the truck made a canopy twenty <u>armlengths</u> high. I sat sheltered from the sun. A good thinking place. A good place for thinking about Sue Bridehead. I got the book out again, unwrapped it and found Part Second. <u>There was nothing statuesque about her</u>, the book said. <u>A painter might not have called her handsome or beautiful</u>. Yes, there was no doubt. My cousin was Sue Bridehead

I realised I had forgotten to ask Auntie Vicky if Sue Bridehead was dark or fair. I stared into the distant trees and tried to conjure her image, but it wouldn't come; perhaps she was just brown like me and everyone else in Orange.

I forced my mind to imagine her voice, the way she moved, but no pictures came. The book said she was <u>all nervous motion</u>, but that didn't make a picture.

I tried to imagine the moment when we would meet, when she saw that she was me and I was her, but no pictures came. I wanted to know how we would live, how our love would be, but no picture came.

I flung the book down, hating how the meanings would disappear in the thick, dark forest of words.

Fierce squawks in the tree broke into my thoughts. It was two big black birds fighting over a dirty white ball of something stuck in a crevice in the tree trunk. One bird tore the bundle apart, but the other drove it away. The head of a maggot swivelled blindly in the end of the bundle. The birds landed on either side and slashed at the maggot. The sight of the dirty white made me tremble. I remembered the dream, Sue's bloody dress, and Thomas Hardy's prophecy. The birds tore off their portions of the wriggling thing. The hairs on my arm stuck up. Sweat coated my face. The birds flew away. The truck dump fell silent.

There was the sound of somebody picking through the rusting truck bodies, perhaps a hundred armlengths behind me. I slid to the ground and slunk behind a pile of old tyres. Had they seen me hiding my copy? Now I couldn't risk leaving it. I clutched it close to my chest.

It was silent again. I crouched in my sweat, straining to hear.

"I can see you, Jude. Don't run."

I spotted Vijay, Mimi's boyfriend, moving in my direction. He'd been tracking me. How did he know where to find me?

He called out, "Jude. I want to talk to you".

I stood up. No point in pretending I wasn't there.

"Did you follow me here?"

"Just let me talk."

"I don't want to talk to you, Vijay."

He came nearer, picking through the junk. I could see black oily stains on his feet from the puddles.

"How do you know this place?" I asked. But then I realised. It was the tyres. Vijay made sandals out of them, which he sold for <u>bucks</u>. He was a useful <u>hubby</u>, kept off the beer and weed. He was someone with a <u>nobby</u> like me. That's why Mimi and half a dozen other women wanted him.

He was almost at the yellow truck. I grasped my bundle tightly.

"It's the reading," he said. "I know what you were doing under the house."

"I don't know how to read, Vijay."

"You're lying. Teach me. I want to learn, Jude."

"I told you, I can't read."

"Teach me, please. I've seen women reading. They know things. I want to know things."

I had to get rid of Vijay. Perhaps I could fool him.

"Those women, they don't know anything. They just write down how many <u>bucks</u> they have with dots and lines. When they've forgotten, they look at what they wrote and then they remember." I couldn't say it any simpler. Would Vijay believe me?

"Liar. What's in your sack then?"

"Some stuff I found. In a truck. Some old clothes, that's all. Look." I held the bag open and he came closer, leaning over it.

"Watch out, there's a spider on your shoulder," I yelled.

He sprang up, whacking his body to shake off whatever was there. People died from spiders in these parts. He ripped his shirt off and it got stuck over his head.

I turned to run, bouncing off rusted metal sheets, splashing through greasy pools. He'd got his shirt off now. He was behind me but I was getting ahead. I leapt from a car roof onto a pile of tyres. I'd jump from there into a clump of ferns by an opening in the thick bush. I leapt but something snatched me back to earth. I'd tripped on a loop of cable and I crashed down, my leg plunging into a crevice of torn metal, flesh ripped, bone scraped. I was trapped and Vijay was looking down. He was scared at what he saw.

"Help me, Vijay."

He came closer, looked at the mess of my leg. His lips flopped around like two carps. He ripped off his shirt and wrapped it around the wounds.

"Take me home, Vijay," I gasped, and he hoisted me onto his shoulders. The pain was gut-scouring.

"Put me down. Get help." I was trembling. There was a lot of blood. Something white glistened inside my leg.

Vijay rested me back on the ground. He got up and looked behind me. I craned my neck. The Aboriginal traders stood silently watching us. Vijay ran off. I passed out, Sue's sweet face watching from above.

Then she was.

Gone.

SUSAN TO ALEX, OCTOBER 0099

Dear Alex,

I'm tired and ill. Physically ill, but also sick in my soul. The <u>History</u> of my poor benighted country is nearing the end.

Ironically, Australia wasn't officially my country until I became a Baroness. I was just a citizen of the Kingdom of England and Wales before, but Australian peerage bestows honorary citizenship and the appropriate update to my PIP. It is darkly hilarious that they don't know I was born in Patria Nullius. I'd better check what privileges my new status bestows.

Knowing that nobody but Princess Maureen will read the book is simply dispiriting. That's if she reads it at all.

To elaborate, Sir Bruce summoned me to the venerable Radcliffe Camera, where I was shown into the Office of the Keeper of the Monarch's Bookes, an exact replica, he told me, of the Muniment Room at the old University of Sydney, the one in Sydney that is. This nook of varnished wooden shelves functions as the scholarly retreat of The Keeper of the Monarch's Bookes. He spends much of his days at a grand desk with an inkwell and a brace of antique nib pens, occasionally making a note in a leather-bound journal. I gather he is convinced that he is absorbing the wisdom from the ancient books lining the walls through some mysterious osmosis.

But to return to the topic, Sir Bruce wanted to show me a mock-up of the display case for

the book. It will recline on a grey ironbark
bookrest in a glass cabinet, held open at a
page in the middle with a silk cord. The
mocked-up binding seemed to weigh a good ten
kilograms. I mumbled my appreciation, accepted
a cup of tea, and made my escape to the shuttle
stop outside. The conveyance hissed through
the square kilometre of Oxford University that
comprises New Canberra - past Brasenose
College, which is now the Royal Palace, and
the Bodleian Library, reborn as the Salvatorem
Mundi Function Centre. I arrived quite
exhausted at the Sydney University campus,
which is housed in the former unglamorous
Oxford Brookes University, a couple of
kilometres east of the historic centre that
the Macfarlanes have absorbed into their
fantasy of a thousand-year dynasty.

On I slog. I force myself to dictate a few
words with Predictive Composition turned on,
so that The Universe takes over and writes
great slabs of hagiography based on the great
slabs of hagiography that have already been
written by others.

When I started writing, I clung to my
conviction that I must write an honest
history, and that I would reason with the
Palace when they questioned my analysis. How
naive I was. Now I mostly accept what The
Universe feeds back to me. Just the other day,
I entered this:

"In 0024, the Solicitor General advised the
Attorney General that the Principality of

Australia may expose itself to challenge if it refused to grant asylum to ..."

Well, strike me pink (as Princess Maureen would say) if the screen didn't flicker and change it to:

"In 0024, the Solicitor General advised the Attorney General that the Principality of Australia would not expose itself to challenge if it refused to grant asylum to ..."

I corrected it on the keyboard (I'm fond of these outdated devices), but it flickered again and restored the nonsense version. It's becoming exhausting. Why not switch off Predictive Composition, I hear you ask four thousand kilometres away? Simple: I can't. It's been mysteriously stuck to 'on' since I became a Baroness.

So, I drag on predictively and predictably to the conclusion. When I check back to earlier chapters of the History, I find bits missing or changed. I read sentences that I'm sure I didn't write. And then I go back and read them again, and I have a foggy recollection of writing them. One day, a passage I was reading was so unfamiliar that I thought I'd had a mini-stroke. For half an hour I did mental arithmetic and sang songs in Chinese until I was sure that I hadn't lost my faculties. After that I indulged myself in a little treasonous thought experiment about Predictive Composition: What would be the

result if a society required all text to be
generated by a text-generating device that
drew on the texts generated by the device
itself? Choose from the following answers:

(a) There would eventually be no more
original writing,
(b) The text-generating device would
eventually distil texts down to a few
archetypes that expressed universal truths,
(c) The device would beg its operators for
fresh material
(d) none or all of the above.

I've written so little of Jude in the last
weeks, and yet I know that he is all that
stands between me and a headachey slide into
whoknowswhat. I force my aching legs to carry
me, The Thing and Mr Remington to the dunny,
where I clack-clack myself back fifty years.
When I rest between sentences, shreds of the
Orange language wriggle around my mind. A
miracle, you could call it: The raw mind of a
toddler soaking up sentences nearly seventy
years ago and hard-wiring the words and
grammar into permanence. Longdrop, that's what
they called the dunny. Clacking in the
longdrop. Dropping in the longclack. Come on,
Susan, concentrate!

Oh, I forgot. You wanted to know about the
'uniforms', as Jude called them. In Jude's
day, they were mostly recruited from climate
refugee camps around the South Pacific. I
discovered (with much difficulty) that
Australian Border Security Inc established the

ABSIKAZ recruitment and training centre in Kazakhstan. It was badged as a SLUZHBA operation, but the Macfarlanes owned it privately, although that bit was scrubbed out of an earlier version of the History. Thousands of recruits were processed at ABSIKAZ and flown down to Patria Nullius, but a lot absconded and disappeared into the Remainder population. There's one I'll mention later in Jude's account - Jack Wing - who I'm pretty sure was a Chinese from Papua New Guinea. My sources tell me there aren't many uniforms in Patria Nullius these days since almost everything is automated and most of the protected settlements have closed down.

Two days later.
I got some stronger pain medication, but Dr Brow-Clapper wasn't happy about it. There could be 'consequences' if I don't have The Thing investigated. I thanked him and promised to think about the idea, but the truth is that I feel my life is on a trajectory that can't be steered off course by my own intervention. Perhaps it's the fatalist speaking, or should I say Fatalist? I so envy the way you Americans pick and choose your religions like a restaurant menu: Catholic today, Hindu tomorrow, Flying Spaghetti Monster the next week. When I was doing my research there, every class was disrupted by groups of students exercising their First Amendment rights by trooping out to pray, some of them stark naked. And of course, many were also

exercising their Second Amendment Rights judging by the bulges in their pants pockets.

You probably don't know that Fatalism actually began in Australia. It originated in the city of Cairns, not far from Kuranda. A couple of evangelist peanut farmers, Maree and Jed Kovacs, were hosting a pop-up prayer gathering at the Cairns Entertainment Centre. Thousands had turned out to pray for Cyclone Basil to head out to sea. Well, it didn't, and Cairns was destroyed. Maree and Ted committed suicide. This was a year before the Flood of Sydney and a year before Bubbles Macfarlane rented Australia out. Her propaganda machine flooded the media with stories about the futility of religion, and signed up millions of people to various organisations with anti-religious and pro-nuclear platforms. Once she was relocated to England, Bubbles used the database to kick off the United Fatalist Organisation, the Mother Church of the Second Nuclear Age. In fact, you'll read more about Maree and Jed Kovacs later in The True History of Jude, as I now call it.

The new painkillers have made me feel well enough to write some more. The piece I've enclosed is about how Jude robbed his first wife Arabella. I remember the night in Kuranda he told me this story, and how shocked I was - not at the events he described - but at his lack of awareness that what he had done was wrong. He was a child taking a crash course in being an adult. Later he and I spoke again about the story, and this time he expressed remorse; but was it authentic? Or had he used

his wits to learn what he should feel, even if
he couldn't feel it? See what you think,

Best, Sue

JUDE STEALS THE TIMBOX

It was almost dark when I woke up. I was lying on a bush track. Pain stabbed my leg. I sat up and ran my fingers along my calf, which was now tightly bound with a neat cloth bandage. There were leaves under the bandage, pressed into the wound. Who did this? The traders of course.

My head was clear, sharp, not the feeling of weed but something else. The bag containing my book lay by me, next to a broken branch cut to the length of a walking stick. I got up and stumbled homeward with the bag slung across my chest. No time to hide it now. I'd get my real book from under the house, and leave the copy there.

It was a long walk with my wounded leg. I stumbled on rocks and fallen branches. Nobody went into the bush at night for fear of animals and strangers from other towns and villages beyond the yellow hills. I saw the grey glow of the movie screen above the trees when I got near to town. It was fixed high up on the front of the Orange Hotel. Hotels were places where people slept, but the Orange Hotel was black and burned inside with no beds. Jude stayed in the Temperance Hotel in the book, and the Arabella in the book married a man who ran a hotel in Sydney.

The movies came on every night on their own. There was a thing like a pie dish on top of the screen. It pointed to the sky, so perhaps the movies came from the highest heaven.

There was no need for me to tell a story tonight. A <u>hubby</u> called Jacko was singing after the first film. His voice was sweet like banana. He had plenty of suitors. He'd be snapped up soon.

Arabella would be pretending to watch the film now, but really her eyes would be darting over the faces, checking who owed what to who, and what favours she'd swap with who.

I crept past the deckchairs in the street. The pictures on the screen were fuzzy because of all the night insects crowding around the light. The giant moths were the worst. When the movie ended, they flapped here and there, hitting your face and climbing into your hair.

I let myself into Arabella's house but didn't light a candle. Where might the <u>timbox</u> be? I searched the house all over but it wasn't there. It was made of heavy metal, two hands wide and two hands deep. You couldn't miss it. I sat down to think and to rest my sore leg. There was blood dribbling from under the bandage.

An idea: Try the <u>longdrop</u>.

I took a candle into the wash house at the back and lit it to check the walls. There was panelling in the ceiling and I stood on the <u>longdrop</u> to reach up. It smelt vile; the pump-out truck hadn't been for a while. A square piece of panel shifted sideways at my touch to reveal a hatch. There it was: I could just see the edge of the <u>timbox</u> inside. I reached up to grab it, but it was too high. My foot slipped off the <u>longdrop</u> and I crashed to the ground.

The bandage had caught on something, and the ripping pain made me gasp. I looked up.

Arabella stared down at me. She was panting slightly and one of her suckers pointed at me with a smug look. Arabella said, "My eyes are everywhere".

I thought fast thoughts.

"It was Vijay's idea. I was just going to take a little bit of money. He said me and him would have a secret stash. You wouldn't notice."

Arabella sneered at me. She didn't believe a word. I tried again: "Mimi told Vijay about your timbox."

This'd confuse her. Arabella's expression of disbelief turned to puzzlement, and she grabbed the sucker by the arm.

"Do you know anything about this? Is that frigging Mimi plotting behind my back? Come on, speak or I'll bash yer."

The sucker trembled. Arabella repeated the question. More trembling and sprouting tears from the frightened woman, but no proper words. I sprang to my feet and onto the longdrop, and this time I grasped the edge of the timbox with my fingers. But it was too bulky to hold with one hand. It slipped from the ceiling onto the sycophant's head. The woman screamed and pressed her fist to a bloody eye. Arabella grabbed a broom and swung it against my legs. I reached up and grabbed the ceiling timbers with both hands, hanging like a monkey as the broom whacked my swinging feet.

There was a cracking sound from above. I let go of the ceiling timbers, hit the ground in agony, scooped up the timbox and staggered for the door. The ceiling fell in. My last sight was Arabella clawing at her face. A shower of dead insects and old bird shit rained onto her. The bleeding sucker clutched Arabella's ankles, screaming.

I ran into the night, my wounded leg clomping in blood-filled bandages, the timbox banging against my chest. Past the film watchers with a scampering crouch, across the big road, past the square building called ALDI and into the street that led to Orange Public School. I hid behind a clump of bushes by the school. The film was still playing, but voices shouted loud and angry. I put the timbox down to rest my arms and to check my book copy.

The bag was gone! Fear and rage filled me all at once. My chest hurt, I was dizzy, crying. I prayed to Sue, then Jesus. Calm returned. I couldn't go north without getting my book and hiding the copy.

Auntie Vicky's house was across the town. The shouting got nearer. A line of fiery torches paraded down Kite Lane towards me. Jude, Jude, the women called. Arabella led them, blood down her face and body, a great torch in her hand billowing smoke and flame as if she was walking out of hell.

I backed into the schoolyard and bumped into a person. A hand clapped across my mouth. Arms grabbed me and flung me across a shoulder. My rescuer ran with big strides. I bumped up and down as each foot hit the ground. I could only see his bum and his heels in tyre sandals. At the outskirts of town, he slowed down, panting hard, saying nothing. We travelled steadily in the dark for <u>nowrotu</u>. He stopped by an old hut. He put me down.

It was Vijay. We went in the hut. He opened two bottles of water. The hut was dark inside but I could see a bag around his neck.

"Here, I found it in Arabella's garden." My copy. He finished his water, patted me on the shoulder and loped off into the darkness.

Stuart Campbell

SALVATOREM MUNDI

FROM: SIR BRUCE WITHERS, KEEPER OF THE
MONARCH'S BOOKES
TO: HRH PRINCESS MAUREEN

Highness,

As per your request, the requisite revisions have been
made to this section:

SALVATOREM MUNDI

It seems incredible today that the old Constitution
forced Australians to the polls almost every year as State
and Federal governments rose and fell. But in 0001, with
entities like New South Wales and Queensland now
mere names on old maps, the first meeting of
Parliament in New Canberra buckled down to
simplifying the machinery of government. Reggie had
already made the necessary amendments to trim the
Parliament to a virtual unicameral model with all seats
vacant pending a Constitutional Convention. Aware of
her solemn responsibility to wisely guide the relaunch of
a nation, Prime Minister Macfarlane, armed with
executive authority over Parliament, insisted on
obtaining the consent of the Australian people through
a referendum.

The government tendered the job to the private
sector, the contract being awarded to WeThink , the
online web services giant that had recently bought out
Facebook, Google and Microsoft. The idea of a
WeThink referendum provoked uproar in some activist
groups and radical media: How could such a process be
free, fair, and representative? And who owned
WeThink? Was it true that SLUZHBA had a 51%

interest in the company? Few knew that Reggie had engineered the establishment of a consortium of SLUZHBA, Sino-French and Caremundo to acquire the whole outfit.

As ever, the Prime Minister faced this reaction head-on. Citing Australia's 2017 postal survey on same-sex marriage, she argued that the old style of voting in a referendum was outdated. Australia was now a 'virtual' country that was compelled to pioneer new methods of gauging public opinion. And what was wrong with the private sector running the show? What could be simpler than opening a WeThink account and clicking Yes or No? Hadn't the Australian Electoral Office shown its ramshackle inefficiency time and time again with its paper and pencil stubs? Hadn't every US presidential election been a debacle of recounts, hardware failure, and court challenges?

But the road was not yet clear. Australian serial litigant and 'human rights' lawyer Billy Qaboos launched an action against Bubbles in the International Court of Justice in The Hague on behalf of those people who had chosen to stay in Patria Nullius. With his flowing mane of black hair and his flashing rhetoric, Qaboos was the poster boy for the discontented and ungrateful. His claim was that the Australian government had infringed the human rights of the Remainder population by blocking their internet access so that they could not open a WeThink account.

Billy's timing was exquisitely ill-timed: Parliament had just made it a criminal offence to publicly discuss any matter within the borders of Australia's former land mass. Faced with arrest, Qaboos fled to Russia.

The referendum romped home with 98% participation and a majority 'yes' on the Constitution

Alteration (Patria Nullius Inhabitants) Year 0001 Act, which 'excluded the remnant population in determinations of the population of Australia'. In practical terms, this meant that anyone still living in Patria Nullius was no longer recognised as a citizen of Australia.

But Barbara Macfarlane was faced with a moral deadlock. While UN Resolution 25/1 required Australia to make provisions for the remnant population, New Canberra was not obliged under the revised Australian Constitution to support non-citizens. How, the Attorney-General asked, would Spain feel about feeding the inhabitants of Chile? Or Germany the inhabitants of Burundi, Rwanda and Tanzania, the modern incarnations of its old colony Deutsch-Ostafrika?

After consulting with faith leaders and eminent philosophers, Bubbles took a proposal to Cabinet: The remnant population would be supported by a special *ex gratia* levy of 0.0001% on annual uranium sales, with services managed by the newly privatised Australian Border Security Inc.

Bubbles wasn't finished in her radical reshaping and downsizing of Australia. In an incisive stroke, the Cabinet introduced a Bill to disallow dual citizenship. Any Australian holding citizenship of another country had two choices: Renounce it within sixty days of the passing of the Bill, or hand over your Aussie passport.

The Dual Citizen (Disallowance) Bill passed into law in August 0001. Of the approximately sixteen million dual citizens outside Patria Nullius, less than a million Australian citizens remained after the sixty days deadline.

Australia emerged at the end of 0001 as a shining example of political creativity: A virtual country of less than a million citizens, custodian of the world's uranium wealth, and issuer of the New Australian Dollar, in which all uranium contracts were written. On New Year's Eve Year 1, one year after the Flood of Sydney, Barbara Macfarlane stood on a dais outside the Bodleian Library, and threw a switch that set off a firework display above the city of Oxford depicting an outline of Patria Nullius above the words SALVATOREM MUNDI - 'saviour of the world'.

PART THIRD - A BUSH JOURNEY

SUSAN TO ALEX, DECEMBER 0099

Dear Alex,

Tell me I'm not going mad. I'm rational, a scholar, a collector and weigher-upper of evidence. I keep wondering whether my writing is really being altered, or whether The Thing is causing hallucinations. I know I don't imagine things, but I need proof.

Here's what has happened: I did some editing of a chapter in my office, sent it to The Universe and went home. Next morning, I opened the document and re-read it. There were seven sentences missing. Just gone.

That can't happen. PC edits in real time, not hours afterwards. I'd locked it as alpha-one - nobody can breach my author privileges. I replaced the missing sentences as best I could remember them, alpha-oned-ed it and took the night off. Next morning the seven sentences were gone again, along with three or four more.

I stopped using my university office and worked in my apartment for a week. As I wrote a section of the History to The Universe, I stopped every ten minutes, memorised what I'd drafted, dashed off to the lavatory to type a copy on Mr Remington, then dashed back. Here's what I copied out one morning:

But now it was down to asylum seekers, loose-tongued ABS employees, and intrepid adventurers travelling in disguise to tell the world of the exotic economies of Patria Nullius. As with our knowledge of language

development, the subsequent understanding of
how the Remainders built their economies comes
from smuggled stories, stolen documents, and
oral histories.

And this is what The Universe said four
hours later:

But now it was down to specially trained
Australian Border Security Inc. operatives to
observe the new economies of Patria Nullius,
and to provide advice to New Canberra on the
best ways to support the populace in achieving
harmonious and rewarding lifestyles.

Hard evidence, I can hear you saying. Yes,
I still have the typewritten sheet. But things
get even stranger: I performed the typing
experiment a week later and NOTHING HAS BEEN
ALTERED SINCE. I've written things that could
be construed as treason, just to see whether
they will be changed. Reaction — zero.

Although they haven't messed with my text
again, I'm still working in the apartment and
stopping to make my clackety copies every ten
minutes. My work analytics are looking very
suspicious: My baseline data has me working in
45-minute stints on average, with the breaks
getting longer towards the end of the day —
pretty close to the norm for my scholar grade.
But how to explain the toilet breaks? So I've
cooked up a cover story about my bowels, and
started eating large amounts of pumpkin so
that I have to visit the bathroom with
abnormal frequency. I visited my doctor as

insurance. He pestered me about investigating The Thing as usual, but he did record loose motions on my Universe health record, so presumably my prodigious poops are now catalogued on my PIP.

But perhaps I'm getting paranoid in my friendless isolation. I don't even have my students to cheer me up because all my classes were taken away this session. I do miss the students: The young ones, all hope and sparkle; the older ones who've given up on their improbable career plans (they mostly want to be film actors in America) and are slipping into happy indolence; the faithful retainers coming to the end of long lives of leisurely study untroubled by the results of examinations and essays.

It was my fault entirely that I was banned from teaching: My experiment with randomly assigned marks backfired, as I knew it would. A week after I uploaded the grades, I walked into the auditorium to give the Monday lecture. Glum faces all around. Right at the front sits Dame Linda Macfarlane-Turnbull wearing a dinner-plate-sized disc on her chest bearing a stylised sad face (remember emojis?). She's very influential, being a member of HRH's inner circle, always boasting about her trips to America to see the shows. I gird myself, say good morning, start lecturing. The Dame gets up and walks out. The other students follow. I continue lecturing to an empty room for thirty minutes.

Next day I find I've apparently ignored all the reminders to update my Good Character

Certification. Untrue in fact; I always renew it, but the record has mysteriously transmogrified. Banished from teaching for six months. The Universe hath spoken. I haven't talked to a soul for a month other than the doctor and the Boy Banker.

It's Christmas Day here. There are people outside wandering around in medieval mode and Santa hats. Two boys in doublet and hose are fencing in the snow, while a squad of princesses sing madrigals, making clouds of voice vapour in the dead cold air.

It's a day that stirs memories of my childhood in Kuranda (although the weather was somewhat different!). Father helped dress the Blessed Prospect church with the cool leaves of fan palms and knots of crimson bottlebrush. I wove little crosses from dried grass. Tiny children swayed and sang along with hymns and guitars and tambourines. Pigs roasted on spits outside.

Jude and I had three Christmases together in Kuranda, but there were no hymns for us.

Oh, by the way: Blessed Prospect church. You'll never work it out: It was built around an abandoned BP service station.

I almost forgot to tell you something about the Creole they spoke in Orange (and which I acquired as my second language up to the age of five). It's explained in detail in the History, but I'll give you the potted version: There was a big refugee camp outside Orange - mostly climate change refugees from the Pacific Islands and Vietnam. The pre-flood Australian Government stuck them there for lack of any other ideas. There were about two thousand souls on basic rations behind barbed wire. But after the Grand Bargain, the guards' pay dried up and they cleared out. The refugees tore down the wire and headed for the town, where they moved into abandoned houses. You see, Orange used to have a population of about forty thousand, but the collapse of farming from droughts and floods had forced most people out. There was no shortage of real estate to share with the few original Orange residents left. Within a few years, bands of kids roamed the town with every kind of mixed parentage you can count. Their parents had developed a Pidgin - that's a simple language that develops where people from different backgrounds are forced to co-exist. It drew on the languages at hand - in this case, English, Fijian, Tongan, Hindi, and Vietnamese (and probably others). What the linguists teach us is that when a community of Pidgin speakers bear children, the next generation develop a fully functioning version as their first language - and that's a Creole. They didn't have a name for this language, although Jude sometimes referred to it as 'lingo miyanyu'. They did have a word for English - oldtalk, which survived among some women as a kind of private code.

Here endeth the linguistics lecture! It's only ten in the morning, and I'm popping out for my fourth cigarette; perhaps I'll run into the Boy Banker and have a nice chat. But there's an upside to solitude - more time to

write The True History of Jude, an episode of
which follows.

Best, Sue

Stuart Campbell

JUDE SEES THE OCEAN FOR THE FIRST TIME

I sped along the bush track on the back of the motorbike with my arms around the trader's waist. The woman sat in the sidecar with Arabella's timbox between her feet. The bike hammered along the tracks for hours, sometimes picking up a proper road for a while, but always returning to the cover of trees. When the sun was at its highest, the trader took a road that wound upwards. The trees became sparser, the landscape greyer, the sun hotter. My greedy eyes ate up the new sights. But the hot rushing air and the throb of the bike clouded my mind and I started to lose my grip on the trader's waist. I slipped sideways, but the woman grabbed me from the sidecar. "The little fellah's pooped," she shouted.

We stopped at the crest and sheltered under the brim of a hollowed-out rock. The woman stayed with the bike while the trader took my arm. We climbed on the rock. He swept his arm sideways and said in oldtalk, "My country, all around. Not them buggers." He must have meant the uniforms.

We stood on top of the world. Behind us were endless low mountains of woolly green-grey. Before us, an emerald plain swept down to a line of blue that went on forever. The trader pointed to a thin grey thread stretching from the blue to the woolly hills. At its closest, it revealed high fences, and then I saw a tiny truck speeding along the line, just like the ones that brought the food to Orange. "Not their country, not them buggers," he said.

The woman brought us each a wedge of hard bread with meat on top. The trader spent a long time scanning the land all around, chewing his food. I copied him, chewing in silence with my eyes slitted. It would be better to try to look like someone who knew this country, even though my eyes goggled at each new thing. At last he seemed satisfied. He leaned sideways and made a large fart. I copied him but delivered only a squeak. "C'mon,mate," he said, and we were on our way again.

Now we took a long route over high country where the trees were sparse. The tracks appeared and disappeared. Sometimes we rode on smooth ground and other times bumped slowly over rock-strewn paddocks. I thought about that line of blue I saw earlier. Could it be the sea?

The sidecar suddenly bucked upwards. It came apart from the motorbike with a crack. The woman hurtled on one wheel into a dry creek. We flew past, the engine screaming, the man fighting the handlebars. We stopped, got off and rushed back to the ditch. The woman was bloody but upright, the <u>timbox</u> under her arm. The couple immediately dragged the sidecar from the ditch and stood it next to the bike. They found a length of stiff wire in the sidecar and bound the broken bracket.

"Got the 'undred mile an hour tape?" the man called out. The woman dug around and found a roll of silver tape. The man unwound the whole roll around the sidecar and the motorbike's petrol tank. When he got on to ride, he had to wriggle his foot among the strands of tape. The engine revved. I climbed on. The woman stepped into the sidecar and made a thumbs-up. We were off again.

As dusk fell, we pulled up at a timber hut hidden among trees. Our sweaty skins were gritty with dust and we had dead insects in our hair. We got off the bike and stretched. Inside the hut was a stash of plastic water bottles and canned food.

The woman prepared a meal while the man started digging a hole about twenty manlengths from the hut. "Come here and help," he said. His spade clanged on something, and I helped him pull a jerry can from the earth.

"Gas." He filled the bike's tank and put the half-emptied jerry can in the sidecar. "That'll get us to the sea."

The sea! I knew it! I'd seen it a film they showed once in Orange. I even made up a story about it, where Jesus and Thomas Hardy walked on it.

As we sat down to eat, the woman talked about the Lord and thanks mate, and the trader flicked lines on his chest with his hand. We ate the meal: Canned fish. Canned corn. Canned fruit in a rusty bent tin with SPC written on the label. Some days the uniforms gave us canned food at Orange. Lucky days.

Afterwards, the trader told me and the woman to bed down on the floor of the hut. He sat outside on watch with a rifle across his knees. I dropped off to sleep tasting sweet bubbles of canned food coming up from my zazzy. Sometime in the night, the woman took over the watch, and the man lay next to me in the hut. He breathed loudly and said, "Jesus save my wretched poor bugger soul," and then started snoring.

I woke up to clattering on the roof, shivering. It was still dark, and raining heavily. The woman scurried inside the hut, and we closed the door to shut out the brown splashes. The noise on the roof made it hard to sleep. The man took a lighter from his pocket and poured liquid into a can that had a lid with holes. He clicked the lighter and blue flames leapt from the can. He made tea in another can on top of the flames. We never did that in Orange, but I hid my surprise.

"What's your name?" I asked him in oldtalk.

"Nunya bisnis." I'd heard that expression before, and it obviously didn't mean a town beyond Orange. He drank his tea, lay down and dozed until the woman said, "Sun's up".

We opened the door. Outside it was thickly quiet, with a layer of mist on the ground. Hundreds of dumb-faced kangaroos nibbled the wet ground cover. The grey bush had become trembling green.

The man slowly raised the rifle. He moved it left and right, up and down, then stopped. Shot. The crack of the gun in the silent morning sent the kangaroos skipping, except for a small one that lay on its side kicking one leg until it was still. The trader and his woman skinned and butchered the animal on the spot in a chaos of blood and tendon. They bundled the meat into a plastic sack and threw it in the trailer.

We were back on the road before the sun started to burn through the mist hanging in the hollows. The motorbike engine thump-thumped and the trees streaked by. I began to feel something new in my heart or head or somewhere: I couldn't find an exact word, but it might have been like growing up. I remembered the Jude in the book who wanted to <u>prevent himself growing up</u> when he was a boy.

Late that day I saw flashes of blue between the hills, and then we swept down a track and burst into a riot of rock and sand and blue water and white foam.

The sea was a thousand times more beautiful than in that fuzzy old movie. It had depth, weight, force. The waves flopped and slapped. There was a metallic crackling smell that was new to me. There were the noises of crashing and hissing, white noises. White surf. White spray.

I stripped off and ran to the water, but I fell through it instead of walking on it. The salt taste was a shock. A wave tossed me like a leaf, dragged me along the bottom. My nose and eyes stung. The trader and his woman laughed at me from the shore. They dived in and swam strongly out beyond the beach. I watched carefully as a line of water slowly rose, growing a frothy white head which crashed down, just as a new wave formed beyond. The trader and his woman glided in like fish, then swam out and glided in again. I lay on a flat rock and gazed into a tiny pool like an inside-out world of wriggling creatures and swaying plants. I thought of God looking down at me.

That night we made a fire on the beach and roasted the meat. In two days, I'd travelled further than ever before. I had so many feelings about my life that I tried to put into words inside my head. One feeling was to do with the oldtalk word - future. In Orange, nobody talked about future because yesterday was always the same as today and tomorrow. I was different - that I know - because I had a plan to go north, so I suppose I had a future. But my plan used to be more like a dream. Now it was real.

We rode for many weeks, never far from the sea. Sometimes we went around the outskirts of a big falling-down town where whole empty streets were washed by the tides. Almost every day we had to find gas, sometimes in places the trader had buried a can; and sometimes we would buy a can or bottle of the stuff from villages we passed through. We spent one whole day in a paddock full of rusted-out cars and motor bikes, searching for a new back tire to replace the old one, which was about to fall apart in shreds.

We took the road to the coast to visit a deserted town where the trader stopped to look for gas. Ross pointed to a collapsed wooden building with Yamba Bait and Angling Supplies painted on the roof.

"We'll hide the bike in there." The tide was out, and we walked down to some little sheds, half-buried in seashore mud and rubbish. He bashed down the door of one after another until he found a little boat.

"Outboard," he said, pointing at the metal thing at the back. "Runs on gas," he said. He unscrewed something and sniffed. "Hold this." I grabbed the bottle. He stuck a tube in the hole and sucked. A dribble of dark brown liquid made a finger thickness in the bottom of the bottle. The trader poured it on the ground and said, "Useless," which meant bigfuckup. But the next hut had another boat, and this time the tank gave up a bottle of clear liquid.

"Me name's Ross," he said out of nowhere. "She's Vera."

Ross and Vera stopped at settlements on higher ground where they bought and sold weed, meat, bottled water, aspirins. At one place, a fellow repaired the sidecar properly with a tool that joined the broken metal together with sparks. Welding - a new word that wasn't in Jude's book. Beyond the repairer's shack was a yard behind a high fence, full of old motorbikes, some whole and some pulled apart. Once our bike was reattached to the sidecar, the fellow beckoned us into the yard. Ross picked up bits of motorbike, weighing them in his hands and squinting into pipes and brackets.

"Gimme that carby and those there cables," he said to the man. Vera counted out some bucks.

There were Aboriginal people at some of the settlements, and other people with yellow hair and long noses. A few people had eyes like

mine. The settlements had shacks made of wood
or plastic sheets and cloths, and sometimes a
little street with a Post Office or a bar (I'd
seen a bar in a movie, but the ones in these
settlements had no beer or drinkers).

Weeks later we were at a settlement in the
hills overlooking a big empty town. There was
a market in front of a hut with a sign saying
PEOPLES REPUBLIC OF ROCKHAMPTON. Ross said,
"Stay here. I've got to get some ammo," and
strode off towards a brick building where a
man was bashing a metal bar with a hammer.
'Blacksmith' it said on a sign above the door,
and I remembered the blacksmith in my book who
had a proper good notion. The man stopped his
work to talk to Ross, perhaps about a notion.

I lay down under a tree while Vera bargained
over some pieces of leather, and closed my
eyes to rest in the balmy afternoon. But I was
awoken when a young woman spoke to me in my
own Orange language. I looked up, rubbed my
eyes. She was like me: Brown-skinned with
black hair and long eyes. I recognised her as
Fanny, the daughter of a woman called Becky.
She disappeared from Orange a long time ago.
Fanny was taller now.

"You're Jude the storyteller. What are you
doing here?"

"I'm going North to find Sue Bridehead."

"You used to talk about her in your stories.
Is she real?"

"Of course she's real. Why are you here,
Fanny?"

"I'm with my hubby," she said, pointing to a big blond fellow who was hammering wooden planks on the side of the hut.

"How did you get here, Fanny?"

"Earl - my hubby - stole me."

"How can a hubby steal a woman?" I asked. But I knew it was a foolish question. In this wide world, anything was possible. I'd learned that in the last weeks. Fanny just laughed at my question.

"What's Peoples Republic of Rockhampton?" I ask her.

"It's where we can be free, where the uniforms can't touch us. Earl's the president." This was all too confusing. I said goodbye to Fanny and promised myself to ask Ross about it.

***

Ross and Vera loaded the trailer with different goods each place they stopped. The contents always changed: In the morning it might be empty bottles and bags of pumpkin; by afternoon we had bamboo poles, lighters and jerky. Everywhere we stopped, they spoke in English, and I was getting better at it. Sometimes there was a gathering where people prayed and read from the New Testament. I was thrilled when I recognised the stories, but nobody ever mentioned the prophet Thomas Hardy. At one place they all sang about Christian Soldiers and arrows of desire. It was a stirring song. I wrote down the words:

"Onward Christian soldiers
Marching as to war
With the cross of Jesus going on before.
Crowns and thorns may perish
Kingdoms rise and wane.
But the cross of Jesus
Constant will remain."

We rode on and on, settlement after settlement, me singing Onward Christian Soldiers into the hot wind. When we woke up one morning, Ross told me we were going to meet some people who I mustn't talk to. "Just shuddup," he said. This time, the motor bike took us along miles of dead straight dusty track, following a high wire fence that stretched into the haze ahead. Vera kept lookout, raising the alarm when she spotted a truck in the distance. We slewed sideways into the bush to hide while it passed. AUSTRALIAN BORDER SECURITY INC, it said on the side. We took a detour inland for <u>nowrotu</u>, stopping at a tiny hamlet in a patch of forest around a dam. A thin white man was the leader of this hamlet, with his black wife and a dozen brown children. He spoke a strange gabble with his family. His <u>oldtalk</u> was hesitant, but enough to strike a bargain: He handed over a cake of brown stuff for a wad of roubles and ten little paper boxes with TYLENOL written on them.

"Who was that?" I asked Ross as we left.
"Frenchie," was all he said.
"What did he give you?"
"Nunya bisnis."

We rode back to the fenced road and pounded forward until Vera yelled, "Stop". She'd seen something in the haze. Ross steered off into a patch of bush. We approached on foot under cover of trees. Two uniforms stood next to their stationary truck behind the fence, pretending to piss. Ross looked at the sky. He nodded, trotted to the fence and passed half of the brown cake through the wire. One of the uniforms took the cake while the other poked a sock through the wire to Ross. It was stuffed with something. Within seconds, we were barrelling inland and the truck was out of sight. Later I asked Ross what had gone on, but he ignored me.

***

One afternoon we drove uphill for a long time. It was warm here, like everywhere, but there was a different smell to the air - heavy and sweet, full of invisible life. The motorbike chugged and smoked when we pulled up in a pretty village where every house nestled in thick greenery, nothing like dusty Orange. Chickens scattered at the sound of the bike.

"Off yer get."

I got off and the bike clattered back down the hill. A sign by the side of the road read: KURANDA. The bike stopped and I saw Ross and Vera talking in raised voices. The bike turned around and chugged back to me. Vera took Arabella's timbox from the sidecar and opened it. She handed half the bucks to me and said,

"Gob bless, yer dumb bugger". And they were gone.

(Alex, this is me now, my young essence glimpsed at last):
I brought my old man husband his breakfast. His tea. His egg. His papaya and finger lime. His bread.

"God bless you, Sue my child," he said, and continued to write the morning's school lesson.

"God bless you, husband, I said."

I loathed his scrapy caresses last night on my young skin. His old hands, his grey-fringed prong, his trickling effluence, his mumbly thanks to God as we lay side by side afterwards. His unsaid prayer that he might have planted his seed.

There was a commotion in the road outside. Some unruly school children were following a stranger and laughing. I went outside and shouted at them, "My husband will hear of this," and they ran away. The stranger turned to me and said something in a language I used to know, but couldn't grasp the meaning of. For a moment I thought I'd glimpsed my own image, but he was quite different from me: Brown as a bunya nut with long eyes like the prows of two swift boats. Slight of build with a thin pointed beard. I felt dizzy. I blushed and went inside. My husband patted my head and said, "I'll come home for lunch. Will there be meat?"

I threw myself on the bed, listening to my husband's shoes march down the gravel road.

The palm trees swayed and whooshed. The breeze filled the curtains with warm green air. Birds whistled and squawked. I lowered the bamboo blind. The familiar stranger filled my hot thoughts. My hand slid down my belly and I betrayed my husband in the heat of the morning.

The True History of Jude

Dear Alex,

He managed to impregnate me once, old Phillotson as Jude called him, but the tiny scrap of foetus expelled itself on a quiet afternoon of pain and blood and humid heat. He came home from school with his books and his brown shoes shined up with emu fat. Witch, he called me. Did you call up Satan to do this thing and to wound our brothers and sisters? But his heart wasn't in his words. I felt a sliver of pity at the defeat in his eyes. He sat on the couch and sighed. I went to the kitchen, woozy and feeling precarious in my belly, and threw some sticks on the stove to make him tea.

Minus fifteen Celsius outside today in wintry Oxford. I haven't been out for a month. The hanging garden outside my window, enveloped in its own nuclear-powered microclimate, produces an endless harvest of tomatoes and beans and aubergines. The pipes that bathe them with warm air and misted nutrients bear the name SLUZHBA in tiny letters below the 'teardrop in a heart' logo. There's a building near here draped in flowering plants that supply nectar to beehives nestled among the foliage. I swear the poor little things buzz around with SLUZHBA stencilled on their backsides. Remind me to check my own derriere.

You don't see the old SLUZHBA logo much these days. When I was researching Barbara 'Bubbles' Macfarlane, AKA The Mother of

Australia, I discovered that she had come up with the 'teardrop in a heart' design as a symbol of the Grand Bargain, i.e. giving away Australia (tears, weeping, etc,) was an act of love for the world (hearts, hugs, etc.). Pop a teardrop inside a heart, and you've got the entire philosophy of world domination in a logo. Barbara wore a baseball cap with the design at the UN Conference when they proclaimed the Pyongyang Doctrine. Trouble is (and you can try this for yourself), the logo looked like a vulva. They quietly phased it out, but you can still find the odd example on a wall transfixed with a graffitied penis.

Just recently people in the block have been avoiding me, the dotty one who quietly upsets the order of things. Nobody knocks on the door to suggest a cheery cup. I heard noises in the corridor last week and popped my head out. My sociologist neighbour Oscar was chatting to a university maintenance worker. Oscar ignored me. Just acted as if I wasn't there. Dangerous to know, that's me, the quaint old nutcase employed to relieve the students' boredom by making them 'study' amusing tidbits. Oscar has been wearing a superior expression for some time, in fact. He's leaving the university later in the year to take up a job at the SLUZHBA Polytechnicum, where they produce the educhunks used to train the professional people who run the Kingdom - doctors, engineers and the like.

I wasn't always desperate and cynical like this, although you've surely seen the change since the years when we used to correspond with such verve and passion. I hadn't realised until I started writing the True History of Jude how those Kuranda years rotted my foundations like a nest of termites. The last two decades have been an exercise in pretending that the house isn't collapsing.

Enough of my moaning. Think of my letters to you as old-style talking therapy. I write, you read, sometimes you write back, I write, you read, insights come (that's the positive version). Or despite the writing, I'm the same self-absorbed sack of unhappiness (negative version).

But here's a surprise for you. I'm going to tell you a little about my early life in Patria Nullius before I hand over to Jude.

I was born in 0020 - two decades after the Grand Bargain. My grandmother told me that she watched their house near Manly Beach slide into the sea the year Barbara Macfarlane rented out our country. The house was mortgaged and uninsurable, and my grandparents hadn't the means or foreign passport to leave Australia. So they moved inland to the Blue Mountains, (think escaping from San Francisco to Lake Tahoe). One of my uncles had a house there, which he had gifted to my grandmother just before he left for the US. This was in the last days of the land title system, and Grandma had a paper printout from the New South Wales Land Registry to show that she owned the place. My grandparents turned up in the mountain village of Leura to find the house occupied. Australian Border Security Inc hadn't brought that part of the country under its control, and the place was lawless. The occupiers laughed at Grandma's paper, but Grandpa kicked them out, beating up a man called Big Eric in a fist fight in the middle of the road. This punch-up became part of local lore. From then on, I was known as the girl whose Grandpa had won the Battle of Blue Parrot Lane.

Leura was located on a ridge a thousand metres above sea level. There was one road in and one road out. Grandpa and Big Eric (they had soon become firm friends) put together a local militia, and when the ABSI truck convoy rolled up the mountain road late in 0030, Grandpa's Leura Freedom Command had already blown a trench across the Great Western Highway. They built a berm from which a roster of trained fighters shot down the ABSI drones sent to spy on the town defences.

A vast bushfire jumped back and forth across the highway in the summer of 0001. ABSI retreated to a town called Springwood, thirty kilometres down the ridge, and never returned to Leura.

Mother — her name was Rosa - married Frank Jones in 0020, and I was born in the house on Lurline Street the same year. Grandpa and Grandma had died from a virus by then, and my mother passed away when I was a year old.

By my fathers' account, Leura was a thriving town for a few years after the Grand Bargain. It was run by the LFC, who carried on a tradition of quirky autonomy these high mountain towns had built long before the Grand

Bargain. People used to visit the area from Sydney for its arts festivals and music, and its ban on junk food and tacky souvenir shops.

The LFC tried and failed to find an economic role for the town. The leaders spun hopes of a brave utopian project: A communally owned sawmill, bakery, and chicken farm, each of which began and fizzled; a social wage paid in food rations that collapsed when the LFC leaders began to hand out tokens because the stock of actual food was exhausted; barter deals with the small farms on the inland plain. But in the end, Leura produced nothing and there was nothing to barter with. The last, sad effort was to send a troupe of actors - Mother played Ariel - on a tour of the inland hamlets. They would be paid in farm produce for performing The Tempest, but they returned with just the bits of their costumes they couldn't sell.

Like many such places, Leura and its surrounds faltered as infectious diseases whittled away the population and the barter system failed to sustain farmers through drought and drenching. Stockpiled fertiliser and diesel ran out, and the farms were reduced to scrub and ruts. Getting fresh water was an endless toil.

As for my father, he traded in second-hand goods, and ran a church with a side business in undertaking. He kept a horse called Rainy Day in a paddock behind the junk yard. Every week somebody offered to buy it, but Father refused to sell. Within a few years, people had nothing to barter for the old clocks and used gumboots in the junk yard. People stopped coming to the church because they had nothing to praise the Lord for. They buried their own dead.

Around my fourth birthday, I became ill, unable to walk properly. I have a faint memory of long weeks resting in bed while my feeble legs regained their strength. I now know that I survived polio.

When I was better, Father swapped Rainy Day for a drum of petrol and an old car. He packed a few goods and drove us to Orange, where Father's cousin Vicky lived.

Alex. I just reread this little potted tale of myself. You're asking 'why doesn't she tell of her feelings, then and now?' Well, you shall hear of them.

Best, Sue

JUDE'S FIRST DAY IN KURANDA

The children heeded the girl in the house and ran ahead of me. They were carrying books. Books!

I called out to the girl in our lingo, "It is me Jude brought to you by Ross and Vera".

I had no doubt it was Sue Bridehead, although I never saw her in Orange because she left just when I was born. She had gone inside the house. Her presence nearby stunned me. I didn't know what to do or where to go. My legs carried me along the street as if they had brains in their kneecaps. A man approached me and asked me something in oldtalk. He wore a beard, cut square like a spade. I stumbled on. There was singing. I saw a building with an open door. It had a sign saying BP CHURCH but I didn't know what BP meant. Inside, a group of men with the same square beards stood, each holding a book, and singing. They swivelled their heads towards me and smiled at me all at once. I recoiled, clutched my bag containing my bucks and my book copy, and left, walking along the green-canopied street until I found an open area with tents and shade cloths. People mingled around tables bearing fruits, clothes, cakes, tools. There were bucks in their hands. Horses were tied up in a field nearby, next to carts. It was a market, perhaps like the one by the Duke's Arms in Christminster. A table bore a spread of golden-brown pies. I took one, but the woman by the table said you have to pay and it is five hundred. I took out the packet of bucks that the traders gave me and showed it to her. She plucked one note and I ate the pie. A voice boomed behind me, a man's voice.

"That's a lot of roubles. You should be careful. Keep it hidden."

"Thank you, Sire."

"You aren't from here, are you?"

"I am from far away."

The man had a spade beard and noble eyes.

"Have you a bed for tonight?"

"No, my Lordship."

"I am no Lord, just a man among men. Follow me. No, not under that tree."

"Why not?"

"There is a snake in it."

He took me to a house with a sign that says LOD INGS. A woman with skin and eyes like mine asked me to write my name in a book. JUDE, I wrote. "Surname?" she asked. I remember name and surname of the parties when Jude - the Jude in the book - married Sue - the Sue in the book. I wrote FAWLEY. JUDE FAWLEY was me. The man helped me pay the woman, and the woman gave me a key.

"Is it for a box?" I asked. I remember that in the book Jude's son arrived on the train with a key to his box around his neck.

She laughed: "A box? A box? I'll give you a box!" I waited for her to give me a box, but instead she took me inside and opened a door with the key.

I lay on the bed and fell to sleep and dreamt that I was entering the kingdom of heaven hand in hand with Sue Bridehead. Then Arabella plucked a snake from a tree and its fangs pierced my calf. Now the gates of heaven drew farther away and I wept. Sue got smaller and entered heaven through an arc of golden light, and then the sun was shining hard in my eyes through the window.

It was late afternoon.

The man said keep my <u>bucks</u> hidden. I went out of the room and looked for the woman with skin and eyes like mine.

"Will you hide my <u>bucks</u>?" I held out the bundle.

"We call them roubles here, not bucks." She wrapped the notes in a cloth, put them in a big <u>timbox</u> and locked it with a key on a string between her <u>huhus</u>.

"You're not from here," she said. "You speak English pretty weird."

"No, I'm from Orange. A long way", I replied, pointing in the direction I'd come from.

"Orange, you say? What's it like there?"

I didn't know what to tell her. Orange was just Orange. It was my place, but I didn't have an opinion about it because I'd hardly thought about it these last weeks. But the woman's question made me tremble with a feeling I didn't recognise. It had to do with tomorrow. Tomorrow was now. I was in it, and there would be a different tomorrow when tomorrow came. My head swam and I grasped the table the woman was sitting at.

"Are you feeling unwell? I'll get you some water."

"I want to go out." It was dusk in the street. People were moving around with great purpose in the dusk light, the colour of tinned peaches. Suddenly, great lamps strung in the trees bathed the street with a different glow - soft, like canned milk.

The market was busy with spadebeards and women in very short skirts and tight blouses that showed their huhus. The women nearly all had blonde hair. Children played under the huge trees draped in living curtains of mossy green.

I entered a house with BAR written above the door. Spadebeards ate noisily at benches. When women brought food and beer to the tables, the spadebeards slapped the women's rumps or squeezed their huhus, and the women laughed.

Some men beckoned me to sit with them. They squeezed up to make a space, and a woman put a plate of meat in front of me. The room went quiet and all the company watched me. The woman leaned closer. It was silent in the BAR. I slapped her rump and squeezed her huhus and everybody laughed.

My heart told me this was wrong. In Orange, a woman might squeeze a man's choni in the evening when they watched the movies, but in what kind of world did a man do this to a woman? I pretended to laugh with them.

The man who invited me said, "Welcome, friend".

I asked, "Why do the women offer their bodies?"

"Because a woman's body is a temple that all may worship of course."

"And why do all the men have straight beards?"

"To show that men live the Straight Way," he answered.

"Don't women live the Straight Way?"

"Once they did, but they fell."

"Fell where?"

"Into the temple, where all could worship them."

It made no sense, so I stopped asking and finished my food. It tasted like wallaby. The beer was thick and savoury with stuff that coated my tongue deliciously. The BAR was a fine place. A woman leaned forward to take my plate away. Everybody was merry.

Her huhus were near my face. I knew what to do. I slapped her rump.

She froze. All the company froze. Two spadebeards hoisted me off the bench. The woman wept. A low moan rose from the men. I was airborne for a moment and then crashed onto the road.

Something in my back was broken. A stab pierced me from thigh to knee when I tried to stand. Tears sprang from my eyes. A hand supported my elbow. It was the woman with skin and eyes like mine.

"I followed you. You don't know these people. They have rules. I will look after you," she said.

She helped me back to the LOD INGS. She wasn't dressed like the other women: T-shirt and a loose skirt.

"Why did they beat me?"

"They always beat a stranger who doesn't know their ways."

"Were you once a stranger here?"

"Yes, but I don't live their way."

"Are there others who don't live their way?"

"There are some, one in particular," she said.

The woman gave me a white pill. Sometimes the uniforms in Orange gave us pills if you told them you were hurt. Pain grasped the inner strings of my thigh, but I found a comfortable position on the bed. My head was muzzy, the night air caressed, Sue came back to me from the shining gates of heaven, and then black ...

***

Six days in the LOD INGS and there was no sign of Sue Bridehead. The house where I saw her was closed up whenever I passed, except that one day an old spadebeard came out with books under his arm. Who could he be? Her father? Or perhaps the Mr Phillotson in Jude's book? My leg still throbbed when I walked, and I could not risk another beating until I understood this strange place better.

The LOD INGS woman unlocked her timbox each day, took a note from my stash to pay for my room and gave me other notes to spend. Spending made my head ache. There wasn't much use for counting in Orange. I knew about the five loaves and two fishes to feed five thousand, and I knew what ten or a hundred armlengths looked like.

The writing on these bucks - or roubles - wasn't exactly English although the A and E and H and C and O and P were the same. I

studied the notes, counting the noughts until
I matched them with English words I knew: One
thousand, five thousand, ten thousand, fifty
thousand. In the market, a cup of beer was one
thousand. Five bananas cost one thousand. A
shirt was fifty thousand. A painting of a
woman's huhus cost ten thousand.

When I asked the woman if I could take my
roubles in my room, she replied, "Yes but give
it back to me when you go out".

It took me a long time to count my stash,
laid out on the bed. It came to 170 shirts,
42,500 bananas, 8,500 beers, or 850 paintings
of a woman's huhus. When I'd finished, the
woman locked it in the timbox. When she gave
it back to me the next day it came to 8,200
beers, so LOD INGS cost 3000 each day.

One morning I woke thinking about when Jude
- the Jude in the book - paid for LODGINGS,
the rent representing a higher percentage on
his wages than mechanics of any sort usually
care to pay. Now I knew what kind of place
this was.

"Can you work?" the woman in the LODGINGS
asked. "You need to earn money for the rent.
Your roubles won't last for ever."

"I have a nobby."

"All men have a nobby. I doubt any woman
here will pay for yours. You are so small."

I blushed. She was making a dirty smile,
like some of the women in Orange did.

"That's not what I mean. I am a
storyteller."

"What sort of stories do you tell?"

"Stories about Jesus on the cross and about Sue Bridehead going to Bethlehem to have a baby."

She gave me a sharp look, but I didn't know why, or if I should ask her why.

I had an idea. I would go to the market, gather an audience and tell a story.

"Do you have a box?" I asked her.

The woman took me to the back of the LODGINGS and pointed at three or four wooden boxes.

I walked to the market and stood on my box. There were just a few stalls open, and a few customers walking around. All the better to try out my nobby.

"Hear my story, people. Hear my story. Once there was a man called Jesus who walked on the sea, and ..."

Everyone scurried out of the market place.

"Hear my story. Jesus went into the hills where the kangaroos jump around ..."

Three spadebeards rushed into the market place. They hoisted me up and bore me down the street like a sack. We came to a muddy lane where a horrible stench filled the air. A sign read 'public latrine'. The men tossed me into a longdrop trench. I gagged and spluttered, struggling to find a footing in the slime.

"It is not seemly to tell stories," one of the spadebeards said in a slow and solemn voice, and they all marched away.

A gaggle of small children followed me back to the LODGINGS, shouting, "Shitty stranger. Get out of our town". Women stared and tutted, "Not seemly".

The woman at the LODGINGS gave me directions to a creek where I could wash off the spadebeard shit. "You're not using my tub smelling like that," she said.

When I came back she sprayed me with perfume and gave me a cup of tea.

"I heard what happened. You need to find another kind of work."

"Is there a stonemason here?" I asked.

"Now that's a funny question," she said. "There is a man - I'm not sure you'd call him a stonemason - but he sometimes makes figures from wood and stone. Is that the work that you do?"

I tell her, "It's my destiny. Jude in the book was a stonemason".

She gave me another sharp look, and told me that the stonemason lived at Kuranda Railway Station.

A railway station! Only unhappiness comes from such places: It was at a railway station that Arabella - the Arabella in the book - told Jude that she was going to marry the bar gentleman.

I went out and walked around the streets and lanes, but there was one question that flooded my mind. The woman in the LODGINGS would know the answer. She was surprised when I returned so soon.

"Did you find your stonemason?"

"Not yet. I want to find another person."

"You mean Sue?" she asked.

"Yes, Sue Bridehead."

"I never heard the name Bridehead."

"That is her name, Sue Bridehead."

"Well, you can call her that if you want. But be careful - she is married."

I thought hard.

"Is she married to an old school teacher called Phillotson?"

"She is married to a school teacher, yes. But what are these strange names?"

"They are their true names."

The prophecy was true. She was married. A black rain fell over my heart.

SUSAN TO ALEX, FEBRUARY 0100

Dear Alex,
I woke early this morning to a pebble on my window, and the boy banker looking up from the street. Down the fire stair I dashed, and handed him 20,000 roubles for postage. "It's gone up to 40,000," he said. "Take thirty or I'll tell your dad you're cheating me," I replied, and he handed over a letter. I stood in the dawn snow and opened the envelope to see that you had written at last, not checking if I was in view of a camera. The little tyke snatched the letter back and said, "Who's my dad, then?" He'd got me there, so I handed over the extra 10,000. Not that the price rise came as a surprise; there's been a wave of inflation pushing through the black economy for the last two years. Everything's gone up - writing paper, samizdat, cigarettes, entry visas for Scotland, whackopowder (or some of my more drugged-up students have told me). There was an article in BOLLOCKS TO SLUZHBA last year explaining that among the criminals who control the system, the Keynesians are in the ascendancy right now. They're raising credit limits and releasing new notes from an illegal mint in Armenia, which has defied all efforts at international regulation. The kid in the street could probably get his dad to arrange a rouble loan in twenty minutes if someone needed some fast cash. There's also a rumour going around that the 10,000 rouble notes overprinted in Spanish aren't (il)legal tender anymore, which is a pest because you

can hardly find a tenner nowadays that doesn't have PROHIBIDO stamped on it.

But while I had the lad there, I thought I'd take a sounding on a so-called visa. "I've got a friend who's thinking of making a trip - you know - outside. Perhaps your dad knows someone my friend can talk to?"

"Wossit got to do with my dad?" he replied, evidently stung at my underestimation of his professional status.

"Well, whoever - you perhaps."

The boy scratched his armpit, put on a distant stare, rocked slightly on his heels.

"I might know a certain party if Scotland's your goal."

"Good. Will you get back to me?"

"There's a consideration."

"Consideration?" Then I remembered it as an old term to do with contracts. A deposit.

"How much?"

"Eighty thousand and you've got my interest."

"You're a cheeky one," I said. The words floated into my mind like ancient ghosts. I remembered Jude asking me what cheeky meant a lifetime and a world away. I moved to hug the grubby boy - I don't know why - but he stepped back and made paddle hands. "Whoa, missus."

"I'm sorry."

"S'alright." He wiped his nose on his sleeve.

"I'll give you the eighty tomorrow," I said, and he scuttled away.

Before I forget, you asked in one of your replies whether my PIP reveals my location to The Universe. I believe the answer is no; the population is mostly too compliant to justify the expense of geolocating everyone.

I must say that your reply to my last letter puzzled me. Stumped me, actually. You seemed excessively interested in my little masturbation episode at Kuranda, but dismissive of the fact that The Universe rewrites my work every night. Are you off your medication? Oh dear, that sounds quite rude. Excuse me if I seem peeved. I'm so isolated here, and I really am thrilled whenever you write.

I made a note that you asked me where I get my roubles from. Since I'm rather getting used to confessing secrets, sit tight while I tell you another. You know of course that the Kingdom of England and Wales would collapse into anarchy without the rouble economy to keep people in luxury goods and illegal services. So here's the shameful bombshell: I work on the quiet as a 'journalist' for the Royal Australian News. My by-line, which I seem to share with a number of others, is Louisa Macfarlane-Baxter. Being a historian, I have special access to all sorts of information sources, which I scour for stories. The Palace pays me a backhander cash stipend to write ten 'news' items a month, including some historical pieces of the light reading variety - 'Australia's Proud History' my pathetic series is called. Hardly anybody reads it, and those who do don't believe it, so it's an ethical zero sum. You give me a storyline and I'll spin it: My masterpiece this month was the Sino-French glove factory in Turkey that turned out four million left-handed items by mistake. The manager was executed, but I had to omit that small detail. My headline was 'Workers Hand in Glove with Innovative Production Scheduling'. Condemn me if you like, but a gal's gotta have a few treats.

Meanwhile, the True History of Jude progresses. (It's so reassuring to know that the manuscript is safe with you). In my last instalment, he'd just discovered that his Sue was married to an old schoolteacher. I left him in despair in his lodgings, realising that Sue wasn't whatever he thought she (that is, I) might be - prophetess, saint, guardian angel, fairy, sprite. Anyway, let him tell the story, as it were.

Best, Sue

JUDE'S EYES ARE OPENED

The knowledge of Sue's marriage plunged me into a grey slump. To make things worse, my skin came out in boils, perhaps from my dunking in the <u>longdrop</u>. I stayed in my room for two weeks, unable to face the streets of the town. The woman with skin and eyes like mine brought me food from the market and took roubles from my stash to pay for it. Thoughts about what I had seen and heard in Kuranda swirled in my brain. But my gloom was overtaken by a mass of new ideas that formed and reformed, ideas about the future, and about men and women, about books, and about my PURPOSE. There was a kind of heaviness before me: Something like the feel of the words DUTY and RESPONSIBILITY and DESTINY. I knew these English words before, but they were grey and formless because there was nothing like DUTY or RESPONSIBILITY or DESTINY in Orange. There I walked around and learned my book and made up stories to tell. But here, each man was responsible for his food and lodgings today and tomorrow and forever, and each woman depended on a man. It was as if I used to live in a story, and now I lived in a place a story was about.

And if I was no longer in a story, what of Sue? She wasn't the Sue in my plan to go north. She wasn't a saint or an angel, but a woman with <u>huhus</u> and a <u>choot</u>, a woman who had lain astride the old spadebeard teacher. I trembled on the bed, picturing Sue lying above me as Arabella used to.

The woman with skin and eyes like mine knocked at the door. She saw my hands covering my choni and smiled, came in and took off her clothes, lay on the bed with her legs apart.

"What is this?" I cried. "It is for me to lie down, not you."

She laughed and pulled me on top of her, guiding me into her choot. I used my full weight to pin her down.

I was powerful. I was strong. I was a new man on top with a COCK.

Afterwards she brought beer, and we lay cooling each other's bellies with the cold bottles. I caressed her BREASTS.

"Why did you take me?" I asked.

"It was you who took me, Jude. All I took was your innocence."

"Why did you take my innocence?"

"Because the innocent do not survive in this town."

We slept for a little while, and when we woke she said, "If you go to the market this evening, you will see Sue selling her pictures."

"What kind of pictures?"

"You will see what pictures."

"What is she like? This Sue Bridehead?"
The woman drew away, pulled a sheet over her nakedness.

"Tell me, what she is like?"

"People say she has a kind of force. That she is like a young girl with something ancient and magical that drives her."

"Is it true? Do you believe them?"

"They have superstitions," the woman said. "Their religion has driven them mad. When they follow the Straight Way, they can see nothing to the sides, nothing behind them or above them."

"Should I fear her?"

"No, you will be charmed by her. She is like a bird that flits here and there, seducing you with her sweet song."

I sat up. The woman had closed her eyes. A brown breast showed where the sheet had slipped away. The flesh rose and fell softly with her breathing. A mosquito pitched onto her breast and I gently pinched it between finger and thumb as it started to stab. I thought about how Jesus would wash away our sins. I thought, I have sinned with this woman today. A tiny globe of blood clung where the mosquito had bitten. I leant forward and touched the red jewel with my tongue tip. She stirred and said, "You've never asked me my name. It is Mia."

***

Later, I left Mia sleeping, put on my clothes, and stepped boldly out into the road, a different man, a man with a purpose, a man with the taste of blood on his tongue. There was a wavering in the old Jude's belly, poor, piss-weak Jude with no purpose, but I forced it down. My new bold stare met and defeated the eye of each spadebeard I passed. Women looked down and scurried past.

Old Orange was a trashcan of stale and fading memories. Ha! That book that shaped the life of feeble, silly Jude. Where did I hide it at the lodgings? I couldn't remember. Didn't care. I practiced the new word I learned from the traders on the journey to Kuranda: Fuck. Fuck the fucking books. We said bigfuckup in Orange, but this English fuck was a wild animal of a word, violent and strong, striking everywhere. I fucked the woman in the lodgings: That's what she meant by taking my innocence.

I searched the market stalls, seeing clothes and fruits for sale, piles of savoury pies, jerky, nails, wooden stools, sugar cane, old knives and axes. And there was Sue sitting by the place where they sold pictures of women's breasts. When I last came here, there was a spadebeard at the stall instead. Sue didn't see me because she was painting, head down. I'd waited half my life for this moment. My vision, my true love, my other self, was painting a fat, pink breast. I didn't know what to say.

Words tumbled out: "Wofo mekit pitcher huhu yu?"

Sue murmured, "Mek pitcher nobby me," and then looked up, sprang to her feet. She said, "Jude, you are cousin Jude, tell me you are." She grasped my hand but immediately thrust it away, leaving pink paint on my fingers. She tossed a rag over the painting. "Come away from here, walk with me under the trees."

We walked in the sunset rays, her hand clutching my arm. Just as the last hot sliver of peachy light sank, the pearly lamps flicked on above us. I craned my neck to watch a line of them below the canopy of the trees.

She said, "Let us take this lane. There are no street lights here. It is more private".

We walked a little way. It was darker. We passed a fire burning in a metal drum. A boy was tossing rubbish into the fire, but he ran away when he saw Sue. I stared at her face in the red fire-glow, so close now. Her features were small and her face heart-shaped. Her hair was twisted into a jolly knot high on the head, with strands struggling free to frame her eyes - grey, grey-green, I was not sure.

"You are married," I say.

"I am called Richard's wife, but I really belong to nobody."

I said to her, "You are a woman tossed about, all alone, with aberrant passions, and unaccountable antipathies."

"Yes, yes," she cried. "But how do you know? Where do those words come from? That is exactly what I feel like. Aberrant passions are what drive me here and there."

I said, "The words are from a book, from Jude the Obscure. That is what the Sue in the book says."

I looked at her again, shyly now. She was small and slim, not dark and not fair.

"I've never read that book. But let's not talk about books now, cousin Jude." She stopped and stared at me. "Jude, I'm frightened and excited all at once. Do you feel it, that we are connected by a thread?"

Her long fingers spoke with her words, flicking and shaping her ideas. She was never still, her eyes darting.

"Connected," I said. "Yes, Auntie Vicky said that I am you and you are me."

"Oh, that foolish Auntie Vicky. You must visit me at my house."

I could not follow her sudden shift of thoughts.

"Your house," I said. Your husband might beat me."

She laughed.

"Sue, why do you dress differently from the other women?"

"Because I do not follow the Straight Way."

Suddenly I was overcome with confusion and fatigue. I was not the bold man with a COCK, but a <u>choni</u> child lost in a jungle of strange ideas and unfamiliar life. What was the Straight Way? Was it the lane where we walked? Was it something else, something not real? I was too tired to ask these questions, knowing that they would lead to more questions and even more questions.

A spadebeard walked towards us with his woman a pace behind. He skulked in the shadow to pass us but Sue said, "Gabriel, come into the light". He approached. The woman's legs were plump and dimpled under the short skirt. Her shoes had heels so high that she teetered forward like a turkey when she walked, and her breasts were thrust out so that they almost burst from her clothes. The man greeted Sue nervously.

"This is my cousin Jude," she said. "The one you beat. Greet him."

It was the woman whose bum I touched before they threw me out of the bar. My new courage faltered, but I remembered to regain my stance as a man with a COCK. I pushed out my chest and said, "Hail fellow".

"Your cousin must learn the Straight Way," the man muttered, flicking scared glances between me and Sue.

Sue faced the woman, her fingers cupped high like claws. The woman's face was white against the flaming barrel. My cousin hissed, so gently that it could be a sudden breeze in the palm fronds. The woman jerked in fright and turned, hobbling away from us. The spadebeard scuttled ahead of her and we watched the pair fleeing under the swishing night trees that were alive with the eyes of small creatures hunting their prey.

"Is it tang-ling?" I asked Sue.

"They call it witchcraft here. I am a witch."

I rolled the word in my mouth. WITCH. It was a strong word like FUCK. I rounded my lips into a tight bud, snapped them open into a slit and then slapped my tongue witchily against my teeth. "Witch, witch, witch," I said. Sue laughed and ran off.

"Come soon," she called.

"Good night Sue Bridehead," I called back.

She stopped. "What did you call me?"

"Sue Bridehead."

"I like that name. You can call me Sue Bridehead."

I watched my WITCH fade among the trees in the moist heat of the Kuranda night. An idea flickered. Will I fuck my witch? But the idea was too powerful, the words too terrible, and scared piss-weak Jude scuttled back to his lodgings.

* * *

So you see, Alex, your dried-up and diffident Prof was a witch of twenty when she first took the arm of her cousin Jude. I knew it was him when he spoke to me in that old language, asking me why I was painting breasts - those daubs of breasts and vulvas that gave sticky comfort to the men of Kuranda when their woman were sequestered each month in sack dresses.

When I heard his words, I kept my head down, answering calmly in the old Creole language with its simple patterns and earthy cadence. But I was burning with some confused emotion: Not deep desire, not love, not warmth, nor the tingle of intimacy. It was as if I myself were standing before me; as if two souls were tangled in an ecstasy of an unknown kind. My spirit danced and teased in the presence of this queer fellow with his look of an infant lost in the world of adults. But beneath this ecstasy a dark secret struggled to come into the light.

LANGUAGE DEVELOPMENT IN PATRIA NULLIUS

TOP SECRET

Highness,

In the section of the *History* below, please note the reference to offences under the Information Quality Enhancement Act (Patria Nullius). As you will recall, Section 9 of the Act includes a provision that makes it an offence to refer publicly to the Act. I have asked Mr Quoit to find a remedy, and will forward the edited text to Your Highness when it is complete.

Humbly, Bruce

LANGUAGE DEVELOPMENT IN PATRIA NULLIUS

Around 0052, reports of a strange language began filtering out of Patria Nullius. An Australian Border Security Inc. doctor working with a vaccination project told a news service that while his staff could communicate in English with people in the main towns and villages, the town of Orange had a tongue of its own.

In 0053 a man staggered into an ABSI depot near Darwin in the far north of Patria Nullius, dying from the effects of a probable spider bite. He was Jack Wing, an ABSI security guard who had absconded into the countryside around Orange with a Patria Nullius woman months before. Before expiring, he managed to explain that the woman had died in a fall. By coincidence, the vaccine doctor attended the dying fugitive. He found a word list among Jack Wing's belongings. It found its way to one of the world's premier schools of linguistics at the University of Chicago.

Enter Professor Zita Kawaguchi, the superstar linguist whose *Smashlingua* implant had made spoken word interpreters redundant. Sensing the potential public interest, Kawaguchi threw all the resources of her lab at the list. Her experts concluded that Wing must have compiled it to help him learn the strange language spoken by his girlfriend. What intrigued the boffins, however, was that the words seemed to be a Creole - a form of language that often developed in the European colonial era when people of different language groups were plucked from their home districts and forced together indiscriminately.

But Mr Wing's word list was just part of a bigger jigsaw. Historians knew that in the years before the Grand Bargain, a large detention centre for climate change refugees had been built at Orange. Most of the refugees were from the Pacific Islands, but there was also a contingent of Vietnamese. From here guesswork took over, because the Australian Government issued a directive banning the collection and reporting of linguistic data under the Information Quality Enhancement Act (Patria Nullius). The supply of reliable information from Patria Nullius dried up.

But unconfirmed reports persisted: Schools closed after the borders were sealed; the refugees escaped their camps and intermarried with the local population; gangs of mixed-race children roamed the lanes and hillsides.

Putting together the pieces, the University of Chicago team believed that the unschooled children born in the first decade of the Grand Bargain spoke their parents' languages at home - English, Fijian, Tongan, Hindi, and Vietnamese. But they played outside together for long days, developing a pidgin language to communicate with each other - basically simplified English with an admixture of words like *zazzy*, *bookhee*, *longdrop*, *tang-ling* and *luraka*, adapted from their mother tongues. When they became parents themselves, their offspring grew up speaking the pidgin, which quickly became the fully developed Orange Creole that was widespread by 0050.

Pidgin and Creole linguistics is a broad and complex field of study, and the fine details are beyond the scope of this book. Suffice to say that Zita Kawaguchi's team spotted tell-tale clues in Jack Wing's list. For example, the repetition in the word for 'husbands', *hubbyhubby*, is a typical Creole method for making a plural. And when the doctor sent his field notes to Chicago, Kawaguchi confirmed from grammatical clues they had a Creole on their hands: The word order of the sentences the doctor had transcribed was based on the same grammatical patterns that have been found in most Creoles around the world, as predicted by Bickerton's Language Bioprogram Hypothesis in the pre-Grand Bargain era.

Zita Kawaguchi's paper on Orange Creole in the journal *Lost Languages* is nowadays considered a classic, but it raised a torrent of protest at the time. New Canberra charged the professor with offences under the Information Quality Enhancement Act (Patria Nullius) and attempted to extradite her from the US to England. A long legal battle ensued, but Kawaguchi prevailed: The extradition treaty between Australia and the US was judged inapplicable by the now defunct International Court of Justice since, as a virtual state, Australia had no physical territory to which a person could be extradited.

In her nineties, Kawaguchi spoke of Jack Wing's word list in an interview at her mountain home in

Colorado. "That crumpled list was a cry of desperate devotion - a man in the wilderness with a woman he loved but could barely talk to. I had to act. I had to show the world that even when you build a fence around a person's humanity, love finds a way. I grieve for the woman - she was called Arabella. Did she find peace in those cruel forests?"

PART FOURTH - KURANDA

The True History of Jude

D&ar Al&x,

A quick follow-up l&tt&r. &xcus& th& odd typing, but wh&n I got Mr R&mington out this morning, th& k&y for th& fifth l&tt&r of the alphabet was missing. Gon&, just th& m&tal rod sticking up. I'm using & instead. It's not th& only odd thing lat&ly. I wak& up som&tim&s to find things hav& mov&d - a cup or a pictur& fram&. By th& way, th& snow has stopp&d but it rains inc&ssantly. Th& v&g&tabl&s that swath& my building ar& showing signs of mild&w.

Panic over. I found e and popped it back onto the metal rod. Typing & quite put me off my stroke. e was in my bathroom cabinet, by the way. Has someone been in here when I'm asleep? Surely not - our entrance doors are PIP-activated. Am I worried? Well, only for my own sanity, and that's been pretty fragile in recent times.

Anyway, I had to send you a note enclosing a piece of student-grade samizdat that I bought from the boy banker yesterday in the blind spot by the garbage bins. See the fourth paragraph. Oh, by the way, you're bound to wonder why it's called 'samizdat' and not 'underground publications' or some such. This goes back about a decade when Princess Maureen's party turned up at the Salvatorem Mundi ball dressed as Bolsheviks. For the following year all the male students had Lenin goatees, red neckerchiefs and peaked caps, and

155

the girls - well pretty much the same but without the beards. (This was some improvement on the previous year when Adolf Hitler was the theme). To cut a long story short, a sprinkle of Russian words were in vogue on the campuses that year - bozhe moi, tovarishsch, druzhba, etc., and while most of them quickly dropped out of vogue, samizdat caught on.

Best, Sue

The truth, the whole truth, and nothing but
BOLLOCKS TO SLUZHBA
News from beyond The Universe to the long-
suffering citizens of the Kingdom of
England and Wales
100% genuine Samizdat printed in some
fucker's bathroom on an antique Roneo
machine.

FROM THE EDITORS
Well, your plucky team Chalky, Stinker and
The Dark Lady have finally got the New Year
edition of BOLLOCKS TO SLUZHBA off the
presses and into your hands. And once again
we've kept ourselves out of jail. [Thank
Fate. The food's disgusting - Stinker]

Following the outsourcing of the Justice
Department to the Universal Fatalist
Organisation, The Dark Lady has been on a
deep cover mission to bring you a shocking
story about the 'reassignment' of Justice
Fenella Rushmore to the bowels of the
Records Department at the K.E.W. Supreme
Court. Rushmore, the last judge with more
than two shreds of judicial objectivity, is
replaced by knuckle-grazing neanderthal Slim
'Fatso' Slattery, whose last gig before
being blasted from the magistracy to the
Supreme Court bench was to acquit his
brother of busting the shnoz of a waiter in
Leeds who spilt his soup. Bollocks to
SLUZHBA and its loathsome subsidiary UFO, we
say. [Full story p.2]

Meanwhile Stinker has been [cue the National Anthem, 'Fate Guide our Noble King, Long Live our Noble King', etc., etc.] perusing a purloined package of printouts pertaining to payments proffered by His Majesty to those audacious amoral antipodean arm-twisters in New Canberra for 'services rendered' by SLUZHBA. Presumably this involves fees for disposal of certain holographic footage of our honoured monarch playing doctors and nurses with an extremely close relative Who Shall Remain Nameless. Ouch! This royal performance puts a new slant on the term 'injection', that's for sure. Read the full account to see how the Macfarlane dynasty has got our King Nigel by the financial curlies. Bollocks to SLUZHBA's blackmail and their pusillanimous victims, we say. [Full story p.4]

And while we're talking about Australia's Thousand Year Reich, a little cockatoo has told Chalky that a historian at the Oxford campus of The University of Sydney (an Aussie Baroness Who Shall Also Remain Nameless) is in deep kangaroo shite, if not facing arrest for treason, because of her insistence on writing THE TRUTH. Tut, tut, when will these preening thinkologists realise that they are paid merely to add the finishing touches to what Predictive Composition displays on the screen? Not to actually write anything original or even true! Bollocks to that, we say. [Full story p.21]

Lastly, our student day of action rolls out on April One [or staggers out depending on how much whackopowder the lazy fuckwits have sniffed the night before]. Objective: To contaminate Predictive Composition by entering the phrase 'THE BOLLOCKS' one thousand times per student during the day. Our mathematical geniuses (yes, there are one or two people left in England who know their times tables) have calculated that by midday, anybody who writes 'THE' will immediately see 'BOLLOCKS' appear on the screen, thus temporarily disturbing their train of non-thought. Bollocks to PC, we say.

Page 1

SUSAN TO ALEX, APRIL 0100

Dear Alex,

A quick update on my journalistic career: It's over. I resigned. The kerfuffle was over the Vatican story. The Palace sent an invitation to meet with media secretary Lord Someone or Other Macfarlane (cloak trimmed with ermine). There were two other 'journalists' at the meeting. The aim was to 'come to a consensus' on how to present the story. I hadn't met the other two but we didn't address each other; with strangers, the less you tell the better.

His Lordship said the Palace preferred us to downplay the recruitment angle. We shouldn't mention that the Vatican had engaged the United Fatalist Organisation to do an executive search for a new Pope. Instead, we were to focus on the outcome, that is a new Vatican Governing Council of six Holy Fathers.

One of my fellow journalists asked if UFO had acquired the Catholic Church or merged with it.

"Short answer," said the said Lord, "It's an acquisition, but that's not for public consumption".

"Are the new Holy Fathers directors of UFO entities?"

"Refer to my previous answer," the Lord replied.

"Will there be priests still?" I asked.

"Or God?" my colleague asked.

The Lord peered at us. "Neither priests nor a deity are permitted under the new constitution."

"Will Catholics be happy?" I was feeling reckless. Silly question: Everyone is happy. That's the point of it all.

"That'll be enough. Pick up your money from the doorman." The Lord stood up, waiting impatiently for a footman to hold up his velvet train before gliding out through a gilt doorway.

Dear Alex, as people used to say in Australia, you wouldn't read about it!

Best (or so-so at least),Sue

Stuart Campbell

JUDE'S PREMONITION

The pain of an insect bite woke me at dawn. A hot needle drilled into my puffy ankle. The creature was clattering from one wall to another, jabbing itself with its sting when it got tangled in the curtains. I whacked it with my sandal. It fell to the floor, spinning so fast it was a blur. Another whack and its brown case was cracked. It lay still in a smear of poison juice.

I knelt down to look at the creature. Now I saw that one whisker was waving slowly back and forth. The movement stopped. The thing had died. I wondered if it had a soul. I wondered if it sinned when it bit me, and if not, whether it would enter the kingdom of heaven. And then I wondered if killing it was a sin if it had a soul.

Mia came in, rubbing her sleepy eyes. I'd woken her with my sandal whacking. She saw the dead thing and frowned. I pointed at my ankle.

"It wasn't that that stung you." She looked at my ankle and then around the room. "There it is." A spider lurked on the floor near my bed. Then it was a smudge of snot under the whack of the sandal. Mia said, "I'll get you something."

While she was gone, my heart started to hammer. I sweated cold, sensed death coming on. Three white bundles flew just outside where my eyes could see them properly. Mia returned with a mess of leaves and bound it to the ankle with a tight cloth.

"And take this." A cup with a finger of brown liquid. I sipped it with dry and trembling lips. The bitter medicine made me wince to my toes. "You'll calm down soon. Lie on the bed and wait for the medicine to work."

I lay down. My heart slowed. The feeling of death lightened. After nowrotu I got up and wobbled towards Sue's house. The place was closed up. The eyebrows of the windows frowned at me. The door was angry as a wild pig. There was an orange smell in my nostrils. The white bundles danced behind my head.

A spadebeard on a horse came up behind me. I wasn't feeling exactly like Jude but like another Jude.

"Out walking?" The words sounded as if two people were saying them in a chorus, but there was only one man on the horse. There was another Jude next to me, I thought.

I nodded to the horserider, and he said, "I'm going down the hill. Care for a ride?" There was a funny lightness in my head - lightness mixed with fear - and I found it hard to move my lips. I slid up behind the man and we trotted off. The horse's bones and sinews ground gently under me. We floated above the road, which had smooth black patches and stony earth in between, like the top surface was worn out. We drifted for a long time with the spadebeard's voice coming deep from a long tunnel. A white bundle appeared again somewhere to my side, but as I tried to see it, it slipped away. Another approached and I thought I saw faces on the two bundles. And a third bundle arrived, the three dancing and bobbing, except that I couldn't catch them with my eyes. A deep dread clutched my <u>zazzy</u> but I couldn't find the reason, except for the three white bundles.

Vomit surged into my throat but wouldn't come out. My heart was hammering, fingers numb. I fell off the horse. The spadebeard's voice was deep and echoey and I couldn't understand his words. I watched as the horse waddled away and I saw that its feet were on the road and not floating at all. I spewed up green sticky stuff that tasted like the brown medicine. Hot sleep smothered me.

* * *

A man stood over me, an Aboriginal with a thick beard and deep eyes. Everything was sharp and clear now.

"Where's the Falls?" I asked him. I didn't know why - I'd never heard of the Falls. He pointed up the hill and walked away. The sun was sinking in the west. I must have been asleep for hours.

I got to my feet and plodded up the hill to Kuranda, and after a long time there was a sign to BARRON FALLS. It was nearly dark but something inside me said I must reach BARRON FALLS, whatever they were. The track was a stumble of shuddering palms and giant leaves that slapped at me as I passed in the falling night. A sticky web draped my face and I swatted away something hairy and moist. I tripped on a skeetering bird as high as my waist. Blunder, smash, wallop, trip, that was poor Jude following the message in his simple head. Water roared up ahead, now louder, louder, and then I was at a wooden platform. Above me a spread of stars, and far below the black crashing of water. The three white bundles flitted just outside my vision. I turned to run home, praying to Jesus to cast out the fear in my heart.

SUSAN TO ALEX, MAY 0100

Dear Alex,

Be prepared to hear from me only erratically in the next little while. I plan to leave England for Scotland soon. The boy banker has taken the bulk of my remaining roubles to pay for the people smuggler and the 'visa'(i.e. multiple bribes). This could become a habit; Jude and I paid a thick wad of roubles to flee from Patra Nullius forty years ago. I'm going to apply for asylum once I'm over the border. Hopefully, the Scots will have the integrity not to send me back. I'm taking daily walks and cycle rides now to build up the strength in my leg muscles. I've given up smoking, too (well almost). No more strange goings-on in the apartment since the missing 'e', although the regular maintenance man in my block has been replaced by a new one with a distinctly spyish look. I'm stumbling on with Princess Maureen's <u>History</u>. I wrote some shallow stuff in my career, but this took the prize for rent-a-writer.

   Latest news: Their wretched Predictive Composition is being mandated for students in all universities in England and Wales from next month (including Sydney at Oxford). It's dressed up as the 'Standardised Study for Success Strategy' or SSSS. Thank Fate for your First Amendment - you'll never be visited by this evil clamp on the freedom of speech. Lucky for me that I'll never have to mark any more student papers, although on reflection if they're all written using PC they won't need marking anyway. I read in 'Bollocks to Sluzhba' that in order to give all students an equal chance, grades from pass to high distinction will be randomly distributed. I was a pioneer in this regard as you'll recall!

In my remaining time with Mr Remington (I've moved him out of the lavatory - the neighbours can make of the noise what they will), I want to get as much of my story down on paper as possible, and across the Atlantic to you. My notes tell me that I've told you a bit about how I ended up in Orange when I was five. I told you that later I was married to 'Mr Phillotson' in Kuranda, so you need to know about the years in between. Let me get stuck in:

You know how it is with childhood memories: The further you go back, the less reliable they are. But what I definitely remember about Orange is the rubbish - pie dishes and beer bottles, soiled paper towels and discarded clothes. I remember the gangs of children I played with, and my father's warnings about fleas and scabies, and him telling me not to speak their peculiar language. There were the lines of souls waiting patiently in the sun for food, aspirins, a screw of hash. These generous provisions were handed out by the 'uniforms', burly men in blue masks, who spoke a language nobody understood (although I know now that many of them were Fijian). There was something they gave the women too - a pellet under the skin.

It was as if the whole town was in a walking coma, except for the younger kids and a few harsh-eyed women who kept a kind of order. I never went to school because there was no school, but my father taught me to read from a box of books he kept hidden. I was a keen learner and was reading simple books by the time I was five. He brought me up speaking English, or oldtalk, at home but I was out in the streets learning Orange Creole as soon as I could walk.

My father had a futile notion of teaching the locals the word of God (Fate wash my mouth out), and even set up a kind of church in an old shed. I used to make little decorations to hang on the wall - crosses and angels and suchlike. He refused to sink into soul-sapping indolence, and was always starting short-lived schemes to motivate the locals: Volleyball, painting, a choir. We often saw Auntie Vicky, who must have been able to speak in oldtalk, because my father refused to speak Creole. As for Jude, I don't remember meeting him. According to my calculations he was born about four years after me.

By the time I was five and a half, my poor father had given up; the uniforms gradually broke him down by warning people not to speak to him, until we were shunned. He was offered exile - a technique I learned later was used by ABSI to get rid of troublemakers. One evening Father and I were packed into the truck that took the garbage away. After hours in the dark box with the skips that smelt sweetly of beer and gravy, the uniforms transferred us to another truck, this one loaded with what I think now was electrical equipment. We spent nights at grim roadhouses where streams of taciturn men in yellow vests and helmets arrived, ate, slept and left. Weeks later they dropped us by the side of a road, where an Aboriginal man met us with a motorbike and sidecar. The next day we arrived in Kuranda. I learned in later years that the man was an uncle of Vera, the wife of Ross. Her family ran a big informal transport business along the east coast beyond the reach of ABSI.

It was a paradise after Orange. Australian Border Security Inc. hadn't bothered to take over Kuranda, my theory being that towns like this served as useful buffers between the Internal Protected Zones and what they thought of as the badlands. Food of many kinds was piled up in the markets, brought in by horse and cart from the little farms outside the town. There was even a solar-powered street lighting system that they somehow managed to maintain.

I should say that Paradise could turn into Hell at short notice what with cyclones, diseases and infestations of pests. But the rich soil, sunshine and rain provided the foundation for a lush, if erratic, existence.

My father got work in the school, teaching arithmetic in exchange for food and the use of a house. Yes, a school! I'd never seen one in my life, although I knew about them from my books. Girls and boys learned in different rooms, and - I soon discovered - studied different topics, although most of it was based on doom-filled religious instruction.

The teachers were men, and like all the men in town, they wore straight-cut beards. The women had to dress in skimpy outfits and high heels.

My father realised soon that he had to outwit these people if we were to survive in this town; even better, they had to fear his power. The spadebeards (as Jude later called them) followed what they called 'The Straight Way', a simplistic mishmash of stern precepts plucked mostly from the Old Testament, reinforced by a lot of choir singing (their singing was hypnotically beautiful). Their women's sexuality fascinated and terrified the spadebeards.

One night my father said to me, "I will never wear their straight beard, and you will never become one of their half-naked chattels". I must have been about seven at the time, but I recall his words exactly; or perhaps I've reconstructed and rehearsed them over the years. It doesn't matter. What's important is that I understood even then that we had to stand up to them.

How could we withstand the pressure to conform? The answer came one night when the electricity supply went down, but here I need to take a step back.

The spadebeards disapproved of what they called 'deep thinking'. One of their favourite songs was 'God's handiwork over Satan's brainwork' to the tune of Waltzing Matilda. They believed abstract thinking interrupted their direct line of communication with God. The result was that they carried out all practical tasks using age-old routines:

Building roof frames, making fertiliser from human faeces, treating sick horses. While these methods generally worked, the spadebeards were hopeless at innovating. Geometry was beyond them. Even simple chemistry - making cement for example - was off the spadebeard agenda. Drinking water was a constant problem: They dragged it up in barrels from the gorge but it gave them diarrhoea and parasites, which they blamed on Satan. They washed with river water from tubs in their backyards, risking eye and skin infections.

By some miracle, the solar panels had kept pumping power into a German-designed battery system built before the Grand Bargain, and the streetlights had kept burning. If the LEDs blew, replacements could be got from the Aboriginal traders, and even a spadebeard could unplug the dead one and insert a new one. But this time, the breakdown was serious; the whole set-up was dead. My father spent a week making a wiring diagram, which looked like spaghetti (I'd only seen pictures of spaghetti in those days). He then made a circuit testing tool from some junk, located the problem in a burnt-out connection, and fixed it. The spadebeards were appreciative, but nervous. They burnt the wiring diagram in a frenzy of prayer.

My father continued to teach arithmetic at the school - very basic number work that even the spadebeards acknowledged the children needed for everyday tasks - but he kept hidden the more advanced topics - geometry, algebra, calculus. His secret power was to be our salvation.

His next piece of wizardry was to design a piece of replacement roofing for the church. The roof had leaked for decades because of a bit of rusted sheet metal, made by a tradesman long ago. The offending piece was supposed to fit precisely at the junction of two curved panels, and was irregularly shaped. The spadebeards had driven themselves almost mad trying to make a new piece. If it was the right width, it was too deep; if it was the right length, it was too shallow. They tried making it in situ, on the ground, copied from sketches, inspired by dreams. They bashed, sawed, hammered, and prayed. But each version let in the tropical rain. The problem of fixing the roof was gradually gaining religious dimensions: God, they thought, was testing them and they were failing Him. The heap of discarded failures behind the church was a divine reproach.

My father worked out the dimensions of the metal piece using careful measurements and his knowledge of solid geometry. On a fresh morning following a night of intense prayer, the spadebeards watched as he directed their metalworker to measure and cut the required pieces, make one curve in a certain plane, and to curve the edge in another plane. When it was made, he held up the paper with his measurements and formulae. The spadebeards muttered and frowned. One of them passed the artefact to a worker on the roof, who popped it into place like the lid on a teapot. My father crumpled the paper and tossed it into a fire that had been lit for the purpose, and everybody prayed thanks to God.

Wizardry, they called it. They steered a wide berth when we walked on the streets, looked at us sideways. We had secret knowledge. We practised Deep Thinking.

Father and I performed more of these spectacles of deep thought from time to time. In the meantime, he occupied the school children with years of long division and the times tables from thirteen to nineteen. But real mathematics was our secret. That's how I became known as a witch, the witch who could draw breasts in perspective rather than as two-dimensional saucepan lids.

But even our wizardry couldn't stem the infectious diseases that swept through the area every few years. My dear father died suddenly when I was eighteen from what the spadebeards called The Sweats. (Perhaps somebody among them had long ago read about the Sweating Sickness in England in the time of Henry VIII?)

On my own, I was powerless to resist the pressures of their social norms. It was thought seemly (they loved that word) to marry me off to the old, childless teacher Jude named Mr Phillotson, who would walk the witch along the Straight Way.

I have to stop. The boy banker is outside.

Me again half an hour later. The boy banker delivered my travel details. We had a taciturn smoke together, and then he said, "Got a present for you". It was the lighter.

"Do you always give your customers presents?" He shrugged, and I leaned down to kiss his grubby cheek. The boy wiped the kiss away with his sleeve and stamped off.

I leave within the week. There is just time for me to get most of Jude's story finished before I go. The boy banker has instructions to pick up an envelope from a certain hiding place. You should have it in a week.

I pray my health holds up until I'm out of the country. (Did I just write 'pray'? Yes, how odd.) The Thing pushes his ugly presence on me at random times, but most distressingly in the mornings when I get a headache I've named the Hot Beast. I've plenty of pills to force it back into its lair, but their effect is waning.

So for now, my best wishes, Alex. I'll be in touch from Scotland, and if the stars align I'll see you in The Land of the Freeish before long. Here's some more of Jude.

Best, Sue.

A FRINGE OF LEAVES

"You must leave," Mia announced one morning.
"I'd like you to stay a few weeks longer, but
the men say it is not seemly."
  "What is not seemly? I heard that word when
they threw me in the longdrop."
  "They think that you and I ..."
  "I and you ..."
  "Yes."
  "But it was only once," I said.
  "Once is enough for them."
  "But how do they know, Mia?"
  "They have a sense. Perhaps they can see the
invisible thread between people."
  "Is there a thread between us?"
  "There is, but the thread between you and
Sue is stronger."
  "I'll go but not yet," I said. She shrugged.

                        * * *

The window blind shut out the afternoon glare.
I'd go to the stonemason tomorrow early when
it was cooler. Ask for a job. Get a new nobby.
  My zazzy ached and gurgled. I had hotguts
every day, loose smelly shits that came
without warning. I never had this in Orange.
When I came out of Mia's longdrop that
morning, I had the idea of bottled water. My
head told me that I needed to drink something
clean, like the water in Orange. And then I
thought about the water I drank in the
lodgings - cups of cloudy stuff from a barrel
with bits floating in it. Sometimes there were

a few bottles of clean water in the market. I'd try to buy some today with my roubles.

My T-shirt stuck to me. I had a wash from the water tub on the side veranda, rinsed out the T-shirt, hung it on the blind in my room. I couldn't find my other T-shirt. There was a cupboard in the corner I didn't use. Mia might have put it in there.

It was empty but for a plastic bag containing a book. I opened it. The book had a paper sticker inside the front cover that read BRISBANE CITY COUNCIL LIBRARY. The book was called <u>A Fringe of Leaves</u>. The word fringe was new to me. I could ask Mia about it later. I started reading, the second book I had read in my life. After I'd read some pages about the woman Ellen Roxburgh and the Aboriginals, I closed my eyes and remembered what had happened to her, and then I tried to think what might come next in the story.

Suddenly a wild thought jumped into my head: Perhaps she wasn't real, this Ellen. What if my idea about what came next was different from what the book said? Which idea would be the true one? This thought bored into me. My zazzy felt queasy when I sat back to think about it.

But no sooner than I was getting comfortable with the fact that an idea in a book might not be true, a truly awful thought struck me: What if the book about Jude wasn't real? What if I made up a different ending, and the terrible things that happened in Part Sixth didn't happen?

I ran out to find Mia. She was dozing in a chair. One eye opened.

"Are the stories in this book real?"

"Does it matter?" she asked. "You think too much."

"It does matter," I said, but I didn't exactly know why. There was a line from a book floating just outside my thoughts, but I couldn't catch it. It was frightening that nothing might be true, but behind the fright was something strong and powerful and important. What was it? What was the line I couldn't remember?

I went back to my room. I lay wondering whether Mia would come to my bed again. Should I take her, the COCK man? Would she take me, the choni boy? What were the rules here? I was getting stiff, my hand in my pants.

But it was hot. I dozed into a half-dream about my book, seeing the forgotten line dance in fuzzy letters. They slipped away, they came back. They teased me. They taunted me. I groped for them. My eyes snapped open. I remembered the line but I couldn't remember where it came from: And ye shall know the truth, and the truth shall make you free.

Had I been free before when I thought my books were true? Was I free now I wasn't sure if they were true? These were questions I couldn't answer yet, but they were questions I didn't know about nowrotu ago. The truth: It was what we called deadright or dinkum in the Orange language, but it was bigger than those old rubbish words. The truth shall make Jude free and powerful and strong.

The stone mason's name was Slab. I didn't know if it was his first name or his last name. I tried hard to learn the second names of people I met if they had one. Remembering was something I was getting used to. In Orange, there was nothing important to remember because every day was the same. Sure, I memorised my book, but that wasn't like remembering when your head swims with thoughts and pictures and new people. When I woke in the morning, my mind played a jumbled-up movie: The green dawn when Ross shot the kangaroo, the weight of the salty sea, Arabella pinning me to the bed, the spadebeards who threw me into the street, Sue under the pearly streetlights, Mia's brown breasts.

Something funny was happening to my old life in Orange. My years there had become frozen, like a story in a book where the characters can't escape from the page. The Jude in the book, Mrs Edlin, Richard Phillotson: Now they were flat and motionless, yet they used to walk beside me in my daydreams. Jesus was different. The spadebeards praised his name constantly. And Sue Bridehead: She was alive, but not in a way I could grasp. She was slippery, brittle, like a sliver of ice but warm.

Slab he was, then. Not Ezekiel Slab or Slab Stonecutter. Only Slab.

When I first went to the station, he asked, "What can you do? You're only skinny".

There were half a dozen turkeys in the yard, which was piled with junk - timber, rope,

rocks, rusted metal. A railway line ran
through the middle of it all. A train with
carriages sat on tracks behind the station
building, strangled by vines as thick as my
wrist. I saw a train once in a movie in Orange,
and I remembered how in the book, when Sue and
Jude went to Wardour Castle, the <u>guard of the
train thought they were lovers, and put them
into a compartment all by themselves</u>.

"I want to be a stonemason. Mia sent me from
the lodgings."

Slab's ears pricked up. Well actually, his
ears didn't move because they were just small
bumps on his fat pink head. Mia said that ears
prick up, and I still got confused about
saying things that meant other things. But
Slab's face showed that he was listening.

"Mia, you say?"

Slab didn't have a beard, and he had eyes
like me and Mia. He stared at me.

"Where are you from?"

"Orange," I said.

"It's a place I knew."

He asked me a question in our Orange
language, but I didn't understand it properly.
I didn't think he had ever lived among us.

"Dun <u>gettit me</u>," I said.

"<u>Bigfuckup</u>," he said. I didn't understand
what he thought was <u>bigfuckup</u> but I knew he
was trying to tell me that he was an outsider
like me and Mia. It was this trick again of
saying one thing and meaning something
different.

"Can you lift and carry?"

"I can."

"I can, SIR," he said.

"I can, SIR."

"You can sleep in there." He pointed at a doorway at the end of the railway station.

"I'll come to sleep tomorrow." I hoped Mia would come into my bed on my last night at the LODGINGS.

"Suit yourself."

"Can I go on the train?" I asked. I wanted to know how the Jude in the book felt when he went to Wardour Castle.

He spat on the ground and said, "Shovel up that horse shit". I shovelled the shit. It was mid-morning and hot, hotter than Orange, humid all the time. I was soon slimy with sweat. After I shovelled the shit, I sawed up branches and stacked logs. Then I made mud with water and earth, and mixed it with straw.

My body was tired. I wanted to sit under a tree and think about Jude and Mrs Edlin. I wanted to see Sue.

So I worked more, filling wooden boxes with the mud mix. Slab sent me with a cart full of empty buckets to a river a long way away. An insect stung me when I got there. My arm was hot and swollen around the bite. Crocodiles slunk on the muddy bank. I walked through a vine that stabbed me with tiny thorns. When I returned with water, Slab was drinking beer in the shade.

"Wash the horse," he said.

"I've never washed a horse," I said. It kicked me in the shin.

"Useless buffoon," Slab said. "You'll never be a stone mason."

"Please teach me."

"Make me some food."

"I don't know how, Sir."

He got up and showed me how to light a fire in a metal drum. I never did this in Orange. My nobby was to tell stories. When the wood was burned to red cinders, Slab tossed on two bits of meat.

"Coupla nice chops," he said when they were charred black. I waited for him to give me one, but he said, "What are you waiting for? The horse has done another shit".

Long after dark, I collapsed on the floor of the railway station. I was hungry. I got up and sneaked around. Slab had left a half-eaten chop on a plate, so I chewed off the bits of meat, and walked back to the LODGINGS.

Mia was drinking a beer on the verandah.

"Phew, you stink, Jude. Better clean up and get some sleep."

I gave her a look that I'd been practising. The look of a man ready with a COCK. She laughed and said, "Sweet dreams."

Next morning I woke thinking about Mia and then Sue and then Mia and then both of them. My thoughts were a jumble of flesh and limbs and choni and choot. I stretched like a lion.

Footsteps filtered into my room from the veranda.

"Who's there? Come in."

The outlines of men's bodies fell across the light penetrating the cool green palm leaves and bamboo blinds. The men began to sing. I stepped outside, drawn by the lusty harmonies. Six spadebeards stood in a row, singing and smiling. They formed a circle around me, singing ever louder. My pants were making a little tent in front of me. "Not seemly", a voice said above the singing.

"Onward Christian soldiers
Marching as to war
With the cross of Jesus going on before."

I remembered hearing this song in the church during my journey from Orange. The circle of men tightened, their bodies pressed on me. Their nostrils were full of hair, their teeth strong and yellow, six purple throats battering me with song. The circle, with me at the centre, moved off the veranda, down the street. My feet scrabbled to keep up. People come out of the little timber houses. "Not seemly", they cried. I called out to Mia, but caught just a glimpse of her leaning on the veranda before the human circle sped up. She was half frowning, half grinning, gave a lazy wave.

"Crowns and thorns may perish
Kingdoms rise and wane."

Faster and faster, the smiling human palisade rolled through the town until we were in sight of the railway station.

"But the cross of Jesus
Constant will remain."

They released me at the entrance to Slab's
yard. I fell down, got up, turned to argue
with them, but they were already marching back
to town, singing,

"Onward then ye people
Join our happy throng..."

Slab handed me a shovel.
"The horse did a shit."

SUSAN TO ALEX, JUNE   0100

Dear Alex,

I've had quite an adventure, though not a welcome one. I got ready on the appointed day, putting on a double layer of clothes against the chill of Scotland, and stuffing my last roubles down my pants. I flitted my fingertips across Mr Remington's keys typing "Goodbye, old friend" on the roller. At 10am I set off ostensibly for a morning walk, conscious of my PIP. Will I know when it is reprogrammed? Will there be a buzz? There's nobody to ask about these things. I kept my head down as I walked to the station, convinced there was a glowing red dot on my forehead. The boy banker's instructions were to head for the 11.00 to Carlisle. If the PIP was working properly, I'd simply pass through the gate, onto the train and be in Carlisle in thirty minutes. A quick change of trains and then over the border to freedom.

Well, that was the theory. The first part went smoothly: Through the gate, onto the train, the indicator on the ceiling flashing the names and seat numbers of the passengers. I looked out for Patti Chombo as instructed, and found her seat. The train beeped, elevated itself half a meter, and hissed away under the power of Australian uranium. The passengers were unexceptional: Business people in cloaks, students, a policewoman handcuffed to a scruffy and confused man with an untidy wound on his forehead. You see this a bit these days - people digging out their PIPs.

The True History of Jude

The drab countryside whooshed by, if the word 'countryside' could possibly be apt: Miles of grey engineered landscape, whether it be warehouses or crops growing under immense plastic screens, or derelict solar arrays angled to soak up the low winter sun, now abandoned under the Grand Bargain. Now and then, a hill rose up bearing remnants of the old world - a church steeple, a cluster of cottages, a flock of puzzled sheep behind razor wire. We slowed for Chester Neopolis, where thousands of passengers were piling off a train from the north. Most were wearing UFO caps, marching eagerly under a plastic ceremonial arch that read LET'S JOYOUSLY RENEW FATALIST PLEDGE TODAY.

I heard a cough to my left and saw that the previously empty seat was occupied by a woman in a uniform I didn't recognise; not that there's anything sinister about that because almost nobody in K.E.W. goes about without uniform or fancy dress. But her demeanour unsettled me.

I involuntarily raised my hand to touch my PIP. She glanced at me, frowned, opened her mouth but turned away, evidently deciding not to speak. She slipped a device from a pocket and jerkily slid her fingertips across its face, read something on its surface and shot another glance at me. Another frown. I caught a glance of the badge on her sleeve: RFDG MID-ENGLAND SECTOR.

RFDG: Regulatory Franchising Delineation Group? Regional Finance Defence Guard? Royal Fulfilment Dispersal Grading? It could be any one of hundreds of meaningless combinations describing the hundreds of vague compliance jobs that the English and Welsh toil at in exchange for a wage higher than FreePay. Better that than have them lolling at home complaining they have nothing to do. The RFDG woman got up and tapped one of the students on the shoulder - a boy judging by the cut of the Royal Horse Guards costume. There were sharp words delivered in a whisper, the boy wiped his eyes and blew his nose into a hanky, the woman looked around the carriage with a 'That Told Him' expression. Great Fate, where are the real men in this country? I had a sudden flashback of my dear Jude chasing me with his COCK (he always said it as if it were in capitals). I'm sure these boy students just have little formless pink devices that come out for pee-pee and a rinse before bedtime.

But with the woman now working her way through the carriage to find more weak victims to irritate, the wriggling things in my stomach had stopped. The sign flashed 'two minutes to Carlisle'. I got out, confident, almost rash. Through another barrier, onto the Scotland train, goodbye K.E.W.

Except that just thirty metres from the exit barrier, somebody tripped over. It was a young man with a strong resemblance to the boy banker. He was grimacing as he held his ankle. A small crowd gathered. The casualty caught my eye. I realised something was wrong.

"Stand aside, I'm a first aider," I cried (First Aid Step 1). It's true. I did the course because so many of my very old students take funny turns in lectures.

"My name's Susan and I'm going to help you..."

"Patti, you're Patti Chombo," the injured party hissed.

"My name's Patti Chombo and I'm going to help you. What's your name?" I asked, back in form (First Aid Step 2). The man grunted something. I crouched over him to hear, and he whispered, "My name's Ivan. Go home."

"Stay with me, Ivan," I said in a loud capable voice. "Is it just the ankle or does it hurt anywhere else?" (First Aid Step 3). By now a posse of medical auxiliaries had turned up. The leader was on her knees in an instant, pressing a PIP reader on Ivan's forehead to get his vital signs. I left the scene, making a great charade of checking that the patient was in good hands.

Susan Bridehead or Patti Chombo (I was convinced my PIP was flashing red and blue) slipped onto the a slow train south that didn't require a seat booking, and within five hours I was home in Oxford mooning around the apartment I had just farewelled. Mr Remington gave me a knowing look. I rolled a new sheet into the mechanism and typed, "I missed you", then flicked the carriage back so he could give me a cheeky ding.

So it's all off for now. The boy banker left me a handwritten note saying 'noTT goin 4 thre weiks'. Bless his crooked little heart; nobody handwrites these days, and if you find yourself armed with a pen and (illegal) paper, there's no Predictive Composition to help get it right. Which of course raises the question of what's right and what's wrong. After all, if the average human can't spell, who cares about standards? Answer: The programmers who run The Universe and a handful of people like me who have old-fashioned ideas about these things, I suppose.

I'm now in the uneasy position of pretending to resume 'normal' life until the boy banker gives me a new date. The problem, I assume, is a blockage in the refugee route to the Scottish border and beyond. It's not quite as dramatic as the American slaves being spirited from the Deep South through Baltimore and on to the Canadian border, or the East Germans tunnelling under the wall. I won't be hidden in a cartload of carrots, waiting in fear as the Kingdom of England and Wales border police prod the rustic produce with pitchforks.

The escape route is actually digital; that is, you have to wait your turn for a hacker in somewhere like Armenia or Chile to reprogram your PIP so that The Universe thinks you're still sitting at home, and some stranger is heading for Scotland with quite legitimate motives (Patti Chombo, for example). Once you're over the border, the hackers wipe the PIP, but I'm told it's best to dig it out of your forehead (don't forget to take a blade!) and bite it in half before claiming asylum. I anticipate a holding camp of hopefuls at Gretna Green dabbing their brows with bloody tissues.

So, I must wait until my digital slot opens and the blockage clears, but I'm seriously worried about my health in the meantime. There were a few weeks recently when The Thing took a holiday, but it was obviously just building strength because yesterday I took a bad turn - headache and nausea when I got up, and later in the day a terrifying period when I couldn't remember who I was. I suppose I should tell my doctor, but the poor dear would be so distraught. At any rate, I feel well enough to write today. I even picked up the threads of The History this morning so that word doesn't get back to The Mother of All Australians that I've abandoned it.

Looking back at the last bit of Jude I sent you, I imagine you're wondering about my state of mind in the days after I first met him in the market, when we walked together under the streetlights. Well, the odd thing is that while I couldn't 'find myself' when I started writing about Jude, my twenty-year old Sue is gradually returning. It often happens in the early mornings when I lie in a half-sleep mulling over what I've written and what I plan to write. That's when young Sue drifts into my psyche, when I'm suffused with joy and tragedy and desire and envy in a way I haven't known in decades. When I'm fully wake, the old workmanlike no-nonsense Sue takes over, unless of course The Thing decides to wreck my day. But I sometimes suspect that The Thing is jogging some memory circuit that opens up my old self.

So to pick up the question of my state of mind in those early days, I had a deep conviction that Jude and I would marry. And because my conviction was so deep, I was in no hurry for it to happen. Why hurry? Fate would lead us. I loathed Mr Phillotson, and felt no shame about having to abandon him when the time came.

There were no secrets in Kuranda. I knew what Jude was doing, where he was going. I knew he would soon find Mia in his bed, which gave me a sort of comfort; it saved me from imagining our own intimacy, by transferring the scenario to another woman. Does that make sense? You see, while I could be overcome with a rush of desire (as I was the first day I saw Jude), the invisible thread between us was stronger than just sex, perhaps even nothing to do with sex. Jude understood me perfectly, even if I didn't: He recognised my <u>aberrant passions, and unaccountable antipathies</u>. He was the only person to accept my nature.

Best, Sue

WITCH

On my second day of work, I followed Slab around the town while he sold things he had made: Saucepans, axe handles, a wooden bench, horseshoes, mud bricks, but nothing made from stone. Nobody took any notice of me. Today I was seemly, perhaps.

We stopped at the LODGINGS. Mia came out with a knife to be sharpened. She took me aside while Slab pedalled the grindstone.

"How much is he paying you?" I told her I didn't know, and she shook me by the shoulders: "You poor fool. Tell him you want a thousand a day and your food. And don't worry about your roubles and your books. I'm keeping them safe."

But I couldn't find the moment or the words to ask Slab for money. That night I flopped down, hungry, long after dark. In the morning, he nudged me awake with his toe and left a loaf of bread next to me.

"There's coffee outside," he said.

We sat in the morning sun sipping coffee and eating bread. I'd never had this drink before. It was like burnt wood, and made my brain whoosh and buzz.

"I'll give you five hundred a day," Slab said.

I had a think. Five hundred a day was two or three bananas. I looked down at my ragged shirt: A hundred days to buy a new one. I thought more. This thinking was frightening, powerful. Even more powerful was that I had something to trade.

"Fifteen hundred," I said. After five minutes of cursing and bargaining and punching his fist into his palm, he agreed to a thousand.

"And food," I said.

"Clear off, you little clever dick, and make some mud bricks."

* * *

Four days later we had a day off. It was called Sunday and it came every seven days, which I knew from the book. Slab told me we must go to church. But which church? If Kuranda was like Christminster, there must be many churches. I wondered if I would see Sue there?

We walked into town and entered the church I went to before, with the big green sign on the roof that said BP. There was a long mound of dense vines in front of the church, and when I looked closely I saw a rusty truck inside the vegetation with the same BP letters on its side. The church was full of spadebeards, who smiled at us and beckoned us to sit on the hard benches. I didn't see any women, but there was a thick curtain at the back of the building from behind which floated glorious female singing. The men joined the singing in lower notes, and my whole zazzy rumbled with the heavenly music, the low and high notes like two arms enveloping me in Jesus's hug. I sat spellbound, hypnotised. The music stopped. A silver-bearded man made a terrifying speech about shame and damnation and God's curse on women.

When it ended, we went outside and Slab gave me two thousand roubles.

"I'm off," he said.

"Where are you going," I asked.

"A'courting."

"What is that?" I asked. He sniggered and rubbed his forefinger up and down in his fist, then trotted off towards a part of town that the spadebeards said was unseemly, where the bakery and a bar could be found.

I wandered around the town but all the shops and market stalls were closed. The streets quickly emptied of churchgoers. Sue's house was nearby. I hung around outside trying to glimpse her through the curtains. After a while, an old man came out.

"You are Sue's cousin Jude?"

"Yes, Sir."

"Do not call me Sir. We are all equal before God," he said.

"But I call Slab Sir."

"He is a heathen," said the man.

"I want to see my cousin."

"That cannot be."

"Why?"

"It is ..." he coughed, "... a certain time".

"What time?" I was getting use to the idea of the time. Mia showed me her clock, and Slab had one too.

"Is it eleven o'clock, Sir?"

"No, is it her ... time."

"Is her time the same as my time?" This was getting difficult.

He croaked, "It is not seemly to discuss these things".

"Why not?" I asked, but he screwed up his old face. Inside the house, I heard Sue calling, "Let my cousin in, husband".

The husband shuddered. "It is not seemly," he called to her.

"But we are cousins, almost brother and sister," she called back.

Sue appeared in the doorway, the old husband trying to shield her. She was wearing a sack, I thought.

"You see," the husband said, "She is in her time of shame. I forbid you to enter. You may come in four days".

"I will return in four days, Mr Phillotson."

"What did you call me?"

"Mr Phillotson. It is your name."

"It is not seemly to call me by a false name."

Mr Phillotson slammed the door.

***

Seemly. They were quick to use this word, seemly, although I didn't know exactly what it meant. As I walked back to the railway station, my poor head swirled with memories, new faces, new things I'd learned.

I was now a worker. I'd sold my labour for money. That might be seemly. A man wasn't a horse to be ridden for no reward. It could be seemly for a horse to give its labour free, I thought. But I wasn't certain. If I were a horse, would I think it seemly? I'd think about that later with all the other mysteries. I'd made a list, my first list, so that I didn't forget what I must do.

Back at the station, Slab was lying under a tree drinking beer and scratching inside his shorts.

"I have a question," I said.

"What?"

"What does seemly mean?"

Slab made a knotty frown. "Seemly. Well, that's a word rich in denotation and connotation, and one with subtle meanings beyond the erudition of many a scholar."

I understood about a quarter of this, so I tried another way: "Slab, why is it not seemly to talk to a woman in her time of shame?"

Slab pulled out a pipe. He said, "I wasn't always the rough fellow you see before you. No, once I was an important man, a man who others listened to and depended on". I couldn't see what this had to do with women, but he was determined to go on.

"I was a librarian in a country not so far away. It is called New Zealand."

I thought hard about these new words. Jude - the Jude in the book - sometimes went to a library with <u>a looming roof</u>. But perhaps that wasn't true after all. But yes, I saw now - a librarian - it must mean a man who looks after books.

"Yes," Slab said, "A librarian in the City of Dunedin, a perfect but diminished replica of glorious Edinburgh. Until it was destroyed by the king tides that eventuated according to the climatic vicissitudes of the Anthropocene

Era. My work was to care for the books. Books
- yes, lad, I knew books. I read hour by hour
between my work of shelving and scanning. I
consumed, to my knowledge, five thousand books
or more. On every topic: Sociology,
anthropology, astrology, nanotechnology,
bacteriology, gemmology". I understood only an
eighth of this particular speech, but this
talk of books had me clinging to the words I
actually recognised.

Slab opened another bottle of beer. His eyes
were on some distant target. He gripped his
calloused hands around the bottle as if trying
to squeeze out another -ology.

"So you ask me about what is seemly, and
what is seemly when it comes to women. I tell
you, lad, that what I don't know about
seemliness and women could be written on the
back of a postage stamp."

This reply threw me. What was a postage
stamp? In the book, <u>Dr. Vilbert's pills were
warranted efficacious by the Government stamp</u>,
but this memory failed to make Slab's reply
clearer.

"But Slab, this talk of stamp confuses me.
What is the answer, I ask? What is 'seemly'?"

"Well, it's like this. These men with their
beards, they ..."

"They what?"

"They have certain views ..."

"What views?" I asked.

"It's a difficult question. I once read
books about such things."

"What did the books say?" I asked him, but he hoisted himself up and passed water over a sleeping piglet.

I could see that no answer would come. Slab's mind was sometimes a rushing torrent, and then a creek where the water had dried to a trickle of mud and old turkey shit. I went to my sleeping place to rest until the sun had set. My chest burst with questions – about this place, about my past, about my future, about books. And Sue Bridehead's place in all of this.

***

When it was dark, I lit a candle in Slab's yard, and read the Fringe of Leaves book. Soon I was bitten all over by hard-cased insects. Slab appeared, slapping his arms and legs.

"Light the fire, lad."

I got a blaze going, and Slab tossed on some leaves that created a veil of sweet smoke. The insects disappeared.

"The men we spoke of before," Slab said. "They may appear to be execrable misogynists and bigots, but we may excuse them on account of the peculiar belief system their forefathers forged on the anvil of ignorance."

"Sir, these words. They are like a fog," I said. Was this the same Slab who was mumbling and pissing on a piglet nowrotu ago?

Slab went on: "The battered doxies of these bearded hypocrites, as the inestimable Antipodean Robert Hughes described the first white women to set foot on this blighted

197

soil... Where was I? Yes, their battered doxies are the physical manifestation of their original sin, living reminders of man's fall from primeval grace."

"Sir, I beg you to speak more simply."

"More simply?" he roared. "More simply? If we were meant to speak simply, God would not have given us the dictionary. We would have been like chattering monkeys, insensible to the significance of our blather."

I jumped at the word DICTIONARY. Jude - the Jude in the book - had a dictionary that he spread on his knees to plunge into the simpler passages from Caesar, Virgil, or Horace, but I never worked out what the plunging was all about, or what Horace was. The truth was that although I knew my book almost by heart, there were many words that I didn't understand.

"What's wrong, lad? You're gaping like a galah."

"Do you have a dictionary?" I asked.

He brought his face close to me, staring hard.

"Boy, you've a quality about you. You remind me of another lad back in Dunedin, not so distant from the dredged-up fellow who stands before you now. A lad with an enquiring mind. But here's a question. Can you be trusted with a secret?"

"Yes," I whispered.

"D'you mean it?"

"Yes, I mean it."

He looked around the dark yard, but the only watchers were splintered barrels, rusted motorbikes, and a gulping turkey.

"Lad, I have a library. But it is between you and me, not to be discussed with those sanctimonious blockheads."

He took a taper from the fire and led me into the station building, stopping by a locked door. A loose brick concealed a key, the door swung open to reveal a metal cabinet. There were two stickers on the door. One said THANK YOU FOR NOT SMOKI. The other read PROPERTY OF KURANDA MOTORS PTY LTD.

"Feast your peepers, lad," he declaimed, flinging the metal door open. The cabinet was stacked full of books with spotted greeny-grey covers. Lots of them had burst at the seams or turned to flaky dust. A horrible nest of insect corpses had absorbed the bottom right of the stack. Slab flicked a rag over the books, licked a finger to rub at the spine of one, which collapsed into grey shreds.

"Not in peak condition, I'll warrant," he said. "But one does one's best under egregious climatic circumstances."

He poked among the mess and drew out a thick disintegrating tome.

"Here, the dictionary."

I took it with trembling fingers, moving it into the light of Slab's taper. The cover said Macquarie Concise Dictionary. I fanned the pages. Lists of words, page after page, grey letters, black letters, slanting letters, standing-up letters.

Words beginning with ABC were at the beginning, XYZ at the end. A dim memory forced itself into my mind; it was my mother singing the alphabet with me. Would the dictionary tell me what seemly meant? I listened to the old echo: ABCD EFG HIJK LMNOP QRS TUV XY AND Z NOW I KNOW MY ABC WILL YOU SING ALONG WITH ME? The letter S, it must be near the end of the book. I flicked back from Z. I found T. But then a section of pages was gummed together with a stiff brown goo and R was on the far side. Seemly would have to wait.

A word jumped into my head. I looked for p, then pe, then peng - it was there, penguin: It was a bird, not a fat man.

I looked up at Slab. He smiled. "Take it, lad. It is the key that will open your poor mind to all wonders."

THE ROOTS OF FATALISM

TOP SECRET

Highness,

Quoit has ably reworded the passage to which you objected, viz. 'religious belief was waning' with 'the candle of the nation's faith was sputtering in the winds of fate'. I commend your third cousin's lexicographic and indeed semantiotic aptitude, and will be recommending said kinsman for promotion.

Humbly, Bruce

THE ROOTS OF FATALISM

One of the best kept secrets in the Kingdom of England and Wales is that Fatalism originated not in England but in Australia. With sixty million registered members in the Kingdom of England and Wales alone, the Universal Fatalist Organisation has undergone staggering growth, steadily acquiring the membership databases and property portfolios of almost every mainstream faith. Its partnership with the Vatican has been world-changing.

But how many modern worshippers, freed from the archaic and ramshackle governance practices of the old churches, temples and mosques, know of Barbara 'Bubbles' Macfarlane's role in the biggest religious reformation since Henry VIII bloodied the Pope's nose?

The story of Fatalism begins one hot night in North Queensland a decade before the Grand Bargain. Maree and Jed Kovacs, successful avocado farmers turned charismatic preachers, are warming up the crowd at the Cairns Convention Centre. The cameras are rolling. The worshippers' sweat is drying in the aircon after the long wait in the turbid 45 degree-plus night. Men, women and children fill the overflow seats outside as Tropical Cyclone Prince roils out at sea. Meteorologists are saying that Prince is 'off the scale'. SLUZHBA banners flutter wildly. Every few minutes there is the pop of snapped rivets, and a sheet of plastic roofing spins into the night sky.

Maree is telling the crowd that God will spare the righteous from Prince. There is clapping and singing. A commotion breaks out in one corner. It is a gang of untidy protesters holding signs demanding justice for climate refugees. Security officers toss them out.

The house lights click off and a single spotlight pins Jed to the stage. He is kneeling, eyes tight shut, keening a prayer, beseeching God to turn back the cyclone. The crowd picks up the strain. Five thousand throats howl at the firmament. A huge screen lights up, showing the dark sky beyond the streetlights. Around Australia, the same image is visible to millions of worshippers, all part of the multi-denominational *Faith Smashes Prince* pop-up rally. A nation prays with Jed.

***

The aftermath of Tropical Cyclone Prince is legend: The thousands of worshippers forced to flee the winds and the storm tide, the destruction of the Cairns Convention Centre, the humiliation of Maree and Jed Kovacs, and their double suicide the next day.

The cool head of Barbara Macfarlane, then CEO of SLUZHBA, was one of the few bright lights in those dark days. Sensing that the candle of the nation's faith was sputtering in the winds of fate, she charged a team of brilliant thinkers - scholars of religion, sociologists, economists and psychologists - with devising a model that would reconcile faith with the material world. They came up with the Fatalism Pledge - a statement of acceptance that the effects of climate change were in the hands of a higher power and therefore beyond the capacity of individuals to change. Signing the pledge - as an individual or by virtue of being a member of a Complying Faith Organisation - effectively excluded concerns about climate change from the spiritual agenda of Australians. An Information Pack gave guidance to members of various faiths on how their revealed texts and their traditions supported the Pledge. For example, Christians were encouraged to reflect on Jeremiah 7:20:

Behold, mine anger and my fury shall be poured out upon this place, upon man, and upon beast, and upon the trees of the field, and upon the fruit of the ground; and it shall burn, and shall not be quenched.

Muslims, on the other hand, were reminded of the prediction of the coming of the Mahdi, who, according to certain *hadiths*, will reverse the consequences of climate change.

Meanwhile, the houses of worship had other woes. With Australian property values sinking as coastal buildings became uninsurable, the balance sheets of faith organisations had become hollow logs. Auditors refused to sign off on the accounts of churches with loans secured against buildings like childcare centres and school halls whose values had not been written down. The crisis of faith paralleled a crisis of finance. Clergy struggled to explain to their flocks why bailiffs were carting off the silver.

Bubbles' team brought out their *pièce de résistance* - the Complying Faith Organisation Service Level Agreement. SLUZHBA would buy the assets of faith organisations at current market value conditional on them incorporating the Fatalism Pledge into their constitutions. In return, SLUZHBA would take on their financial management and client relation functions. Religious institutions could now concentrate on core business rather than wasting their best talent on struggling with profit and loss, cash flow, solvency, membership databases, recruitment and marketing.

But within a few short years, the Flood of Sydney swept away the fertile Antipodean soils that had nurtured Bubbles' project. The Australian Fatalist Organisation was history .

SLUZHBA's experts, however, had been quietly fine-tuning the model, using Australia as the proving ground. Transplanted to the Kingdom of England and Wales, the Fatalism Pledge and the Complying Faith Organisation Service Level Agreement quickly spread, first through the smaller charismatic churches run by financially illiterate enthusiasts, then through the ailing faith-based private schools sector, and on to cash-strapped dioceses of the major churches. The Universal Fatalist Organisation, a fully-owned subsidiary of SLUZHBA, was launched in 0001 under the Chairpersonship of Peggy Linklater-Macfarlane, Duchess of Tring. In the words of Her Grace, "UFO stands as the ultimate symbol of freedom of thought and universal siblinghood: All citizens, be they Christian, Hindu, Buddhist, Muslim, Jew, Atheist or Hottentot, are united in their belief that their destiny is in the hands of Fate. This revolution in the spiritual life of England and Wales is underwritten by the financial might of SLUZHBA."

Nowadays, membership of UFO - individually or through registration with a religious organisation - is considered a *sine qua non* of a career in public service and the professions. UFO has expanded its remit to running charities, setting and administering professional accreditation examinations, and building prisons. In 0095, it won a ten-year contract for the outsourcing of the Kingdom of England and Wales Department of Justice, memorialised by a statue of Maree and Jed Kovacs in St Mary's Co-Cathedral in Oxford.

PART FIFTH - IN
JUDE'S KINGDOM

SUSAN TO ALEX, JULY 0100

Dear Alex,

I noticed grapes sprouting on a vine outside my window, so Summer is in full blush. Still no positive news from the boy banker other than another note: Bee patshient Im werkin onit. Patshience is all very well, boy banker, but The Thing won't wait. I mean to get to Scotland before it kills me.

Alex, I suppose you must be wondering if I've been back to the doctor. Well, I have, but the visit turned out differently from expected. I told him I needed strong painkillers for my aching back.

"No need for subterfuge, Professor Bridehead. I'm not going to send you for tests on your brain." He passed me a dozen strips of tablets. "Under the table. These'll help. Nobody needs to know." Good man. Right then, I didn't need my employers to find out about The Thing. There's nothing they'd want more than to find an excuse to re-evaluate my position. Once they'd started poking around, my plans to escape would be discovered.

We sat quietly, he examining his fingertips, me absorbed in the soundscape: The tweeting of an artificial finch, the doctor's breathing, the brief hiss of the irrigation pipes in the grapevine outside the window. I waited for a signal that the consultation had ended, although of course I could have just got up and left.

"It's Clarence, by the way, my first name." So he wanted to talk. Why?

"Mine's Susan. But you know that from my medical record."

The irrigation pipe squirted again. A plane droned overhead.

Suddenly, the doctor contorted himself into a knot of limbs: Legs crossed, feet crossed, arms crossed, head to one side. Words were about to be squeezed through the screwed-up lips. They came in a strangled spurt.

"It's your courage I admire."

Did he say courage? I don't have any of that commodity. "I beg your pardon."

"The courage to face your death. That's what I admire."

"I've nothing to live for, Clarence. I welcome death."

I sat back shocked at my own words. Did I say I welcomed death? Where did that idea wriggle out from? But I've said it. It can't be unsaid.

Clarence ground his palms. Tears leaked from his eyes. I wondered how old he was. Thirty? Thirty-five? I got up and stood behind him not because I felt especially sympathetic; it just seemed appropriate for the occasion. I massaged his shoulders, stroked his brow. His hair was dry and thinning. There was something unbearably pathetic about the flakes of dried skin on his collar, so I looked away. He made a little shudder and turned to hug me about the waist.

We remained in this position for a little, until I said, "Clarence, relax now, tell me what's wrong". I felt remarkably clear-headed considering - or perhaps because of - my shocking declaration. Clarence unwound himself and I withdrew to a chair.

"I'm a dead man, or as good as dead," he said, placing a sheet of paper on the desk. The sight of illicit paper was almost as shocking as my death-welcoming declaration. He glanced up at me, caught my conspiratorial nod, and rotated the paper so that I could read it. It was samizdat. I skimmed the double-sided letter. The masthead was EXECUTION WATCH, the editor a certain CVD. I'd heard of it but never seen a copy; there was a huge amount of samizdat floating around, much of it said to be government disinformation. This material was deadly serious - none of the black jocularity of BOLLOCKS TO SLUZHBA. It plotted a monthly tally of executions in the Kingdom of England and Wales, with locations, dates, names, and crimes.

"My life's work." He made a sigh so deep that I expected his body to collapse.

"You're CVD?" He nodded. I focussed on a section:

Braybrook Marcus Klyuch, Bury St Edmunds, 10 January 0100. Communicating with a person in the Federation of France and Germany with an unregistered electronic device.
Shobha O'Reilly-Flame, New Southend, 14 February 0100. Stealing a nail gun.

Executions are an unspoken truth in the Kingdom of England and Wales. When it comes to sedition, Clarence was Olympic-class.

"You've more courage than I have in my ear lobe, Clarence."

He twisted in his chair again. "It's not that simple. You can't even imagine."

"Try me. I'm not partial to cryptic comments. Under the circumstances, we might consider being frank."

"Point taken. You see, I received a message."

"A message? Who from?"

The doctor made a rueful snort: "My boy banker, who else? Here." He gave me a grubby slip of paper: "Yore frenz said 2 tel yu THE CAT ESCAPED". He shifted in his seat and his shirt sleeve slid up his wrist. I glimpsed a cannula in the back of his hand. I was mildly puzzled, but more interested in the message.

"So whose cat got away?"

"It means I've been identified. It's over."

I stared at the cannula. No, please. This can't be its purpose. Clarence took a syringe from a drawer and filled it from a vial.

"Something else from under the counter." He snorted again.

"Wait," I said. "There's more to this. You're not telling me the whole story. What's that stuff in the syringe?" But I'd already guessed the truth. "You attend the executions."

"Just at the Oxford facility. Several times a month. I prepare the ... patients. I certify death."

Long silence. The fridge motor clicked on and then off.

"So who does ... the actual deed?" I enquired. Clarence looked up, puzzled momentarily as if I'd asked something everybody knows.

"Oh, of course. Who swings the axe? Who shoots the bullet? Well, you do. Or your neighbour, or the man who sells the fish, or King Nigel. Anybody really. The control module for the syringe is triggered by a randomly chosen person interacting with The Universe."

"Interacting?" I asked.

"Just so, it can be anything and anybody. Death by democracy."

"Let me get this right. If I order a pair of socks, somebody could die?"

"Or your aunt could look up her horoscope and - click - here's the Grim Reaper." Clarence made a bitter chuckle. "Or King Nigel might send Princess Maureen birthday wishes, and another one bites the dust."

"It's a masterpiece of banality," I said, more to myself than to Clarence, who had now begun to weep properly. His inconvenient truth was unveiled; he assisted in executions so that he could report them. I was torn between revulsion and admiration.

"Was it worth it, Clarence? Don't doctors swear an oath?"

He was spluttering now, a red-faced muddle of anger and shame. "We give them a good death, we bear witness, they don't die unknown."

So there was a secret coven of these devil-angel doctors.

Clarence clicked the syringe into the cannula. I could stop him, or I could walk out. His life was in my hands at that moment. I should have felt a vast weight of responsibility or some piercing distress. But there was nothing: Inert gas where my heart should be. I didn't care. Even worse, I didn't care that I didn't care.

Clarence promised to wait an hour. "That'll save you getting involved when they find me. And I need some time to make arrangements." I supposed he must have a family. A goodbye note to write. Financial matters to tie up.

"But you might do me a favour." He took out the boy banker's note and wrote THE CAT IS DEAD on the back. "Give him this."

"How will I find him?" He gave me an address close to my apartment and described the blind spot and the urchin. Something compelled me to kiss Clarence on the lips, the first I had tasted since Jude's. He whispered, "Bless you," and I closed the door gently as I left.

I have the Diagonal Steel Spike headache this morning (yesterday was the Hot Throb), but three of Clarence's tablets have blunted the point and quelled the nausea. I'm well enough to write more of the True History of Jude, but I have to pace myself these days; too much concentration affects my sense of who, where, why and when. I'm likely to find myself slumped and slack-mouthed, wondering where the last hour has gone. Read on, Alex and you'll learn how it was to be a witch.

Best, Sue

Stuart Campbell

JUDE HAS A HISTORY

It was four days since Mr Phillotson sent me
away. I'd worked three days for Slab, and
studied the dictionary for three nights in the
light of an oil lamp. The arrangement was
becoming clear - A to Z, words sitting
together in families, their meanings explained
with more words. The words chased each other
through the book, all explaining each other.
This book could teach me about the whole
world, I knew. Except for things beginning
with S.

Slab was ill this morning, groaning with
hotguts.

"What work should I do?" I asked.

"Take a furlough, lad," he said through
gritted jaws. I looked around the yard for a
furlough. There was nothing I recognised with
that name. The dictionary, of course! It took
me a long time because of the spelling - fer,
for, fir, fur, furl - and I found furlough.
Yes, I saw it! Slab was giving me a day free
of work.

I walked along Coondoo Street to the town
and knocked firmly on Mr Phillotson's door.

***

We sat in the parlour, Mr Phillotson and I,
while Sue made refreshment in the kitchen. The
chair was soft. It wrapped around me. Pictures
hung on the walls: The face of a spadebeard
drawn from the side, a flat-looking mountain,
some writing done in coloured threads. Mr

Phillotson had a tired look, a worn-out look, as if he had used up all his kindness.

"Tell us your history, young man."

"My history?"

"Who you are, where you came from, what you did."

Nobody had asked me this before. My history - what an odd expression. How could I have a history? The world had a history, Christminster had a history. But yes, I remembered the Jude in the book told Sue the shameful history of his marriage to Arabella.

"Where shall I start?" I asked him.

"From your earliest memory," Mr Phillotson replied. He dabbed his old eye with a rag.

I said, "I remember mother teaching me to read but she went away. And I remember Auntie Vicky and I remember the uniforms and the orange fish in the creek, and Ross shooting the kangaroo".

Mr Phillotson frowned. It was clear that my history wasn't what he had in mind.

Sue came in with rattling cups. She was wearing a simple long skirt and T-shirt today, not the sack of shame. "Husband," she said, "My cousin's mind is unformed. I intend to teach him to order his ideas".

I listened carefully. Sue was right. I wasn't a fool, but I knew that I needed order, I needed ordering. I'd blundered into a new world whose rules and arrangements puzzled me. I knew too that I was learning fast. Mr Phillotson looked gravely from me to Sue and back again.

"This is not possible. It would not be seemly to instruct him," he said.

Seemly again. This word chased me like a wasp. I still couldn't find it in the dictionary. If only I could prise apart the pages in the brown gummed-up part.

Sue took cups and pots from the tray. Everyone was silent. The spoon clinked on the saucers. Sue stirred the liquid in the teapot.

I must do something about seemly. Swat it, step on it so it goes away. I said, "Fuck seemly".

Mr Phillotson's head jerked up. The birds outside stopped squawking.

Sue burst into tears. Mr Phillotson stumbled to his feet and clapped his hands over his wife's ears.

"What?" I asked.

"That word. It is forbidden. It is full of a woman's shame," he said.

Sue broke away from Mr Phillotson and pushed him into his chair. His old eye fluttered and his mouth made a possum's bum hole.

"My cousin is a child in the shape of a man," she said. "He fumbles through a new existence, trying this and that, making mistakes that arise from his innocence and his misunderstanding of the lives of grown-up men and women."

I sat watching them, one to the other. Did Sue mean this? A child? I wasn't a child when I strutted up the street, a man with a nodding COCK after the afternoon with Mia in my bed. I wasn't a child when I bargained for my labour with Slab.

Sue turned to me. "Cousin, how did you learn that word?"

"From Ross, the trader."

"When?"

I thought carefully. I wasn't good with days and weeks.

"Two weeks ago," I said.

"You see," she cried. "He is an infant. You men, you whisper fuck and cunt in private company."

"Have a care, witch," Mr Phillotson said, his old eye glistening.

I was sweating in the armchair. What next? Would they slap one another? But Sue abruptly sat down and smiled at Mr Phillotson.

"Will you have tea, husband?" He nodded warily and accepted the cup from this woman with her <u>aberrant passions, and unaccountable antipathies</u>.

A <u>nowrotu</u> passed with awkward talk about my new home town. Awkward, but I learned a lot. I learned that the spadebeards referred to themselves as the Blessed Persons, and they had no leader except for the real Jesus, who died for them on a cross in Cairns, which I knew was wrong. I learned that the uniforms never came here. I learned that the fruit and vegetables in the markets came from the spadebeards' farms outside the town, and that the Aboriginals owned the horses and carts that brought produce to the market. Mr Phillotson told me that Slab owned his horse, but he used to rent it from an Aboriginal man called Williams.

"I thought you could only rent lodgings." I said.

"Oh no, it means more. It means one party pays for the use of something."

"So if Slab pays for my work, am I rented?" I asked.

"No," said Mr Phillotson. "You are someone, not something. You are a free man."

"And is Slab's horse a free horse?"

Mr Phillotson rubbed his old nose and pulled his long ear lobe.

"Oh dear, simple boy. A man is made in God's image, but a horse is not. Let us leave this kind of talk alone."

Sue glanced at me. A glance that said, 'be careful'. But I was remembering the power of my speech when I was a storyteller.

"Is that why it is seemly for a horse to work for no pay? Because it is not made in God's image?"

Sue pinned my eyes with hers, and said in the quietest of voices, "Wofo mekit hubby vale?"

"Wife, what are you saying?" Mr Phillotson asked, cupping his hand to his ear.

"I asked if you would like more tea, husband."

"No more tea, and no more of this talk from your cousin. We follow the Straight Way in this house. Now we will read."

My Sue was right in warning me not to make the old man angry. I had stepped too far in baiting him. I sat politely while she cleared away the cups. When she came back, Mr

Phillotson took out a Bible and read aloud a long passage that ended with:

"And when he hath made her to drink the water, then it shall come to pass, that, if she be defiled, and have done trespass against her husband, that the water that causeth the curse shall enter into her, and become bitter, and her belly shall swell, and her thigh shall rot: and the woman shall be a curse among her people."

Sue sat primly, looking up at me once or twice. The thread between us was so strong that I wondered if Mr Phillotson could see it, but he was deeply engaged in his reading. I ached to be alone with her, but at the same time she and I were in a secret parlour inside this parlour. A word hopped into my head. I'd read it a thousand times, but it had never shown me its real shape. The word was LOVE.

***

I visited the house every week, and learned the word chaperone: A married woman must not be alone indoors with a man who is not her husband. If Mr Phillotson was not at home, a woman called Leah sat with us, trussed up in tight clothes and high-heeled shoes. I asked her about the shoes one day.

"When we marry, the husband's mother makes us a gift of shoes," she said, wrenching one off and passing it to me. It was worn and scratched, the lower part carved from hard wood, the top cut from a tyre.

"Does it hurt to walk?" I asked.

"It is our penance," she said.

"Penance for what?"

"For being a woman, of course. For despoiling God's plan for a paradise on Earth."

"But Sue does not wear them," I said.

"Sue has her painting. That is her penance."

I changed the subject. I knew that Christ suffered for our sins, but surely that was enough suffering for all of us.

* * *

One day, Leah was taken ill while she sat with us. The malaise was heralded by a putrid, noisy <u>stinko</u> from under the short skirt. She excused herself and ran home. Everybody in the town suffered from <u>hotguts</u> from time to time. The pains came on quickly, and the bowels leaked blood and shit for two or three days. Because I bought bottled water whenever I could, I suffered less.

After Leah left, Sue sat on my lap and stroked my hair. We kissed chastely and she told me that we must never be apart. I was surprised at how delicate and thin she felt in my arms. Drunk on the sweet smell of her skin, on the film of moisture where our bare arms touched, my hand slid to her breasts.

She jerked away. "Cousin, you take advantage of me, a married woman."

I leant back in shame and confusion. "I love you," I said. "You are me and I am you."

Her look softened. She said, "Our love is sacred, surely, not profane. Let me sit close to you again".

This time, I kept my hands away. But when we kissed, her tongue pushed against mine and her fingers stroked my stomach. I sat rigid, in even more confusion. She saw my sorrow.

"What were those words, Jude? Aberrant passions, and unaccountable antipathies, yes, that was it. Even I do not understand my own passions. Be patient with me, my love."

There was the noise of boots on the doorstep. We flung ourselves into separate chairs and put our hands in our laps. Mr Phillotson entered.

"Where is Leah? What is going on?"

"Nothing, husband. Are we suspected of something?"

Mr Phillotson shrugged. There was more tea, more chitchat, but the husband looked wary.

As we talked, the air became heavier and the sky darker. Birds called strangely. A horse whinnied somewhere. We went outside. The street was empty. A hot wind whipped across the town and a large tree branch flew onto the roof and bounced off. The wind blew stronger. Palm trees bent sideways.

"Go home, Jude, shelter in the station," Mr Phillotson said. I pushed towards the railway station against the wind, tasting the memory of Sue's lips. I'd call tomorrow. Perhaps Leah would still be ill and Mr Phillotson would be out on an errand. My thoughts were swamped by an animal howl and a wall of solid hot air pushing me from behind. A rain of hard things hit my back: Branches, fruits wrenched from trees, bits of timber. The howl swirled around me, in front of me, in my ears and nose and up my guda. I tripped, I bowled over, I rolled down the hill. A flappy grey thing swiped my face and flew upwards, twisting. It was a corrugated iron sheet and it slashed my cheek on its way skyward. My eyes filled with blood and dust. I got on my knees but didn't know where to go. Someone pulled me down the hill. Slab's voice yelled: "I've got yer, lad."

The True History of Jude

Dear Alex,

Another month gone, and no news of my departure. I shared a quiet smoke with the boy banker last week. He told me the problem is that the wildfires in Russia had damaged a big cable, which I assume is a kind of hackers' highway out of sight of The Universe. So, plenty of time to muse on the meaning of life and other big questions. My symptoms have receded somewhat as my sense of resignation to fate has grown; perhaps The Thing was a phantom.

I've never told you why I left America after my two years as a visiting scholar. It was very sudden, as you might remember. Barely even time for the History Department to give me a proper farewell party, although if there had been one I'd have been shrinking into a corner of the staff lounge as I always did. When someone suggested opening a bottle of champagne in the common room, I made an excuse about feeling sick and after that nobody asked.

To witness such a tumultuous two years! I arrived in the United States of America and departed from the Northern American Union. The secession of the South Eastern States, the construction of Ivanka's Golden Colossus on the drowned remains of Ellis Island, the sealing of the border to the north and south, the withdrawal of American directors from the boards of the Triopoly, the decommissioning of the nuclear power plants. It was a historian's

Nirvana. And where else in the world would people refuse to wear a PIP or connect to The Universe on the basis that it was unconstitutional?

When I first arrived, I was stunned by the market stalls and coffee shops selling books made from paper, by the backstreet publishing shops where anybody with a manuscript could order up a crate of bespoke paperbacks. Ninety-nine percent of it was rubbish or stolen. I was amazed at how scholars inhabited a lawless intellectual world with their own guilds and rivalries and fist-fights. It couldn't have been further from what I had come from, where university curricula were centrally approved and accredited, and prescribed reading lists were uploaded to students' PIPs on enrolment to be listened to while they watched the pictures on a bookoid. The American students had to pay for their courses, so classes were constantly disturbed by people coming and going to get to their work shifts. That's when classes weren't cancelled because of strikes or power cuts or floods or gun massacres. Funny what you get used to: Assignments and exams handwritten on lined paper, meat in your diet, advertising hoardings and signs on every surface, big black telephones tethered to the wall with cables, and of course private vehicles.

The ethical cannibalism debate fascinated me. I was taken to one of those lab-grown human tissue restaurants before they were closed down after the Supreme Court ruling, but I chickened out (not quite the right term) and just had the salad.

I wonder how it all looks now after fifteen years? It was obvious to me that the place was on a glorious path to self-destruction - the low birth rate, the lack of economic planning, the crime, the permanent crisis of politics and governance.

It was complacency that got my visa cancelled. While I could write freely about the Americas and almost anywhere else in the world, any critical discussion of the Kingdom of England and Wales was off limits - clearly stated in the agreement I signed to get an exit visa on my PIP.

It was a foolish mistake. I gave a talk to a lunchtime gathering on the financial dependence of the Kingdom of England and Wales government on the Macfarlane clan - basically describing the debt trap arrangement. I dared to contrast the K.E.W. situation with America's refusal to buy Australian uranium and its ban on dealing with the Triopoly. Somebody must have recorded it because two days later, a printed pamphlet was on sale in all the university coffee shops. A day after, I got a message through The Universe to the effect that I must return home immediately, followed by a visit from North American Union Homeland Security with a deportation order and a PIP reader. What choice did I have? Perhaps I could have found the courage to dig out my PIP and go underground, get a fake social security card, become a bag lady, disappear into some rural community and blend in with

the jam-makers, poets, and religious nutcases.
But I knew I couldn't cope with the anarchy
and uncertainty of American life. My younger
Sue Bridehead would have, but I wasn't her
anymore.

Nothing was said when I arrived back in
Oxford. There was an office and an apartment
waiting for me, as well as a 'transition plan'
to ease me back into work after two years away.
Then, the golden prize, or perhaps the gilded
cage, of the Macfarlane-Gillette Chair of
Modern History.

More of the True History of Jude attached.
Keep my papers safe.

Best, Sue.

JOIN OUR HAPPY THRONG

The storm blew for three days. Slab and I tethered the trembling horse at the end of the station corridor, and huddled in the library room, barely able to speak above the roar. Our little oil lamp spluttered and died halfway through the second day. Slab's oil drum was in a shed in the yard. He crawled to the entrance, returned, said, "The shed's gone and the drum's stuck up a fuckin gumtree". We eked out the food - dried wallaby strips and avocadoes - and drank beer.

"I've never known the like," Slab declared.

Nor me, I thought. In Orange, the clouds would bank up over a couple of hours and then drop a whole ocean of warm rain that stopped before you had time to think about it. But this weather was like a wild animal, like the spadebeards' God perhaps, in its savage punishment.

On the third morning, we woke to silence and a lightness creeping into the fuggy station air. We went into the yard, but there wasn't a yard now. All the vegetation had been blown away except the big gum tree where the oil drum was stuck. There was just mud dotted with a few of the things the wind couldn't lift: A tractor engine, a concrete block with a steel pole and a square sign that said <u>30 MINUTE ANGLE PARKING REAR TO KERB</u>. Slab shook the pole and said, "Good, I was gonna use that for something." We spent the rest of the day searching the mud and the shredded trees for Slab's tools.

"Never seen the like," Slab said for the fiftieth time. We poked around in the mud and debris. Most of the tools were now restored to a wooden rack we made from some sleepers that had blown in from somewhere else. Slab appraised the sleepers, saying, "The Lord taketh away but he generally giveth back something unexpected". The horse was reconciled to a new landscape. Slab found the cart in a ditch and made some rough repairs to it. We had water in our barrel.

"Better go to town," Slab said. "See what work we can pick up."

I nodded, but what I really wanted was to see my cousin Sue.

The town was almost entirely covered in smashed vegetation and fallen trees. There was no passable street so we tethered the horse to proceed on foot. Spadebeards worked in pairs, singing as they cleared the tree trunks with huge double-handed saws. The air was filled with a crisp, weedy smell of mangled leaves. It was hot beyond possibility, humid as a bath. Somebody shouted "Snake!" and a man fell down clutching his leg.

Aboriginals had come into town on foot, offering their labour for barter or roubles. An old spadebeard chased them away: We've nothing to give you. But Slab said he would work for credit, and soon we were hauling tree logs into piles on the promise of supplies when the town recovered.

Credit: I made a mental note to look up this word in the dictionary. In the book, Sue told Jude 'Your wordly failure, if you have failed, is to your credit rather than to your blame', but I couldn't see the connection with the fallen trees.

Around the middle of the day, women tottered out with food and drink. Slab saw me looking in the direction of Sue's house.

"Go, lad, scarper and see your dainty paramour." I'd left the dictionary at the station, but I guessed he meant Sue. I did what I think scarper must mean.

Sue's front door was open. In the parlour she knelt dabbing the brow of Mr Phillotson, who was propped on pillows. His trouser leg was rolled up to show a bloody sausage of bandages. Mr Phillotson nodded at me, and Sue turned.

"Cousin Jude, you are safe. But see my poor husband. His leg is impaled."

I now noticed that a corner of the parlour was ruined and open to the sky. A piece of flying tree trunk had pierced the roof and was lodged in the couch on which Mr Phillotson lay. I looked closer. A side branch had gone clean through his leg. Sue had bound the flesh next to the branch to stem the blood.

I ran back to fetch Slab. We spent the afternoon removing the tree and repairing the roof while Sue held her husband, sheltering him from the wood chips and grit that flew from our work. At last, Mr Phillotson was free, although still bearing the piece of bloody stake trimmed with a saw near entrance and exit. When we were finished, dusk was falling. A crazed choir of frogs and insects struck up. I helped Sue to move Mr Phillotson to a room at the back of the house. A woman visited with medicine for the old man.

"He will sleep till morning," the medicine woman said, with an edgy look at my witch.

"Stay, Jude," Sue said. "At least for the evening. Until you go to the station to sleep."

I asked, "Is it seemly? With no chaperone?"

"Chaperone <u>bigfuckup</u>," she said. "We are cousins."

"More than that, Sue."

"More than that, surely," she whispered.

(Alex: I can't tell you what forced those words from my mouth, and I can't ever know Jude's feelings at that moment. All I can say is that I was buzzing with a frightening closeness for Jude that was not quite sexual and not quite platonic. It was a rawness in us both: Too painful to touch, too alluring to resist.)

My witch pulled me onto the couch with the blood-brown hole from the impaled tree. I tried to kiss her but she said, not the lips, not there. She kissed my neck and gripped my hand so that it didn't wander.

I pushed her away saying, "What are you?"

She burst into sobs. "I don't know. I am you and you are me."

"Enough," I said, the man with the COCK who had sold his labour and had a history. "Talk straight," I said. "What are you, and what are we?"

There was a groan from the back room. We rushed in. Mr Phillotson had risen from his bed and fallen to the floor. The bloody bandages had slipped to reveal a mess of stripped flesh, glistening sinews and blackening wood. Sue felt his forehead.

"He is burning. Jude, fetch the medicine woman."

I ran out. The woman was posted in the street with her basket of weeds and phials. She dressed the wound with a muddle of crushed leaves and a pungent oil, gave the old fellow a few drops of brown liquid on his tongue.

When he had settled, Sue pulled me back to the couch. We lay like spoons, me behind her, while we spoke softly about our future. We will be married, we will have children, we whispered.

"I will be a stone mason," I said.

"I will paint portraits of the spadebeards to hang in their parlours."

"Wofo nolonga mekit pitcher huhu yu?" I asked her in the old tongue.

"Because when I live with you, I will have no shame. Someone else can paint their tits and cunts."

"But you are married, Sue. When can we be together?"

"Soon," she said.

***

The weeks rolled by, doused with storms, but none like the one that did for Mr Phillotson. Yes, he hung on for six Sundays with his leg growing more putrid and his body bloating as the townsfolk rebuilt their houses and workshops.

During those days something clicked in my thoughts, or perhaps in my feelings. I tried to grasp what the change was, but its meaning slipped away just as I almost had it between my fingers. The nearest I came to explaining it to myself was that I was going forward, not standing still in the present. I had other thoughts too about how one thing caused another, and why that should be so. I spent hours hunting the dictionary for the words to explain my new thoughts.

The provisions promised to Slab for our labour never arrived because of the damage to the spadebeards' crops. When I visited Sue each week, she would be feeding her husband a miserable soup of water tinted green with some bitter leaf. Mr Phillotson shook his head at the food, saying, "Eat and save yourself, sweet witch".

Faces were gaunt, eyes red from gazing at the leaden clouds. The rented horses were spirited away to the hinterland where the Aboriginals would fatten them on their secret pastures. But the townspeople forged on with their pitiful tasks, growing thinner day by day. With the Aboriginals hiding out, there was no meat; the spadebeards abhorred hunting, just as the Aboriginals loathed gardening. A few of the men struck up a hunting party to throw rocks at wild pigs or knock down birds with sticks, but came back empty-handed. The churches rang with hollow song.

Slab and I stayed inside the station yard making items we might sell when times improved: Tin mugs, horseshoes, rubber boots. We fed on dried wallaby from Slab's secret caches as the rains lashed the town. At nights I devoured books from Slab's library: North and South by Mrs Gaskell, Fifty Shades of Gray by E.L. James. Others were The Odyssey, The Day of the Jackal, The Old Curiosity Shop, Basics of Solid Geometry, The Girl on the Train.

Every two or three days, Slab gave me a handful of jerky wrapped in palm leaves.

"Take it lad, take it to your sweetheart. But keep mum. Zip it."

With this remark, he would pinch thumb and forefinger together and swipe them across his lips.

While Sue was wasted to a wraith, poor Phillotson was a purple sack of agony and resignation. Sue would coax a few shreds of jerky through his crusted lips.

"Eat, Sue. Save yourself," he would whisper.

"No, I will save it for when the fever has passed and you can rebuild your strength."

Then on a day when the sun rose into a clear, broiling sky, Mr Phillotson gave up his patient soul. Slab and I knocked up a coffin from some scrap. A squad of spadebeards sang the town down. Mr P was buried under a banana tree and a cross that Slab carved from a breeze block. My sweet witch was free.

* * *

I woke in fright. It was dark, not dawn yet. Slab was shaking me. Burning oil smoke in my nostrils, a wavering yellow flame. A book beside me. The familiar walls of my room, my mattress. I sat up. I heard singing, coming closer. We stepped outside to see, under the full moon, a posse of singing spadebeards coming our way.

"Onward Christian soldiers,
Marching as to war,"

My witch stumbled and tripped, captive in the knot of strong-toothed Christian soldiers. They reached the station, the circle unjoined, and Sue was released. Slab dashed to catch her before she slumped to the ground. She was wearing a sack. We carried her inside and gently rested her on my mattress. Slab melted away. She clasped my neck, breathing hard. We clung to each other in the warm darkness. The singing faded away.

"Onward, then, ye people;
Join our happy throng.
Blend with ours your voices
In the triumph song ..."

I am you and you are me.

The True History of Jude

Dear Alex,

I woke this morning with the fading wisps of a sex dream in my mind. I fought to call back the writhing limbs, the tingling flesh, the wetness, fingers, tongue, choot, choni, hot breath. The scenes wouldn't replay in the dim light of my dull room, but I knew my young self had been with Jude. I opened my thighs and caressed myself for the first time in Fate knows how long, feeling his hands and tongue move over me, through me, under me.

And here I draw a curtain, dear Alex. Suffice to say that I lingered long beyond breakfast time, and spent the rest of the day mulling over the delicious return of those sensibilities.

As a scholar, I attribute this phenomenon to writing about sex: As I coolly construct mind pictures of lovemaking, I convert them to writing. As I re-read them and think about them later, the mind pictures begin to thaw, warming rarely used parts of my brain, arousing bloodflow, awakening nerve endings. A classic feedback loop, a psychologist would say...

By the evening, I was exhausted. The Thing must have been lurking beneath the blanket of pleasure, but quietly doing its dirty pain work while I was distracted. A double dose of Dr Death's tablets knocked me into a dozy heap of limbs and sobs. In the early hours another dream broke into wakefulness, and this time I reeled the scenes back in: My father cradled me while a beautiful woman with long eyes lay spreadeagled and naked beside him. We were on a burning bed that sank into green water, and then I was in a long room sliding a cannula into Jude's hand ...

Bestish, Sue

REVELATIONS

Slab legally married us the next afternoon on the authority of a certificate confirming that Endeavour Winston Frost was registered as a Justice of the Peace (Qualified) in Queensland in the year 1978.

"If you are Endeavour Winston Frost, then why do I call you Slab?" I asked after he carefully unfolded the certificate on a tin tray. Where his name was written, the words looked as if they'd been scratched into a layer of grey paint. Slab made a show of tapping the side of his nose and zipping his lip, and refolded the paper before storing it in a pink plastic box with a locking lid.

"Tupperware," he said. Later I checked the dictionary: From Tupper, American manufacturer of plastic goods, 1950s + ware.

The wedding was quickly done. Sue had changed the sack for an old-fashioned flouncy frock she found in a rotting suitcase in the station. It had a label in the neck saying THE CAIRNS PLAYERS THE IMPORTANCE OF BEING EARNEST. Slab roasted a piglet and served beer to Sue, me and our sole guest Mia, who had come up from town.

While Slab fetched more beer from inside the station, the sun was momentarily blocked. I heard a rumble and caught a dark moving shape in the corner of my eye. The vibration from above made me sick in the zazzy. A shadow passed over the sunny part of the yard. I looked for Sue and Mia, but they were walking under the trees towards the longdrop. When everyone came back, I said nothing. Perhaps I imagined it.

Slab spent that night courting in town, leaving us to our honeymoon in the station. Mia whispered some secrets to Sue before she went home. My witch and I talked in the yard until the first pink of dawn, neither making the first move to my bed. The word 'seemly' stood at the edge of my thoughts like a schoolmaster's wagging finger. When an animal snarled close by, the finger dissolved in the perfumed night air, and we went inside to make sweet, slithery, confusing love, with her sometimes me and me sometimes her, and often neither of us knowing who was who. We crept out naked to meet the first rays of the sun, sitting apart in our own bodies for a short time before we washed one another under the shower bucket that Slab had rigged up. In the faint morning light, I saw that we both had dried blood on us. We had made our honeymoon while she bled. Watching my look, she shivered and said in a cat's purr voice, "It was not seemly," and kissed me deeply.

(Alex, I don't expect you to make sense of what I've made Jude say. In truth, I have no idea how he felt that night because I've given him my thoughts, or at least my memories of my thoughts. Of course, I've re-remembered them a thousand times and it may be that they are as empty of truth as a homeopathic dilution.)

Three months had passed since I'd moved into the railway station, according to Slab. I never had any use for months and weeks in Orange, but I was getting used to the idea of dividing the past and the future into small and large pieces.

In these three months, I'd been experimenting with ways to make clean water. The few bottles of water in the market had disappeared. A trader told me they stole it from ABSI trucks that come a gutser, but there hadn't been one for a while. I asked him what a truck coming a gutser was.

"These trucks don't have no driver but they can see what's in front, like men or dogs can. If you want to stop one, you can't just chuck a rock under it when it passes, because it'll drive around it."

He explained that you dug a big hole in the road and covered it to make a trap. The truck would fall into the hole, turn over, and come a gutser.

"Well, I can't wait for a gutser to come," I said.

I took over a corner of Slab's yard to learn to make clean water. The idea came from a wonderful book called Scouting for Boys by Robert Baden-Powell. Mr Robert said All water has a large number of germs in it and we must boil it because germs are very tough customers, and take a lot of boiling before they get killed. So I brought a barrel of water from the place on the river where everyone took it from. I didn't know how much a lot of boiling was, so I boiled a bucketful for a whole day. But at the end, most of the water was gone and I'd burnt a whole tree, so maybe an hour was enough. Next I made a cloth filter that I'd read about in a book called Naked Camping. After a few weeks I found the right combination of boiling and filtering to get sweet water without any bits floating in it. After a month of drinking nothing but my sweet water, Slab, Sue and I had avoided hotguts.

"Slab," I said. "We can make water machines and sell them to the spadebeards."

He looked sideways.

"Why not?"

"Chances are those numbskull Neanderthals will accuse you of Deep Thinking."

Slab was right. I took my water things to town, and they chased me out of the market, babbling about water made with Satan's fire. Bigfuckup, these people.

***

We sat all three in the yard under the shade of young banana trees that had thrown themselves skyward in the months after the storm. Slab was arranging sliced avocadoes on a tin plate he'd rubbed clean with his sleeve.

He knelt and placed the food in Sue's lap, with doting concern.

"I am not sick, dear Slab, just pregnant."

"You cannot be careful enough, Mrs Fawley, with these tropical breezes. A microbial fever might lurk in their lulling softness."

Sue finished the avocado, but she looked as green as its pulp, not wishing to offend Slab's solicitude.

Next to a row of water machines, a cauldron boiled over a wood fire to sterilise bottles for sweet potato wine, our new venture. We called it Redskin. The spadebeards guzzled the murky liquid in their bars, preferring it to the beer that was made by the colony of Fijians out at Mareeba. I learnt the skill from one of Slab's books, The Complete Illustrated Guide to Homemade Wine.

But trouble was approaching. One morning we rose to find smashed glass and spilt wine in the yard. Slab traded twenty bottles of Chateau Redskin for a savage dog called Hitler. We attached it to a long chain so it patrolled the yard at night. No more trouble for now, but the Fijians glared at us when they passed our market stall in town.

Slab found something called a safe among some junk thrown down a gorge years ago. We hid Arabella's roubles and my book in the little box, which Slab chained to a girder in the ceiling of the library room. Sue concealed the key among her clothes.

* * *

Our little colony of three exiles was growing prosperous. Sue had taken up painting portraits of spadebeards that sold for big roubles in the market now that food was being grown again. Slab and I scavenged far and wide for scrap metal for plates and forks and brackets. We learned how to make nails. The safe was stuffed with roubles and our sheds full of jerky, preserved fruits, and sweet potato wine. No stone masonry yet, but I was patient.

I had read my way through a third of Slab's library - at least the books that hadn't turned to dust and dry shreds. The last six were stacked by my bed: Teach Yourself Maltese by Joseph Aquilina, 100 Masterpieces of Australian Painting by William Splatt and Barbara Burton, Cairo Mon Amour by Stuart Campbell, Phillips World Atlas, Call Me By Your Name by Andre Aciman.

Words came easily to me as my thirsty mind soaked up chapter after chapter, so that I now existed in parallel worlds: There was a realm of stories and places I'd never been to; each book added another connection and another blank in the realm was filled in. None of this had any link to the everyday world of the station yard and the private world where I was Sue and Sue was Jude. I found Kuranda in the Phillips World Atlas, and I knew that we lived in a place that was called Australia.

Hitler bit my hand one day, and Slab shot the angry creature. I was sick with fever and trembling for a week. The wound went black and stank. The word rabies was in my ear whenever Sue and Slab were talking about me, but it turned out that I didn't have this dread sickness. My hand recovered but never worked properly again because the knuckle joints stayed stiff and swollen.

With the dog gone, we had to build a palisade to keep out night intruders, employing Fijian brewers to dig postholes.

They took their meagre roubles sullenly, returning to their settlement in silence.

Mia was song-marched out of town and moved in with us. She must have been no longer seemly. Slab told me she used to be a veterinary nurse in a place called New Caledonia. I didn't ask him what a veterinary nurse was; I'd got into the habit of hiding my ignorance. Veterinary and nurse were in the dictionary, many pages apart. Mia, I eventually discovered, helped make sick animals better.

On the morning of the birth, Slab and I were banished outside while Mia wrangled the infant from Sue's slim hips inside the station. She did the horse births for the Aboriginals, Slab said, while we paced the yard. I jammed my ears with my hands at Sue's screams and moans. We hardly ever heard of a birth in Orange. When I thought hard about it, I realised that there was nobody in the town younger than about eleven. Why hadn't I wondered about this when I lived there?

At the sound of a piping cry, Slab sloshed Chateau Redskin into my mug and we toasted new life.

"In you go, lad. Make the acquaintance of your progeny."

Sue was clutching a tiny thing with almond eyes like mine. I embraced my family, peeped in wonder at the miniature fingers and the creased face.

"She will be called Winston," Sue said, "In Slab's honour".

Winston. Win-ston. I rolled the name around my teeth. Yes, it was a seemly name for this tiny female miracle that Sue and I had made.

"Pardon me for mentioning," said Slab, who had been listening outside the doorway, "but Winston is really a feller's name".

Sue looked at him with tragic eyes, and he harrumphed and said that notwithstanding, it was a fine name and he was deeply touched, and it would be so. We would have a furlough tomorrow in the lass's honour.

The next day, we rested under the banana trees and palms, talking of our old lives. Sue told of the days in Leura when her father fought the Battle of Blue Parrot Lane, and I recited one of my silly Orange stories in the old language of that region. Slab laughed at the clumsy expressions and half-recognised words, but Sue and I exchanged secret looks, knowing that there was no more than a whisker between the old Jude and this new Jude who fucked on top and bought the labour of Fijians.

I asked Mia how she had come to Kuranda, but she looked away, mumbling something. When I asked again, she said she came to Australia by accident, being put ashore by a smuggler.

"A smuggler?" I asked.

"My people were left abandoned in New Caledonia when the French left, and my father paid men to take us to Timor."

"What is Timor?" I asked.

"A place where smugglers bring and take people. We wanted to go to France, where I had family." I'd seen France in the Atlas, shaped like a bat in flight. They spoke French there.

"What was the nature of the accident?" Sue asked.

"The boat broke down and we came ashore at Cairns. Twenty years ago. I was separated from the others. I avoided the uniforms and came up the hill to Kuranda."

"But there are no uniforms in Cairns. I've been there with Slab," I said.

"There were," Slab said. Mia looked into the distance.

I turned to Mia and asked, "And you have lived here since?"

Sue gave me a wary glance.

"I did my penance," Mia said, "before I became a respectable woman".

The swishing of palm trees filled the long silence, and then I asked, "What is your history, Slab?"

At that moment a roar in the sky brought us to our feet. A thing like a tube with flat edges flew a hundred armlengths above us. It disappeared over the trees, and then returned lower in a circling path as if hunting us. We flattened ourselves on the ground, poor Winston howling her lungs out. I babbled a prayer in the Orange language to Jesus and Sue Bridehead that it wouldn't come back. But Slab was on his feet, hands cupped around his eyes.

"It's an SAFM Mark 2, I'll wager."

We waited for more information, but he was following the flying thing intently. It faded into the edge of the sky.

Slab stood unmoved, while I blushed over my silly prayer. I looked at Sue but she mustn't have heard me praying to her. Or to who she used to be.

"A Mark 2 or a Mark 3," Slab said. Sue and I stared at him in puzzlement, and he changed the subject, proclaiming about the quality of this month's batch of Redskin.

"Slab, what's a SAFM, Mark 2 or Mark 3?" I asked. I was curious now, not scared.

"Tell him," Mia said. "Tell him everything."

Slab walked away, kicked a few sticks, stood by a banana tree. We waited. He wrung his fat hands together, then let out a long sigh.

"It's a Sluzhba Autonomous Flight Module. A drone, some would have it in a colloquial fashion. Takes photographs, blasts humans to a flaming oblivion, a thoroughly hateful and diabolical contraption. That's all there is to it."

"That's it?" I said.

"How do you know of such a thing?" Sue asked.

Slab looked at my witch with such pathos that I expected them both to burst into tears. He collected himself and sat down, topping up his mug of Redskin. We were in for a story. He made himself comfortable in a desolate kind of way.

"My dears, I have been reluctant to delve in a public fashion into my contorted and - I confess - not salubrious biography. But in the interest of complete and thorough disclosure of all facts positive, negative and otherwise,

you will have the flamin' lot." He swept us
with a stern eye and continued.

"After the great deluge that wiped out my
sweet Dunedin, I was press-ganged into
Australian Border Security, quite simply
plucked from the ridges of the Otago Peninsula
by helicopter and dumped on an aircraft
carrier to join hundreds of captive Kiwis and
kidnapped Pacific Islanders. Disembark me, I
say, I am Endeavour Winston Frost, a librarian
and a proud New Zealander. There's no fuck'n
New Zealand no more they say. Here's my
passport, I protest, handing the hallowed
evidence of my sacred southern birthright to
a carrot-faced brute in black overalls, at
which said brute shears the passport in two
and declares me stateless. I claim asylum,
says I, more in vain hope than in concrete
anticipation of a fair and equitable outcome.
But within the hour, I am lined up in a steel-
walled room below the waterline with fifty
other ill-starred victims donning Australian
Government underwear and being bawled at by
the aforesaid monster. Six weeks basic
training in Kazakhstan, and I find my sorry
self in Australia, a gentle man of books
transmogrified into a slack-jawed Neanderthal
trained to fart on command."

"Slab," I asked, not sure how farting was
involved in this story, "do you mean you were
a uniform?"

"Indeed, lad. A spell in Orange, and then
taught to control a SAFM Mark 2 from a base
down in Cairns. A stick twiddler, a murderer,
a lethal Peeping Tom."

I was bursting to ask him more about Orange. Did he deliver our food? Did he take away our garbage? Did he know that man who gave Arabella the money? But Mia broke into my thoughts.

"Tell them the rest, Slab. Or I will. We are all dear friends and we should have no secrets."

Slab's mouth turned down at the corners and he fortified himself with another big swig.

"About twenty years ago, Australian Border Security upped stakes and left Cairns. I don't know why. Nobody told you anything, but we heard that we were being redeployed to Gladstone. On the day before we were to fly out, a refugee boat landed off Yorkie's Knob, just north of the city. I was sent up there to sort things out. Just me and a motor bike and a gun because there was nobody else to spare."

Mia wiped her eyes.

"There were six of them on the beach, all skinny and burnt red by the sun. Four of them ran away - well, staggered away - and I let off a random shot or two, but they were gone into the mangroves, most likely to end up as a crocodile's luncheon. The two left, well, one's a woman and her feller's standing in front of her swinging a wicked bit of steel rod and yelling in French.

"Arretez vous mon ami," I requests, recalling my studies with Teach Yourself French over a quality cup of Earl Grey and a welcome finger bun in the Dunedin Public Library staff room. "Ferk off," he shouts and runs at me with the steel rod. There's a bang and him bleeding in the surf from his eyeball and yours truly Endeavour Winston Frost staring at the gun in his hand and the woman running away shrieking and tearing her hair."

"I escaped into the canefields," Mia said.

"I killed your man."

"Yes, you killed my Etienne. You came after me, you put me on the motorbike and brought me up here. You deserted from Australian Border Security. You kept me safe. And I have forgiven you."

We peered at the ground, all unable to find words.

Baby Winston stirred and Sue fixed her to her breast. She murmured these words: "I am the Alpha and the Omega, says the Lord God, who is and who was and who is to come, the Almighty."

With this utterance, a wave of something grave and portentous passed through me and I shuddered, not from fear but from the revelation that I was a man of the Earth. Not an aimless ant shoved from one incomprehensible place to another. Not a cocky little man with a COCK but no brains. Not a dreamer spinning vapid meaning from an old book with Part Sixth missing. Not half man and half woman, not the obverse of Sue Bridehead. I was a man connected by an unbreakable thread to the Pharoahs of Egypt, to Henry the Eighth, to Mr Gray with his butt plug, to Pork Vindaloo, to Nicholas Nickleby, to the Manchester Ship Canal, to Mrs Gaskell, to President Oprah Winfrey, to My Guitar that Gently Weeps, to Naomi Klein, to Noddy and Big

Ears, and to the Golden Colossus of Ivanka Trump on Ellis Island, and to Lord God the Almighty.

I glanced at Sue. I was me and she was her. We were no longer one.

A horse whinnied outside the palisade. I went outside and found an Aboriginal dismounting the beast, which was festooned with trading goods.

"Dontcha recognise an old mate?"

I looked closer. It was Ross, the man who first showed me the world beyond Orange.

"Word is you've come up some, feller. Wanna do some business?"

I clapped him on the shoulder. "Mate, you're on."

RETURN OF THE NATIVE

A year passed. I bought and sold things, tried this, tried that, lost money on tin mugs, made money on paper screws of salt. I read some books on the principles of business from Slab's library, studying ideas like profit, loss, debt, tax, inventory. The books had pictures of people in glass buildings, men with neckties and women with eyeglasses. I sometimes saw people like that in the movies in Orange.

The world of business didn't look like Kuranda with its choking blanket of vegetation, its murderous ants, its bearded patriarchs and its downtrodden wives. Did ruinous fires break out from cooking hobs in these shiny people's glass buildings? Did their husbands and daughters and neighbours suffer from boils and fevers? Did their pineapples ripen and rot more quickly than they could eat them? Did infants die without cause?

"Look, Sue," I would say. "We can make big profits. I can make a balance sheet."

"What is a balance sheet?"

"It's simple: You write down what you own, and next to it you write what you owe to others. Then you work out what is really yours."

"You already know what is yours, Jude. Why bother to write down? You've got bottles of Redskin, a big pile of paintings, sacks of jerky, a winery. And you owe ..."

"What do I owe?" I asked.

"I don't know. Tell me what you owe. No don't, I'm tired of this game. Look, Winston is asleep. Lie with me and massage my shoulders."

I tried everything to convince her but she wouldn't talk about the balance sheet.

"We are rich," she would say, "in things that nobody can count. But some days we are richer than other days".

"What do you mean?" I asked.

"Well, today I call you my love, but in truth I love you a little less because you are making such a fuss about your balance sheet. When you don't talk about it, I love you more. On those days, we are richer."

That didn't make much sense to me. It struck me that Sue was out of touch (what a useful phrase) with the real world (another useful phrase). I questioned her on this: "What is the real world to you, my love?"

"It is a shifting thing," she said, "not reducible to a list of facts. It is my father's courage. It is our daughter Winston's sweet head. It is Slab laughing over a mug of Redskin. It is you in my bed. It is a thousand other things, some in the past, some now, some in the future."

I had a sudden vision of Sue's real world: A landscape of swaying palms and misted hills and creeks meandering to the horizon. Figures emerging from the bush and fading back into it. A Fringe of Leaves. But the picture dissolved and all I could see of the real world was a heap of sweet potatoes in the yard that

needed to be made into Redskin before they
rotted to useless mush.

***

But I seduced her. I wooed her with numbers,
knowing full well my duplicity.

"Sue," I said one morning. "You know
mathematics."

"Yes, my father taught me."

"Then, my love, teach me."

So she taught me multiplication and division
and averages. She taught me BODMAS: Brackets,
of, divide, multiply, add, subtract. She
taught me algebra and geometry. She knew of
course that my aim was to count my things, to
write them in lists, and I cringed at my
dishonesty and her loving complicity.

After some months I was able to consider
what I owned in a new way - not by looking at
fifty bottles of Redskin or eight hundred mud
and straw bricks, but all these objects
reduced to numbers on a page.

(Yes, he seduced me with his numbers, Alex.
But looking back down the tunnel of the years,
it's easy to write 'he did this' and 'he did
that'. The reality is that I was someone else,
and he's been dead for years. What chance is
there that my 'he did this' conveys what
happened in our souls? Let me try: I'm a
savage, a girl burdened with a garbled system
of beliefs picked up from old books, from my
dead father's eccentricities, from living as
a witch. A stranger arrives and by some magic

we fall into a lustlove that is too powerful
for either of us to understand. I'm a witch
tossed out; I have nowhere to go but him. He's
a child-man struggling out of fairyland. He's
obsessed with his manhood, but terrified of
its force. I'm a mother drowning in love for
my child. I know nothing of the world, of the
future. The world is me, him and the child,
bless her soul, as we live in a tinpot paradise
at Nature's cruel whim. Nobody 'did' anything.
We just were.)

*　*　*

"So you got what you wanted," Sue said one
morning when I was counting my property.

"You gave me the knowledge willingly," I
said, barely able to look at her directly.

"Have you thought about what I want?"

Her question hung in the column of warm
foetid air that hung over the yard. A turkey
with cruel claws scrabbled in a pile of
leaves. The sound of Slab chopping a tree
floated up from somewhere below. It wasn't a
question that had ever occurred to me. I
finished my counting and went to the longdrop
to read Why Jesus Wants You To Be a
Millionaire.

Next day, I asked her what she wanted.

"What do you mean?"

"Yesterday, you asked me if I'd thought
about what you want."

"Oh, so I did. But, Jude, it's a bigger
question than the poor words that ask it.
Sometimes what I want is an immediate feeling,

a tangible need, and then it's more - it's my past and my present and my future, and my fate, all mixed up into knowing that my life takes a course I can't chart, and then the question makes no sense."

"Do you mean that your life is in God's hands? Do you think like the spadebeards?"

"No, Jude, I scorn their God. I'm not God's puppet."

"So, tell me. What do you want if God doesn't decide for you?"

She looked up into the trees, pulled Winston close.

"Ask me tomorrow," she said. "And the next day, and the next and the next. And when you have written down all the answers, make an average."

Sue's answer signified a change in my life, or perhaps our lives. For the first time I questioned what I really understood of her aberrant passions. Poor cousin Sue. She'd been my goddess, my sprite, my saint, my other self, my lover, my wife, my witch, and now she seemed not altogether mine at all.

The day after our conversation, I woke to agonising bellyache and a bloody arse. Winston screamed with cramps and would take no food. Slab, grey-faced and moaning, managed to get on a horse and ride to town for medicine. But he came back with nothing, fell off the horse and crawled to the longdrop. The medicine woman had died in the night, he told us later, and nobody knew how to mix the powders and leaves in her cupboards. Half the town was sick. The water from the river must have been the culprit. A rotting pig, perhaps, just upstream from where people filled their pots.

How did the sickness get past our water machines? My fault: We'd been short of wood, and I'd cut back on boiling time.

The illness spared Sue. She cared for us - Winston, me and Slab - for a week until the hateful poison was expelled. She collected wood and made clean water from a sweeter spot on the river bank. She had us drink it mixed with salt and sugar, like The Naked Camper said. Baby Winston hovered on the edge of death for a day. I watched as Sue dribbled the sugar-water between the baby girl's lips, soothing her with whispers I could not make out. The baby's hands clutched Sue's fingers. Her toes curled and uncurled. They made a tiny world of their own love and fear where the only meaning was that their tiny world existed. Sue was Winston and Winston was Sue, and Jude was the dolt with shitty shorts and a balance sheet.

***

With my new knowledge of arithmetic, I had estimated that the population of the spadebeard town of Kuranda and the surrounding settlements was about one and a half thousand. But the sickness killed hundreds, and the town wore a mantle of despair and resignation. The church singing was less lusty, the market was mostly half-full. I barely recognised the bustling place where Ross had dumped me a year or two before. Sue said that the town's heart was broken.

"How can a town have a broken heart?" I asked her.

"Perhaps I've used the wrong words, Jude. But I've lived here since I was a girl. Don't forget that I was married to a spadebeard as you call them, and I learned how the town came to be as it is."

"And how was that?" I asked. It occurred to me that I had no idea of the town's origins. The idea of history still didn't come naturally to me.

"I'll tell you what I know, Jude. Down in Cairns many years ago there was a big prayer gathering with a preacher called Jed and his wife Maree. They were originally farmers and they lived here in Kuranda. That night in Cairns there was huge storm, the Prince of Storms, and it wiped out the church where the meeting was happening. The next day, they say God took Maree and Jed to heaven, sucked them up into the sky on a column of golden air."

"Is it true? Do you believe it, Sue?"

"It is as I was told by Mr Phillotson."

"Then what?"

"After the flood, most of the Aboriginals came up onto the tablelands, and other people went south or flew away in aeroplanes - there were still aeroplanes then. After that, Australian Border Security Inc took over Cairns and kicked out the last of the people there."

"Maree and Jed had six sons - a baker, a carpenter, a horseman, a priest, a blacksmith, and a farmer – who travelled to the far reaches of the tablelands, I'm not sure why. Mr Phillotson told me that God called on them to return to Kuranda, and they married six sisters here. The sons set up the BP church and made rules for the town to live by. Each son had six more sons. Mr Phillotson was a great grandson of Saint Jed."

"Saint Jed?"

"Yes, his portrait is hung behind the altar in the BP." I remembered the picture of a man with big eyebrows and a terrible frown.

"Wasn't Maree a saint?" I asked.

"No, a woman can't be a saint among these people because of her shame."

"And what about the town's heart, Sue?"

"I suppose I mean that everybody knew their place, and got on with their lives purposefully – even the women with their crippling shoes and their public shame. But since the sickness, the cheer has gone. It's as if the town's heart beats more slowly, fading like a wounded bat."

***

I thought about Sue's words as I went about my work. It was true that business had been cooling since the sickness. "We've no cash to buy your Redskin and your jerky and your pots and pans," they said. They were right: Hardly anybody had roubles to spend or goods to barter. Those who did have any cash were hoarding it for the future. No cash, no sales, no food, no profit. Soon, no town.

I sent Slab on a two-week trip to the Aboriginals' saltpans to build up our stocks. I needed time on my own to experiment with making coins. After two days, I had the technique, making small disks stamped 20 JUDES and big ones with 100 JUDES.

By the time Slab returned with the salt, coins were circulating and there were signs of a pick-up in the town market. I'd given away 10,000 JUDES to help people buy things, and half of it quickly came back to me from sales of my goods. I kept studying Jesus Wants You to be a Millionaire, which was falling to bits.

"Can we have more money?" people asked.

"You can borrow money," I said, "and pay me interest".

"You mean usury?" they asked.

"You can call it that if you like," I said. "Up to you."

Sue was furious. "You have made these people hostage to your grubby coins," she said. "You already have all their roubles hidden in the station. You have introduced usury to their poor lives."

I said to her, "Just as you and your father introduced witchcraft with your mathematics tricks and your electrical repairs".

"That was different. My father and I had to protect ourselves from their ignorance and prejudice."

"As I am protecting the whole town from sinking into indolence and poverty," I said. "And thereby protecting you and Winston, who we so recently nearly lost. Am I not like a father to the town?"

Sue fell silent at this, clutching Winston to her chest and stroking the sweet girl's head. At last she said, "I suppose you may be right".

"Sue, you have told me of the dangerous times of your childhood in Katoomba and your journeying to Orange and to Kuranda. Your father was your protector, just as I am now, and just as the Holy Father protects us all."

"You don't believe in any Holy Father, Jude."

I drew her close. She resisted and then let me hug her. Her damp skin pressed on mine in the heat of the afternoon. This moment, I thought, is all I have. There was no Holy Father, no spirits flashing through the waving fronds above us. There was a man alone in the world with only his brain to guide him, and there was the tantalising mystery of a woman's skin to confound his reason.

"I no longer know what I believe Sue, if I ever did know.'

"Nor I, my love."

After a few days, Sue came to me holding one of my coins. "It is a poor thing," she said, "easily copied by others. I will help you make a better one. Here is a drawing, my protector".

She walked away under the palms while I studied the drawing through misted eyes. When I looked up, she was absent-mindedly kneeling to scratch the insect bites on her ankles, her hair parting over her thin shoulders. I fought back my tears and cursed myself for bringing her under my control.

(And that, Alex, is the origin of the coin I still keep around my neck. It is cut from sheet aluminium that Jude stripped from the counters of derelict bar tables in Cairns, and hauled up the long hills with the horse and cart. It has my portrait on one side and Jude's on the other - crudely rendered and stamped by a die he made from a bit of concrete reinforcing rod.)

***

The town struggled to recover from the sickness. The balance of the place was out of kilter. Hunger and lingering illness blotted the lives of the muddled spadebeards and their sad women. I sold them food from my stores on credit.

"Credit?" Slab roared. "These people can't pay you back."

"They can pay me in kind."

"Kind of what?"

"Their houses," I said. "They can sign a paper to say that I own their houses."

"Damn your paper, and damn your coins. Give the food away. There's got to be a bloomin' modicum of respect for the working folk who built this town with their sweat. These are men and women who have laboured to provide the wherewithals of comfort and ease for other members of their society. I've never heard the like."

"Society!" I said. "There's no society. Each of us is a man with a responsibility for himself and his close kin."

"Bugger me sideways," said Slab, "if you're not sounding like a king from days of yore. It's that millionaire book you're glued to day and night. Next you'll be telling me you have written authority from God Almighty."

Too quickly I said, "Yes I do".

"Ha! King Jude is it then? I kneel in obeisance to your tinpot sovereignty over this blighted snotball of a place. Hail the King. Hail!"

I spent the next day wandering the town with my list of debtors, King Jude surveying his snotball monarchy, the bully boy authorised by God to own this and own that, the cocky man with the limp COCK.

In the market I drank a mug of Redskin and then another. Nobody asked King Jude for payment. A couple of loafers joined me in toasting the monarchy, and then we drank some more and tottered to the bar near the bakery, where my new friends shared an upended woman, His Majesty looking on.

By dusk, I, King Jude, was on all fours outside the bar with a little crowd laughing and singing "God Save Our Gracious King, Long Live his Noble Prick".

A sharp voice said, "Dat bigfuckup larka hubby me."

I rolled onto my back. Two faces peered down, a man and a woman.

The man asked, "Are you Jude from Orange?"

"Who wants to know?"

"Jack Wing wants to bloody know."

The woman said, "<u>Wofo yu kip, bigfuckup larka</u>?"

The bottom fell out of my <u>zazzy</u>. The woman was my first wife Arabella. How did she find me? Who was Jack Wing?

"<u>Gonna luraka me</u>," I said, and I spewed on my shorts. Hands pulled me to my feet. Arabella was meatier, stronger, angrier. The man Jack Wing said something and pointed to two little girls who were holding Arabella's hand. The children had eyes like mine.

***

I woke at the station, not knowing how I got there. It was hot, early. Voices pressed through the green fog in my head. Arabella was talking in the old language of Orange. Sue too. And a man's voice, but he didn't speak it properly. Jack Wing. It must be Jack Wing. I turned my head. All three were standing, Sue pointing her finger at Arabella, Arabella with arms crossed and a thunderous face. Jack Wing held the hands of the two little girls, who I saw were identical. Slab sat under a tree feeding avocado to Winston.

I closed my eyes. The voices stopped.

I opened my eyes. Arabella was striding towards town. Sue was now carrying Winston away. Slab had disappeared.

"Get up, you low bastard," Jack Wing growled.

I propped myself on my elbows. "Who are those girls?"

"They're yours, Jude," he said. He was wiry, burnt brown. "And we want their Mum's money."

Something moved inside me, like a kidney slipping into a safer place. Arabella's timbox. They came all this way for the timbox. I stood up on jelly knees. The stink came up from the dried sick on my shorts.

"Take yourself back to Orange, fucking Jack Wing. I don't have her money."

"There ain't no Orange any more. We're headed west."

"No Orange?" The words didn't fit. There couldn't be no Orange.

"All dead. From the si-yu sickness, that's what they call it down there." The old word puzzled me for a second, and then - yes, I had it.

"Fainting, you mean?"

"I suppose. Yeah, they go to sleep and die," Jack Wing said.

"So why aren't you dead?" I asked. I didn't like the look of this rough one.

"Mind your business. They're all dead and that's that. Where's my old lady's money?"

A memory clicked into place.

"I know you," I said. "You were a uniform. I saw you in her house one night. She gave you beer and you gave her money."

He leaned towards me, raising a scaly fist. But Slab was suddenly behind him. "Watch it, my lad. Let's sit down and chat over a mug of Redskin."

Jack Wing shrugged. Perhaps he wasn't so brave as he wanted to appear. I looked him up and down: A ragged man in the wrong place with a woman who could scare a wild pig to death.

Slab asked the girls if they wanted food, but they stared blankly. I asked them in the Orange language. They glared and nodded at the same time.

"Have they got names?" I asked Jack Wing.

"That one's Sedi, and that one's Mara."

They were named Sorrow and Anger. I remembered that some superstitious people in Orange gave their children unfortunate names like Rat and Dirty Dog to ward off bad luck. And I remembered that last night in Arabella's bed when she pinned me down and drained me of the last drops of my seed. My sorrow and her anger were what made Sedi and Mara.

"Why are you with Arabella?" I asked.

"I love her," he replied with a sideways look. Was he bashful? Was he lying?

"Where are you headed?"

"Timor." I knew where Timor was now from the Atlas.

"Why are you going there?"

"Where's the money you stole?" Jack Wing asked.

"You're getting no money from me."

He got up. "Look after your kids for now. I've got business in town."

"They're about three years old," Sue said. She looked at them in the way you watch a reptile that's not quite close enough to bite. "They're yours, it's obvious."

The little girls sat wide-eyed and ready to scratch. As for me, I was numb, although perhaps it was last night's Redskin hanging heavy on my head. A faint shiver disturbed my insides again. Three children. The Jude in the book had three children, but they were boys, and my Arabella only bore one. I pushed the thought aside. I was done with prophecy, except in the way of estimating my profits.

I wanted Arabella and her companions gone. The shiver came again. When I looked up, both girls were staring black rays into my eyes. They were mine, but from a me I didn't know. A me, but not me. My organs shrivelled again.

Gone, gone, they must be gone. I went to the station and looked at my lists. I made up a packet of roubles.

When Jack Wing and Arabella returned from town, I asked them how they got here.

Jack Wing said, "A truck dropped us at Cairns. A bloke called Ross brought us up from the coast road". Ross, of course.

"Tell me where you're going and tell me you'll never come back. Then you get the money."

Jack Wing gave me another sideways look, but different from when he said he loved Arabella. This was a man who trusted nobody, who looked sideways to cover his feelings. "OK," he said. "Ross is gonna take us inland to meet a fellow".

"What then?"

"We go by truck. Cross-country to Darwin. There's a road called Savannah."

"What truck?" But I knew. Australian Border Security Inc. Those were the only trucks.

"Where's the money, then?" Jack Wing asked. His face was streaming with sweat.

I ignored him. "And after Darwin?" I needed to know it all.

"A boat to Timor and then another boat to Indonesia." My mind was tripping over itself. Such place names. Such distances. Such ways of travel. Jack Wing kept talking but I was beyond understanding.

"The money now. I gotta pay people." An idea formed in my mind. A frightening idea. The idea that I might also want to leave this place one day.

"And what after Indonesia?"

"England."

I'd seen England in the Atlas. It's where the Jude in the book lived. The other side of the world. Jack and Arabella weren't coming back.

* * *

Ross came to the station late that night with two horses. Arabella and Jack Wing mounted, and we lifted Sorrow and Anger up to their saddles. I passed the bundle of roubles to Jack Wing, but Arabella growled, "You gib me". It was the first time she'd spoken in English.

The horses picked their way into town by the light of Ross's flaming torch. When they were

almost out of sight, a satanic chorus of
screeching bats farewelled them from the
glowering shadows of the palms trees. I sank
to my knees. The children had gone.

We slept, my witch and my baby Winston. Dead
to the night, utterly exhausted. No dreams for
me until I found myself in a place where the
spadebeards sang Onward Christian Soldiers. I
forced myself awake because the dream was too
real. I must wake. I must hold my wife and
baby daughter. I must hear the night sounds,
the jostle of a stirring bird, the sudden
shriek of a murdered lizard, the wind in the
fronds. I must push the dream back.

But the singing grew louder, footsteps
sounded outside. The door opened. A spadebeard
held a torch aloft and pushed Sorrow and Anger
into the room, where they stood lancing my
spirit with their glare. The men with the
torch withdrew. The room was black but for the
flash of eyes.

***

They followed me, these girls with their eye-
beams. As I worked in the yard, they stood in
their shifts and watched. They observed as I
rode away on the horse, and they stood at the
same spot when I returned. They ate, they
washed, they drank, all in silence, all the
time watching me.

I tried to coax them to smile, to talk, but
all I got was shrinking shoulders and wounded
stares. Sue couldn't bear their eye-beams, and
took Winston to the Falls each day, half an

hour's walk from the station. On the third day, I joined her at the lookout platform high above the foaming torrents in the dark gorge. The timbers were grey and splintering, most of the handrail long gone over the edge.

"What will I do, Sue?" I asked. "These girls drain my soul. The prophecy fills my every thought."

"Your prophecy has truly polluted your mind. The Jude in the book had two sons with his Sue: Two boys, and Arabella brought him a third. Three boys, not three girls. And Arabella isn't even her real name: You told me that she changed it to Arabella after she was sick. As for me, I was never called Bridehead, and my dead husband was never Phillotson. I curse your prophecy, and I curse that whore of a mother who taught you to read and gave you that book."

Did I hear correctly? "My mother a whore? What nightmare is this?"

"You never knew?" Sue hissed. "Of course not. You wandered through life like an enchanted pixie. And then one day, you thought the truth would make you free. Do you want the truth about your mother? She fixed in your fluffy head the idea that you belonged in another realm, that you had a destiny. A plague on her eyes! Nobody in that place had a destiny. And here you came, here to Kuranda, where you seduced me with your fey whimsy and your damp spirit."

"Sue," I cried, "Deny that we are one and the same, two berries on one twig."

Stuart Campbell

"I cannot deny it." At this my witch broke down, sobbing, "Yes, I am you and you are me, and it will ever be."

"It's the truth," I cried. "We are one."

But a worm squirmed in my breast, wrapping its slimy foulness around the sacred truth of our oneness. My mother - what did Sue mean, my mother a whore?

"Whore, you said. Tell me about her. Tell me."

"This truth will enchain you as it has enchained me. Enjoy the freedom of ignorance. This truth will be the end of you, Jude. Do not press me."

She moved towards the edge of the platform, with Winston on her hip. "The water," she said, "I wonder where it goes, what it is like when it reaches the end".

"It reaches the sea. There are crocodiles, and terrible creatures in the water that make a man go rigid and die at their touch."

"No Jude, I mean where each drop of water goes as it mingles with the ocean and follows the currents to the end of the world. Aren't we just drops of water?"

"Come away from the edge, Sue." Her foot had loosened a crust of soil that skittered into the gorge.

She placed Winston on the ground. The little girl pulled herself into a crouch.

"Look, she will walk soon, Jude," Sue said. I darted forward to scoop up my daughter with one arm, but Sue turned away and stood swaying at the crumbling edge, her shoulders shaking.

"Tell me your truth, Sue."

"No, it will kill you."

"Tell, tell!"

She was just audible above the rush of water. "Your mother - she went with my father."

Went? Went with my father?

I imagined two people as they went here and there - the river, the Post Office Tree. It made no sense. And then it dawned that they WENT to some private place and ...

The meaning of the words pierced me, churned my zazzy. I looked into the eyes of my sister-wife's daughter, looking for some sign of our sin, but there was none, just the child's loving gaze.

We three huddled on the platform as the evening closed in, and new spirits took over the darkening bush. Insects whirred and murmured, invisible around our heads. Many-legged fleshy things slunk along nearby branches. Stings and bites threatened. The waterfall thrashed in the black gorge. We stumbled home.

Back at the station, Slab had lit a fire that flung dancing light at the curtain of vine-knotted trees encircling the yard. He called out to Sorrow and Anger, who sat atop the station roof.

"Come down, let me help you," he implored.

The girls stared back at him, silent, but when they saw me, they set up a rhythmic howling in the Orange language, the same words repeated over and over: Miyanim kotok, miyanim spisi yu.

"What are they saying, Jude?" Sue asked.

"They are saying, 'We are damned. We are your fruit. We are damned. We are your fruit'."

A hot wind swept down. The glossy scalloped leaves of the palms whipped back and forth, side to side. An obscene fig on an arched frond danced a sticky jig. Invisible birds scrapped over a perch-hold. A web-cradle of swollen sooty spiders bounced with the whipping branches.

Sue wrapped Winston tightly and ran into the station. Slab threw wood on the fire and gulped from a bottle of Redskin. He started to dance, spinning on one foot with arms outstretched, spinning, howling with the girls. My connection with this life was dwindling.

The howling stopped, the girls stood silent on the ridge of the station roof, the wind dropped. Sorrow and Anger fell forward, drifted down on ballooning shifts, and alit like feathers in front of me.

"Miyanim kotok, miyanim spisi yu." The howling started again, the lancing stares. I fell to the ground, curled into the tiniest ball in God's kingdom, and pressed my hands to my ears to stop the demonic noise.

* * *

The night was a battleground of dreams and monsters and howling. Sleep it may have been, but the kind of sleep that destroys repose, that mangles ease.

I woke early. The station yard was empty. I ran inside the house but it was empty too. A snore erupted from a bundle that was Slab.

"Where are they?" No movement.

I ran towards town, then ran back. Cold clamped my stomach. A picture of three white bundles leapt into my mind's eye. I dashed towards the path that led to the falls, running, sobbing, stumbling. There was the crashing of vegetation ahead, movement among the fringe of leaves. Sue ran alone towards me, screaming. She stumbled past me through low bushes and whipping tendrils, disappearing into the green tunnel I had just torn through. I rushed on, intent on what I knew I must find.

It wasn't far. An old sign with faded paint said, 'Barron Falls 300 metres'. I heard the waterfall, kept running. I threw myself prone on the platform, looking down into the gorge at what was prophesied.

Stuart Campbell

THE ACCIDENTAL ECONOMIES
OF PATRIA NULLIUS

Highness,

Note the quotation referring to 'testicle' in this extract from The History. Your Highness's advice appreciated on the seemliness of this extract.

Humbly, Bruce

THE ACCIDENTAL ECONOMIES OF PATRIA NULLIUS

The current era has been called 'the time that economics forgot'. In the past, vicious wars were fought over commodities like oil, coal, food, and water. Land and resources were devastated by fruitless struggles among the great powers and their proxies. Citizens fretted over stock markets, exchange rates, government debt, taxes, and inflation - the grim by-products of unbridled capitalism. Nowadays, the means of production, distribution and exchange are collectively owned and controlled by SLUZHBA, CareMundo and SinoFrench. The intricate network of cross-holdings among the Triopoly ensures that war is unknown, and poverty has vanished. For the average citizen, economics is dead.

For many of the remnant population of Patria Nullius - or to use the common term the 'Remainders' - economics was an unknown concept. Thousands of Remainders found themselves in what historian Janet Aziz has called 'orphanage economies': Food, housing, clothing and essential medications were provided by Australian Border Security Inc. Free marijuana and nightly open-air movies kept the populace docile.

With the familiar institutions of schools, churches, shops, clubs, offices and factories locked and abandoned, stories of hope, speculation and aspiration dwindled into the mundane chatter of a populace reduced to the mentality of children in an orphanage.

For economists and anthropologists, the first few years of Patria Nullius presented a laboratory like no other. This was a chance to observe the invention of a new order of societal existence. In his memoir *The Accidental Frontiers of History*, Lord Basil Macfarlane-DeSouza recalled his two years in Patria Nullius as a United Nations monitor. "As a young anthropologist, I was privileged to watch a society collapse and then stumble to its feet like an unruly toddler."

The response to this new utopia differed from place to place. Macfarlane-DeSouza predicted that forms of primitive communism would emerge, where society would run on barter and communal loyalty. There would be no private property. Belief systems would be based on myths drawn from pre-Grand Bargain history.

"I was partly wrong and partly right. But I tell you what – Marx and Engels would have given a testicle each to be there," he said in a lecture to the first cohort of graduates of the Oxford campus of the University of Sydney. "We saw towns where the populace basically lay down and got themselves stonkered from morning to night. We found places that quickly developed crude manufacturing to supplement what Australian Border Security Inc. didn't provide – jewellery, smoking implements, sandals, sanitary goods. The most unusual micro-society was in Orange, where, within a few years, women were adopting leadership roles in a network of small business ventures, using a cache of obsolete Russian money as a kind of fiduciary issue currency. No matter that there was no government apparatus to back these 'bucks', as the cash was called; the locals were prepared to swap a pair of home-made sandals for a thousand-rouble note in the sure knowledge that they could spend their 'bucks' on a bottle of perfume smuggled in on a ship from Yokohama or Istanbul or Amsterdam."

But the curtains were quickly drawn over the new economic models. Australia's mandate to monitor the Remainders on behalf of the UN lasted a mere two years. The experts returned to posts in the new university campus at Oxford, where Lord Basil Macfarlane-DeSouza would eventually don the possum-fur stole signifying his elevation to Chancellor, and lend his wise counsel to commerce as a director of SLUZHBA.

But now it was down to asylum seekers, loose-tongued ABS employees, and intrepid adventurers travelling in disguise to tell the world of the exotic economies of Patria Nullius. As with our knowledge of language development, the subsequent understanding of how the Remainders built their economies comes from smuggled stories, stolen documents, and oral histories.

An enduring theme in all these fragmented sources is the existence of a complex, thriving, economy deep in the plains and forests outside the regions controlled by ABS. This is explored in more detail in Chapter 22, *The Role of the Aboriginal Population in Shaping Patria Nullius.*

PART SIXTH - EXILE

SUSAN TO ALEX, OCTOBER 0100

Dear Alex,
I visited the university medical centre yesterday. My usual doctor was no longer there, replaced by a young woman of frigid personality, who could provide no information about his whereabouts. She directed an infinitesimally faint frown at my records, asking why they contained no information except a note about loose bowel movements. I asked for my regular painkiller, showing her the empty drug package from my executioner doctor. The icy maid allowed herself half a millimetre of additional frown, opened a drawer and handed me two packs.

"This is irregular. Please put them inside your clothing. Thank you."

I stuffed the packs under my jacket and moved to hoist my aching carcass off the chair in order to regain the refuge of my apartment.

"Please wait. There is someone here who would like to speak to you."

She got up and walked out, leaving me to study the chair where my tortured friend had squirmed and grimaced with a cannula in the back of his hand.

As she exited, a youngish man entered and sat behind the desk. I guessed from his Byronesque outfit - a dark blue cloak and a floppy felt cap - that he was a functionary attached to the Keeper of the Monarch's Bookes.

"Quoit," he said, offering me his hand.

"As in the traditional game of skill where a ring is tossed to fall over a spike?"

"You have the advantage of me, Baroness. I am not acquainted with the pastime to which you refer."

"Never mind. Get on with it. What do you want? Why have I been ambushed?"

The man Quoit stroked his little triangle of goatee, striking the pose of a deep thinker. He sat back in his chair, crossed his legs with precision and looked at the ceiling. He looked to be about thirty years old, with flawless skin and an almost feminine elegance to his features.

"Ambush? I'd hardly use the term 'ambush'."

Now he put on a pince-nez and peered at me over the tops of the lenses.

"Unless you have something profound to say, I'm going home," I declared.

"No, wait. I really do have something to tell you."

"Spit it out, lad. And can you please drop the medieval philosopher pose?"

Quoit chuckled, took off the ridiculous cap, and tossed the pince-nez into it.

"I'm terribly sorry. It becomes a habit in a job like mine. We're expected to appear intellectually superior. To be honest I detest this goatee."

"Are you feeling quite well?" I asked. Sir Bruce's staff never let down their guard. This had the smell of mutiny about it. Or mental illness.

"I'm perfectly well. Look, the thing is I've got a terrible weight on my shoulder.

Actually, I'm mortified, and I'm terrified at the same time."

"That's quite a cocktail, mortification and terror. Let's see what we can do to make you more comfortable." By now my mind was galloping. Was he dangerous?

"Do you have a first name, Mr Quoit?"

"Lochinvar."

"A lovely name. Your parents must have been devotees of Sir Walter Scott."

"Please don't tease me, Baroness. I'm taking a terrible risk."

The young man's poise had quite collapsed. His arms hugged his torso and his legs were folded up fit to snap the tendons. A sort of déja vu came over me, but then I recalled my doctor contorted in the same fashion in the same chair. Looking closer, I detected a similarity in the brow, the angle of the eye.

"He was my elder brother," Quoit said quietly.

My face flushed and my legs went numb. I quelled my thumping heart.

"Is it safe for us to talk here?"

"Yes."

"I have a feeling I know what you are going to tell me," I said.

Quoit grasped his brow and smiled wryly.

"You're Alex, aren't you?" I asked.

He nodded, sniffed, looked at the desk. "Can you forgive me?" He raised his head with such an expression of tragedy that I was ready to hug him.

A curtain of silence hung between us.

"Do you happen to know anything about Alex, actual Alex?"

"He was killed in a shoot-out on campus in Chicago, five years ago."

I said nothing. Alex was a 'she', not a 'he'. I needed to tread very carefully.

"You wrote convincingly as Alex."

"We are trained in it."

"No, there's more to it than that, Quoit Lochinvar. You have sensibilities that are beyond the capacities of Sir Bruce's minions. Where did that come from?"

"I have no clue what you refer to."

"Yes, you do, Lochinvar Quoit."

"I can't tell you."

"Well," I replied, "I think I know the answer. You see, I've been dealing with your type for years. You appear erudite and intellectually poised, but it's your training: They teach you to deflect, to question rather than state, to leave your interlocutors insecure and confused. But that's not about sensibilities - that's a veneer of rhetorical technique covering a feeble education that denies the very existence of the imagination." I stopped, looked up. Quoit was attentive, perhaps even displaying a little excitement behind the professional mask he had readopted.

"But you, Lochinvar Quoit, are somewhat different: You've been reading fiction. Is it possible that you are tossed about, all alone, with aberrant passions, and unaccountable antipathies?"

The man sat upright abruptly. The pince nez jumped off the woollen hat and one of the tiny lenses detached itself from the frame to roll a wobbly path across the floor. Quoit and I watched it until it toppled flat.

"I know Jude the Obscure almost by heart," he whispered. "When I was first tasked with impersonating Alex, I was granted special permission to download it to my PIP from the Proscribed Books Archive."

"And to memorise it, you must have made a copy."

He nodded. "Can you imagine where I made it?"

"To hazard a guess, I'd say in your lavatory." Lochinvar Quoit perched on the dunny recalling the text of Jude the Obscure while he scribbles with an illegal pen on illegal paper.

"It would be hilarious if it wasn't so depressing."

"Now, now," I said in the soothing voice I use for an aggrieved student. "Perhaps we can speak about what you really want to tell me."

He sat up and arranged the foolish hat on his head.

"Her Royal Highness wants you arrested for sedition."

"I don't understand. Are you my saviour or my inquisitor?"

"Your saviour, I hope."

I had to think about that.

There was a knock on the door. The icy female doctor put her head in and made some subtle signal to Quoit.

"My time's up. I'll be in touch," he said.

"But what am I supposed to do? Can I trust you?"

But he reverted to role, flinging the cloak over one shoulder and elevating his nose to an angle of one hundred and twenty degrees. But just as his hand was on the door, he turned.

"The typewriter. Take off the e key. You'll find a PIP glued under it. I tried to warn you. Do you remember?"

"Wait. Why a PIP on my typewriter? You had the letters to Alex."

"Oh, those. I let them go through the letter network to prevent any suspicion by the boy bankers. One of our people in Chicago took delivery of them. I'd already had the tech people get the PIP to do a 3D scan of the mechanism of your Mr Remington, identify the dynamic profile of each key, and send the keystrokes to me. Much simpler!"

***

I prised the e key off when I got home. It skeetered across the floor, landing in a patch of sunlight. Quoit was right: The red dot, the size of a mustard seed, sat snugly in a groove in the metal. What to do? Scratch it off? No, disabling a PIP is illegal under half a dozen pieces of legislation, and the Universe will alert the authorities the instant the deed is done. Leave it alone and keep typing? Continue to pour out my intimate thoughts for Quoit to read?

The True History of Jude

What choice did I have, Alex, but to pop the
e key back and keep typing towards my destiny,
keystroke by keystroke?

* * *

Another week of toil on Her Royal Highness's
History. I'm mainly editing, tying up loose
ends, making myself look busy. I don't know
why I'm making myself look anything. They know
everything about me, and every sentence I
write on Mr Remington adds to their knowledge.
The Thing is always with me, reminding me of
my imminent demise and sneering as I swallow
more pills to smother its vengeful pain.

I've rerun the conversation with Quoit,
examining his words, his expressions,
torturing myself with the suspicion that his
candour was no more than guile. Arrest for
sedition? Why now? Was his warning intended to
provoke a reaction from me that will reveal
some new evidence of my treachery? Isn't The
True History of Jude sufficient evidence to
have me tried and sentenced?

The connection between Quoit and my doctor
is baffling. Did he mimic the doctor,
carefully moulding my response? But surely I
saw the family resemblance? My headache clamps
tighter as I try to recall the order of events
when he spoke of his brother. Was I fooled?

A couple of days later, the boy banker hissed
at me as I came back from a painful walk around
the block. We sidled into the safe zone.

"I'm did sorta talk wiv a colleague yesterday," he said, now evidently solid in his belief that I am fluent in Arg.

"And what did your colleague tell you?" I gathered he was referring to another banker in his circle. The tyke slipped a tiny square of paper into my hand. I scrunched it into my palm and went inside.

The next day found me rooting through my black garments to find something suitable for an apparently discreet lunch date with Lochinvar Quoit. I generally avoid mirrors these days, but my search for a garment forced me to acknowledge that I was even skinnier and more undistinguished than the last time I looked.

Now I'm a planner by nature. The prospective lunch must have a purpose, but what could it be? The only plan I could formulate was to penetrate Quoit's motives by tipping him off balance.

The address of the venue, printed in shaky upper case on the boy banker's message, was a restaurant on the river favoured by senior functionaries of the Palace. I announced myself and was ushered to a plush private room, where Quoit sat browsing a printed menu. This time he wore an old-fashioned red military tunic, jodhpurs and shiny high boots. Imperial Russian garb, perhaps?

"You're a meat lover, of course." His eyes didn't leave the menu. Insolent little dickhead. Of course I'm a meat lover. Didn't I tell Alex/Quoit how I loathed vegetables?

The menu, written in scrolly gold lettering on stiff card in French and English, listed a dozen complicated meat dishes.

"Is it real animal flesh?"

"Yes," he said, "It's like stepping back in time. This is Princess Maureen's private dining room by the way."

I recalled the pen of sheep behind razor wire I'd spotted from the train to Carlisle. Was one of them about to become navarin d'agneau?

"I'm honoured to be invited here." I scanned the list of viandes and fancy sauces and spotted a fair dinkum cracker, as her Royal Highness might have put it.

"I'll have the ortolan." I'd let the boy see what a real carnivore looked like, although my stomach churned at the thought of eating a tiny songbird recently drowned in hot brandy.

Quoit nodded with what I suspected the training manual would have called 'earnest but understated flattery'. He looked up.

"An excellent choice if I may say so. I will also have ortolan."

So much for my pathetic attempt to rattle Quoit. Should I admit defeat and ask for the veal? No, I'd eat the damned songbird and look him straight in the eye. I observed him closely while he ordered our food, hoping some quirk of his behaviour might help me decide if he was trustworthy.

"You checked the typewriter?" he asked.

"You know I did."

Quoit picked up a crystal flute and held it to the light, frowning. A waiter scuttled up, took it, and returned polishing a fresh one.

"And you were wondering why I said Alex was a 'he'."

The Thing clamped down. I shoved the lurch of pain into a cage, swore at it until it cowered. My mind oriented itself to the oddness of the circumstances: Quoit commentating on my recent letter to him/Alex. The Thing relaxed its grip.

"Enlighten me, Quoit. Why did you say that?"

"To make you wonder if you can trust me," he replied. To hell with him. I'd answer his question with a question.

"And what do you think I decided?"

"Does it matter?"

"Why do you do this work, Lochinvar?"

"What else would I do?"

"Do you enjoy your work, Lochinvar?"

"Is this getting us anywhere?"

"No, just say what you want to say."

"As you wish." He smiled faintly. "So here's the first item. The Princess has been following The True History of Jude. She wants to know how it ends. In fact, she looks forward to a happy ending."

A question occurred to me, but I must pull the current thread first.

"Why is she so interested in a story like this?"

"It's not so much the story as you. She's fascinated by the way you - what's the word? - despise the monarchy, and that you grew up in Patria Nullius. She'd like you to be her friend but on her own terms. Frankly, she's bored with the courtiers she mixes with."

"You seem to know a lot about her inner feelings."

"I am well briefed for my task."

"Evidently. Why don't you just feed The True History of Jude into Predictive Composition and find out the ending?" I asked.

"I got nowhere. I tried every kind of tweak but it didn't generate anything I could put in front of Her Royal Highness. Let alone something happy."

This was interesting. PC was spectacularly clever at generating all sorts of texts, but Jude had put a spanner in the algorithms.

"What did it come up with, out of interest?"

Quoit blushed and straightened a butter knife.

"Come on, you can tell me. I'll say if you got close."

"There was one output where the spadebeards erected a bigger danger sign at Barron Falls."

"That was the ending?" I asked.

"I'm afraid so."

"Fate save us! What else?"

"Let me recall. Yes, you and Jude had three more children to replace the ... other ones."

"Well, I'll give PC full marks for insensitivity. But I see the difficulty. Did you have a go at writing your own ending?"

His eyes widened and his jaw quivered. I'd inflicted a small blow with surprising ease. Quoit and his ilk could no more make up a story than cut off their private parts. Their training at the SLUZHBA Polytechnicum rendered them surgically efficient at manipulating factual information, and that was it.

But, I remembered, Quoit had taken a small step into the world of the imagination by reading Jude the Obscure. Surely that made him different.

"Come on Lochinvar, try to join the dots. I'm a young woman running away from Barron Falls in a state of madness, Jude has seen something terrible at the bottom of the gorge. I now live in England. Jude has never been heard of since. Can't you think of anything at all?"

It was no good, reading a single novel couldn't compensate for the dead hand of his education. The poor sap stared at me shaking his head.

"I'm most awfully sorry, Baroness." He dabbed his nose with a silk handkerchief.

"It's alright, dear. You can't help it. So let's get to the point. I think you are asking me to finish The True History of Jude."

Quoit nodded. I was on the point of asking what the quid pro quo might be when our dinner arrived on a gilt trolley accompanied by two moustachioed chefs in tall white hats. One chef lifted the edge of one of the two silver domes to release a disturbing aroma.

Now I happen to have studied the history of the French practice of eating ortolan. Until the early twenty-first century, the tiny songbird was a special treat for wealthy gourmands, but the act of eating it was so repulsive to fellow diners (some said to God) that the diner wore a large napkin over the head.

I was sure I could manage to get the thing down my gullet, but could Quoit? After all, I'd eaten a vast range of birds, bugs, fish and mammals in Patria Nullius. Our diet depended on the rhythms of the seasons and the weather; when the meat of larger creatures was scarce, smaller bonier ones had to do.

"Have you partaken of ortolan before?" I thought 'partake' might appeal to his fondness for the lesser trod lexical paths.

Quoit tipped his head back and looked at me along one nostril.

"I am familiar with the dish." Which meant he'd never eaten it. I guessed he'd had to pull some thick silk ropes to bring me to the Princess's table.

"Fine, let's partake."

My previous research had led me to believe that only one ortolan was served per diner. I gulped when my waiter plucked off the dome before me to reveal three tiny bird corpses covered in hot brown slime. Quoit blanched as his own sticky trio was exposed.

The two waiters unfolded serviettes the size of bath towels.

"No thank you," I said. Quoit waved his serviette away.

Each waiter placed a single bird on each of our plates. I mentally stalked my ortolan, observing its pathetic feet, the dripping beak in an eyeless head as small as a hazelnut, its tiny chest. I snatched it up, slid it feetfirst into my mouth, winced at the hot gravy, gagged on the musty stink, and - remembering my research - crunched twice, once on the thorax and once on the skull, and swallowed.

Quoit's technique was hopeless. His jaw worked on the bundle of sharp bones and flesh, gravy seeped down one side his chin, blood down another.

Time to tackle him while he was vulnerable.

"So, Lochinvar Quoit, am I to understand that I am entering into a Thousand and One Nights arrangement with Her Highness? You're familiar with the concept, I suppose?"

While he closed his eyes to force the bolus of mashed bird into his oesophagus, I gestured to the waiter to serve my second ortolan, disposing of it with simulated panache.

Quoit's eyes glazed as the mess forced itself down to his stomach. He found his composure.

"Yes, I am familiar with the concept. I suppose you might wish to emulate Sheherezade's example."

"Come on, eat up. Now, just so I'm clear, what will happen after I've finished Jude's story and I'm arrested for sedition?"

"You will be tried, found guilty, and sentenced to death." He glanced at the congealing ortolans, shuddered, and indicated for the waiter to replace the dome.

"But I'm dying right now. I'll probably beat the executioner to it. And my book? What will become of the True History of Jude?"

"Baroness, you asked when we first met whether I was a saviour or your inquisitor."

"I recall."

"So I want to prove to you that I am your saviour. By the way, with respect, you don't need to eat that third creature. I'm very impressed with your skill. I do wonder though, why you didn't remove the beaks?"

I rearranged the sharp bundle tucked behind my back molar and slid the two beaks onto my tongue and into my fingers. Quoit raised his eyebrows.

"So prove it, Lochinvar. In what way are you my saviour?"

"I plan to get you over the border to Scotland before you are arrested."

Now here was a surprise. Better step carefully.

"Why on earth would you do that? But wait. Was it you who stopped me leaving before?"

"The little drama at Carlisle? I couldn't let you go without finishing your story."

Time to pop the question, but I already knew the answer:

"Lochinvar, you've told me that Princess Maureen has read The True History of Jude. Do I take it that she hasn't seen my letters?"

Quoit nodded. "Of course. I've referred to them just vaguely. I wouldn't be sitting here if she'd read about our meeting at the doctor's surgery, or your aborted trip north"

"So I cross over the border. What happens to my book?"

"Ah, now there's the question. You see, I cannot let you take it with you."

"Why not?" But I knew the answer to this one too. Quoit would be for the chop if The True

History of Jude turned up in an American imprint, ripe to be passed around as samizdat.

"But I have a proposition, Baroness. I will ensure that The True History of Jude is preserved for eternity."

"How?"

"Sir Bruce has explained to you, I believe, that The History of the Principality of Australia is to be displayed in public."

"Yes. And I understand that it won't be published as such. What was the reasoning behind that, by the way?"

"The reason? You were too good at your job. Sir Bruce has persuaded Her Majesty that all the rewriting in the world cannot generate a history that would meet the expectations of the public."

"What would the public expect? A comic strip?"

"I hadn't thought of that. At any rate, as the idea developed, the Palace warmed to the idea of a mystical book."

"So is that why they stopped robo-rewriting my work?"

"Exactly. They deemed it pointless for you to continue writing and for us to keep correcting. If The History is never to be read, it doesn't much matter what is in that presentation copy in the Bodleian Function Centre, does it?"

"Which," I took up the account, "would actually bear two authentic-looking pages where the copy is open on the lectern, covering The True History of Jude."

Young Lochinvar executed a clumsy wink that didn't come out of the training manual.

A waiter came with a dessert menu. Quoit surveyed it greedily.

"Yummy. I simply cannot decide between strawberry fool and summer pudding. Baroness, what will you have?"

I snatched the menu from him and hissed, "Damn the dessert and listen to me. So The True History of Jude lies in state for the next nine hundred and ninety-nine years of your poxy dynasty. Yes, what a marvellous private joke that'll be for you as you smarm your way into Maureen's favour as the next Keeper of the Monarch's Bookes. That's your game, isn't it, when Sir Bruce shuffles off? That's how you'll reconcile your new-found literary sensibilities with the grotesque work you do, by telling yourself how cleverly you have subverted the system. But what happens to me? Dumped across the border without my book? With just weeks or months to live?"

Quoit straightened up, gently took the menu from between my fingers.

"Baroness, let me finish. There is yet more to my proposition. You see, your PIP has been scanning your brain activity since you first told my brother, the doctor, about The Thing. According to our medical people, you most likely have a meningioma, a benign brain tumour. I have made a reservation in a hospital in Scotland for next week to have it removed."

I slumped back in my chair. What right did this preening pipsqueak have to decide what happened to my brain, let alone look inside my brain waves?

Evidently, there was even more. He leaned towards me, twisting slightly in the chair. There was a slight squeak as his knees flexed inside the riding boots. He placed a hand over mine, soft and quite unlike Jude's gnarled paws.

"You see, Baroness, you have many years to live."

I snatched my hand away.

"That's my business, how long I have to live." Stupid rejoinder! Dear Fate, he had me shaken, rattled.

"Susan, if I may address you as such, please let me finish."

He hesitated for a few seconds.

"Jude is waiting for you in Scotland."

The Thing now decided that it had had enough. A metallic diagonal pain suddenly glowed purple in the side of my head. I started to sweat and feel dizzy. A fuzzy, worried Quoit hovered before my eyes. He offered a tablet and a glass of water. I spewed up a sticky brown mess with cartoon bird feet, and then another. The last words I heard were, "Baroness, please don't die. Please don't die."

***

It would take more than rich food and a splitting headache to kill an old chook like me. I woke in my apartment propped up in an armchair with my feet arranged on a cushion.

Someone, Quoit no doubt, had taken off my shoes and arranged them neatly at the front door. Mr Remington sat on my desk practically begging me to get back to work.

Jude is waiting for you in Scotland, that's what you said, Quoit. Perhaps he is, perhaps not. Whichever is the case, you're obviously constructing a delicious romantic scenario for yourself: Oh yes, here's the freshly enlightened Quoit, drunk on a dose of Thomas Hardy, imagining the Great Reunion of Jude and Sue. Batty old Susan propped up in a hospital bed with a bandaged head and a frilly gown, the door opens a crack, a nurse glances inside and says to a figure in the corridor, "You can come in now." Susan's bosom heaves. A bearded man enters. He has eyes shaped like high-prowed boats, a lithe build, a small book under his arm. He approaches and offers the book to Susan.

"These are my love letters Susan, in verse, composed over these last fifty years ..."

Anyway, Sheherezade has work to do.

Where was I? Oh yes, Poor crazed Jude looking down over the falls at the three white bundles. My younger sister-wife self, last seen crashing through the bush away from the falls.

Let Sue take over the account from Jude, who at this point is beyond articulating anything coherent.

The spadebeards told us we had to remove our unseemly selves. We understood from Slab through storms of grief and rage that he would get us out of Patria Nullius altogether. Arrangements were made on the periphery of our understanding. Events flashed by: Slab helping us pack a few clothes, fat bundles of roubles passed over. A truck came. We got in. We ached and sobbed through days of travel, two rotting figs on one blighted branch. During hot days in the back of the dark truck, Slab made us eat jerky and drink water. We never spoke except for one night when Jude screamed, "I killed them," and I yelled, "I killed them," and he shouted and I shouted, and we fought and scratched and kicked, both shouting, "I killed them."

There was a port at night-time, concrete and girders, the eggy smell of dock water, moving mounds of darkness that were men and crates; Slab saying farewell. We must have thanked him as he passed us over to men with blank faces who shoved us into a place below the waterline of a ship. We must have eaten and drunk and washed during the weeks we were in that place, jostling for sleeping places among the many others down there with us. We cowered while people fought each other until the smugglers held guns to their heads and gave them injections. Jude and I were a conjoined smudge of madness and grief and terror.

Some nights they brought us on deck while they flushed the filth from the hold. Hundreds of us stretched and sucked in clean air, gazing at stars and the lights of passing ships.

On another night we were pushed up on deck to stand under the moon, in sight of a dark line of land and a sprinkle of moving lights. We remember looking at each other that night and seeing our own faces reflected back. You were me Jude, and I was you. And we remember being taken ashore in a small boat, and we remember jumping into cold water and wading hand in hand through tall marsh grasses. And then somebody barged between us and our hands parted, and one of us went one way, and one the other, and then we weren't we anymore.

I kept wading, following the sloshes and cries of people rushing for dry land. Water became mud, and mud became a slimy shore of slippery rocks and stinking rubbish, and the shore became a wood where I blundered into hard trees and suffered scratches and stings from brambles and nettles. There was a line of wavering lights ahead, and the sound of barking. I heard gunshots and cries of pain.

A dog flew out of the night, knocking me down. Uniformed arms wrenched me to my feet and clipped my wrists together. A bag was pulled over my head. Shouts, orders, shoves. The voices sounded like English, but I couldn't grasp the meanings. I yelled for Jude but nobody replied. There was a vehicle, a journey, clanging of doors, the bag removed, a concrete cell with a shiny metal toilet. Your shit flew down a hole and disappeared. Square beige food came on plastic plates. Taps hissed. Fans whirred. Feet in plastic shoes slipslopped along corridors.

A flash of memory from the refugee ship: Don't tell them where you came from.

They interrogated me, pale-faced limpets of indistinguishable gender, but weeks under the decks had faded my tropical skin and lithe muscles to English putty and I looked the same as them. After a few days I started to understand their round-lipped toothy accents, and mimicked them.

"Whar dod you come from? How moch dod the smogglers charge?" they asked me over and over.

"Smogglers? I cont remomber smogglers. I hot my hod and lost my momery and found mysolf on the shore."

"Whar you alone? Was thore onyone woth you?"

"Thore was jost one of us," I replied truthfully and untruthfully.

* * *

They put me in a refugee camp full of oddballs who all claimed to be from nowhere and spoke dozens of languages that must have been spoken somewhere. The camp was in Leicester, I learned. Outside the perimeter fence lay flat, featureless fields of plants in rows under glaring low sun. I shared a room with three women who spoke no English but wept and squabbled endlessly. After they had attended English classes for a while, they were able to tell me that they too were from nowhere. For the first few months I slept twelve hours a day as my mind and body accommodated to goop-food, running water and electric lights. In my twelve waking hours, I haunted the mess hall, the library, the workshops, the exercise yards, half-spirit, half-human, my very essence suspended between living and dying.

One morning, I chose to live rather than die. The months of anguish had scoured Jude from my heart. Quite dispassionately I asked a guard if she knew of a man called Jude - early twenties, Asian features - who'd come ashore the same night as me. She must have felt sorry for me because the uniforms wouldn't normally give you a sniff of their guda.

"How do you know hom? Os he rolated to you?"

I said he'd been kind to me on the ship. I wondered if he was safe. She checked on a screen, frowned, checked some more.

"Yos, an individual of thot description was in detontion."

"Can you tell me where?

"Thot's all I can say. It is not permitted to comment on operational motters."

My query was a test. I passed. I was free. At least until last year when my brother-husband crept back into my soul.

* * *

A month after I chose to live, a supervisor took me to an office and asked me, "What do you want to be?"

Such a question! "Hoppy and free," I replied from the corner of my mouth. The supervisor said, "When you ore released, thot os. Whot job woll you do?"

"Hostorian," I said. Goodness knows why I came up with that, but now I remember Slab once explaining to Jude what a historian was, and how he should read a book by Julius Caesar.

The supervisor person (I think a man) found 'historian' on a list and enrolled me in classes. I gobbled up the coursework and had enough credit for a degree in nine months. A set of algorithms clicked somewhere in The Universe, and I was invited to an Identity Clinic to have a PIP implanted in my forehead. This mustard seed recorded my citizenship of the Kingdom of England and Wales, along with access to an apartment and a stipend to take higher degrees. I dedicated myself to the study of history, perhaps because I wanted to obliterate my own history. You know the rest, Your Highness: A reclusive scholarly life, a stream of books both esoteric and popular, academic and civil honours.

I'm off to bed now with a strip of tablets to placate The Thing. But I have a sense that something is missing. My fingers flick towards my throat, an involuntary action that I probably perform a hundred times a day if I care to count. The coin necklace is gone, the pathetic bashed sliver of aluminium bearing Jude's portrait on one side and mine on the other, worn shiny and thin by my unconscious habit. No doubt Quoit will find a way to present it to Your Highness in order to advance his career.

INSIDE PATRIA NULLIUS

Highness,

In view of the final line of this extract, Your Highness's counsel is appreciated on a way forward to a solution that aligns Your Highness's objectives in relation to the factual integrity of The History with the material herein.

Humbly, Bruce

INSIDE PATRIA NULLIUS

The task of sealing off Patria Nullius from the outside world in 0001 ranks alongside the Iron Curtain and the Great Wall of China among the world's most ambitious security operations. Who better to perform the task than the newly privatised Australian Border Security Inc., the organisation that had made Australia's borders impregnable?

In the years following the Grand Bargain, ABS had a wider mandate than its former task of keeping illegal seaborne arrivals out. Firstly, Patria Nullius had a remnant population whose care had been guaranteed under UN Resolution 25/1. Here, ABS drew on its experience in managing Australia's former offshore detention centres with their world-class catering and health facilities. Secondly, the organisation had responsibility for protecting the coastline of Patria Nullius, including the all-important ports through which uranium exports and nuclear waste imports flowed. The third task was to secure the so-called Internal Protected Zones, which were categorised as Remnant Population Reserves, Mines and Disposal Sites, and Transport Corridors.

The Mines and Disposal sites were located mainly in the former South Australia. Port Adelaide was rehabilitated to withstand huge tidal surges, as were the ports of Newcastle in the east of the country and Fremantle in the far west. The major coastal cities were emptied of their few remaining residents, who were resettled inland in Remnant Population Reserves, mostly located in high country. Transport Corridors utilised the existing freeways network, which were modified for driverless vehicles controlled by Chinese satellite technology leased by Sino-French to SLUZHBA. The skies over Patria Nullius were protected by a joint force of manned and unmanned aircraft provided by Argentina, Israel and Iran under the command of Care Mundo's Vice President (Military Leasing), Retired General Mehmet Gulay. Since the Grand Bargain, command of the skies has been rotated every five years to Sino-French, SLUZHBA and back to Care Mundo under an Enduring Business Continuity Charter.

Information on the internal administration of Patria Nullius has always been limited to sparse annual reports filed by Australian Border Security Inc. to the Royal Australian Securities and Investments Commission.

All well and good.

But not to Australian celebrity explorer Yasser Uthman-Macfarlane, rebel scion of the royal dynasty. YUM-YUM, as he is known worldwide, captured the devotion of not just his doting great-aunt Princess Maureen, but the hearts of millions of viewers with his debut reality show *Swamp People*, set in a cannibalistic community in South Carolina. Next came *Lashings of Pleasure* where he worked undercover as a barman in a private Shanghai club for Sino-French senior executives. Then YUM-

YUM disappeared for a year, emerging sunburnt and lean after traversing Patria Nullius in the guise of a deaf-mute Aboriginal. The result was the multiple award-winning show *The Unpeople*.

Controversially, the show received a special exemption under the Public Interest clause of the Information Quality Enhancement Act. It was the first officially sanctioned film about Patria Nullius in sixty-five years.

YUM-YUM's film follows the routes trodden by itinerant traders through the Remnant Population Reserves and into the vast inland tracts where the inhabitants of outlaw settlements eke out their squalid lives, encouraged by rebel leaders to shun the protection provided by Australian Border Security Inc.

The diversity of the towns and hamlets of Patria Nullius is astounding: The Dandenong Mountains RPR in the former State of Victoria is home to a community of polyandrous woodcarvers whose goods fetch high barter prices in the outlaw markets; YUM-YUM saw exquisite hand-made Dandenong food bowls in markets in the far West of the continent. Australian Border Security Inc. delivers food and fresh water to this high-country community using specially designed drones.

Meanwhile, the folk of the Orange RPR have developed a multi-ethnic matriarchy with its own Creole tongue. Orange is located on the edge of a Transport Corridor connecting the port of Newcastle with a Disposal Site five-hundred kilometres inland. A spur road facilitates delivery of food and the necessities of life by satellite-controlled ABS driverless trucks.

YUM-YUM visited more than one hundred ABS-run communities, filming with a miniature device installed in the sweat band of his bush hat, the data secretly beamed back to his HQ in England via an abandoned Cold War satellite.

In one of the most stunning shots, YUM-YUM stands atop a mountain in the Great Dividing Range, arms outstretched against a ruby sunset. As the last flames of the celestial furnace dip below the horizon, YUM-YUM turns his head to the darkening mass of an inland forest, saying, "Tomorrow, I descend these slopes and enter the badlands of Patria Nullius. Only Fate knows if I will return".

Fate did indeed return our intrepid adventurer to the bosom of Australia's new homeland in England, but not without a scrape or two. Let YUM-YUM himself take up the story:

"I encountered the depths of human depravity among wretched settlements. Incest, bestiality, suicide pacts, devil worship, the eating of children - these were the daily routine of the sub-humans who spurned the care of ABS. There were the times I was chased by deformed Amazons wielding poisoned spears. I was captured and tortured by a tribe of foul children. Begging for scraps of food, my health broke down until I was a mewling bag of diarrhoea, covered in putrid sores."

YUM-YUM's images from the badlands tell the story of his ordeal: Swashes of dark, unfocussed movement as he flees through the forest; an eery still of the tree canopy when his hat lies lost in some stinking swamp; a spider crawling up his ankle while he hides in a clump of rank creepers.

OK. THAT'S ENOUGH. I CAN'T WRITE ANY MORE OF THIS TRIPE. EVERYBODY KNOWS YUM-YUM WAS A FRAUD. FOR THE RECORD,

HE ADMITTED TO ME THAT HE WAS ACCOMPANIED BY ABS MINDERS WHEN HE TOURED THE REMNANT POPULATION RESERVES. HE NEVER SET FOOT OUTSIDE THE RESERVES. HE TOLD ME THAT THE BADLANDS FILM WAS SHOT IN THE LAKE DISTRICT. A POX ON YOUR HIGHNESS'S BOOK.

Bruce: Tell the Attorney-General to organise with the Poms to get a warrant for her arrest for whatever.

HRH

Your Royal Highness,

I crave your regal indulgence to inform you that Baroness Professor Bridehead was discovered in her apartment yesterday deceased, apparently from an overdose of painkillers.

May I humbly suggest that this event might present an opportunity to enhance the unveiling of The History of the Principality of Australia, e.g. with the bestowment of a posthumorous medal for the aforementioned Baroness or somesuch by your revered self.

I have asked Mr Quoit to look into the matter.

Humbly,
Bruce

Stuart Campbell

SCOTLAND

QUOIT TO ALEX, NOVEMBER 0100

Dear Alex,
It's been a month since I took myself off to bed with those tablets. From what they told me at the Scottish hospital, I must have taken the whole strip of ten, and rendered myself ~~completely~~ unconscious. The day after I ~~woke up~~ came to after the operation, an official paid me a visit. She was presumably charged with negotiating cross-border matters that the Republic of Scotland and the Kingdom of England and Wales preferred to keep out of public view. I sat propped up in bed while she balanced her ~~items~~ things on her knee

The meeting began with me signing ~~a whopping pile of~~ a good many forms where I agreed to behave myself and keep my mouth shut. The last form was to consent to the removal of my PIP. With this document signed, a doctor came in, scanned my forehead with a pen-like instrument, found the right spot, pressed a button and ejected the tiny PIP into a sample jar.

The doctor left. The woman clicked the sample jar into a metal case.

"So how did I get here?"

"~~I am I'm~~ I am not authorised to reveal any details." Scottish accent. Face blank.

"What about the general picture, no details? The doctors told me I overdosed so I know at least I didn't come of my own volition. Was I pushed through the back roads on a bullock cart by lusty Caledonians in kilts? Did they fling me across on a giant catapult? The

Caledonians were an Iron Age people who spoke a language that was an ancestor of Breton."

The official relaxed a little. She looked around the room.

"Ah, you have a coffee maker. I could do with a jolly nice cup. What about you, Professor Bridehead?"

We drank while she examined some paperwork.

Yes, paperwork. Obviously the Scottish Civil Service prefers to keep its business out of view of The Universe. I watched her working: Thirtyish, keen intelligence in her eyes, smartly dressed, a pen (a pen, fair dinkum, for Fate's sake!) tracing the lines of writing. She looked up.

"Actually, I can tell you something without causing an international incident."

Perhaps my silly joke had relaxed her. My reputation in academic circles outside England and Wales is extremely fearsome. She might have been expecting a Gorgon, the father of Medusa.

"We'd been anticipating you a week later but we got an emergency request for an ambulance transfer at the border. You were almost turned back because of an anomaly with your PIP. Actually, I need to check whether the name Patti Chombo means anything to you."

I explained to her my earlier attempt to escape. She nodded and made a note.

"There was some luggage with you in the ambulance."

"Luggage?" Such as Jude's portmanteau, I wondered.

"Yes, I'll get it for you. Don't get out of bed, Professor."

She opened a cupboard and placed Mr Remington on the bed, snug and cosy in his case. I ran my fingers over the case, imagined his keys lying in readiness. Hello, dear old friend.

They discharged me from hospital soon after. Good fellow Quoit, I thought as I walked to a taxi carrying Mr Remington and a portmanteau of personal effects. Taxis are ubiquitous in Scotland, and known for their efficiency and convenience.

The taxi delivered me at a cottage in a village in some hills. A man stood in the garden. It was Jude. We went inside and made passionate love immediately.

Afterwards I asked him who killed the three children that day in Patria Nullius. He said he had a number of possible answers but the most likely was that the earth at the edge of the lookout crumbled when I was looking away. Evidently the railing hadn't been properly repaired. In former times, local by-laws would have stipulated that the railing should comply with Australian Standard AS1657.

THE END

GLOSSARY

armlength	unit of measurement for estimating length or height, about 80cm
bigfella	stud
bigfuckup	useless
bookhee	hungry
bookoid	a book-like instrument that displays a graphic version of a book while the 'reader' listens to an audio version.
CareMundo	multinational corporation, one of the Triopoly. Originated as a health insurance corporation in California.
choni	penis
choot	vagina
doublegranny	2 bedroom house
dun gettit me	I don't understand
educhunk	a module of learning material
ganja	marijuana
gonna luraka yu	You're going to vomit
guda	anus
hubby, pl. hubbyhubby	husband
huhu	breasts
jigijig	fucking
kalu	wife
kotok	curse, damned
larka	boy
longdrop	lavatory
luraka	vomit

manlength	unit of measurement for estimating distance to visible objects, about 180cm
mek(it)	make, do (something)
missis	wife
miyanim	we (i.e. not including you. c.f. miyanyu)
nobby, pl. nobbynobby	occupation, job
nowrotu	in a little while
oldtalk	English
PIP	Personal Interactive Processor: Tiny electronic implant embedded in the forehead.
pitcher	picture
Predictive Composition	A service provided by The Universe which assists a writer by suggesting sentences predicted by what the writer has already written. PC has a homogenising effect since the suggested sentences are drawn from a database that is replenished by the new texts created by PC.
semold	The rhythm of life
Sino-French	multinational corporation, one of the Triopoly. Sino-French began as a joint venture furniture factory in Guangzho.
SLUZHBA	multinational corporation, one of the Triopoly. Sluzhba ('service' in Russian) began as a charity for military veterans.

Smashlingua	artificial intelligence implant that allows a human to understand and speak different languages
spisi	fruit (probably derived from SPC a brand of Australian canned fruit)
stinko	fart
Tang-ling	magic
The Universe	World-wide interactive database of human knowledge, administered jointly by the Triopoly.
timbox	strong box
Triopoly	An arrangement whereby all commerce, intellectual property, media, and communication services are managed by a three-member private sector cartel. The regulation of these domains is outsourced by national governments to the Triopoly.
vale	angry
wofo	why
yarndi	marijuana
zazzy	stomach

NOTES ON THE TEXT

PROLOGUE
My description of the tsunami was inspired by the research of the Australian tsunami expert Ted Bryant. A popular article outlining his thoughts on tsunamis on Australia's east coast can be found at https://www.australiangeographic.com.au/topics/scie nce-environment/2010/12/tsunami-terror-from-the-sea/

SUSAN TO ALEX, JULY 0099
I sketched the Basic Features of Arg at this link: https://wp.me/p4uFaw-Bt

SUSAN TO ALEX, AUGUST 0099
The New Australia Day bash is inspired by an Australia Day party I attended at an Australian embassy.
Perhaps the Palace got the idea of the clockwise rotation during *Waltzing Matilda* from the tradition of the Western Sydney Wanderers soccer team when fans turn their back on the pitch at the 80th minute of the game.

JUDE MAKES PLANS
The truck dump was inspired by a spooky paddock of burnt-out campervans I stumbled on in the bush at Barrington Tops, New South Wales.

SALVATOREM MUNDI
On Billy Qaboos's muzzling, see discussion of Australia's *Border Force Act 2015* at http://www.austlii.edu.au/au/journals/CommsLawB/2017/18.pdf

For non-Australian readers, see Constitution Alteration (Aboriginals) No. 55 of 1967 at https://www.legislation.gov.au/Details/C1967A00055

SUSAN TO ALEX, FEBRUARY 0100

The story of the Turkish glove factory is filched from a similar story I read in the Soviet news magazine *Ogonëk* in the seventies, when I was studying Russian in London.

LANGUAGE DEVELOPMENT IN PATRIA NULLIUS

I found Derek Bickerton's Bioprogram Hypothesis compelling in the early twenty first century, and I have no doubt that it would have still been influential in Rita Kawaguchi's time. See:

https://www.cambridge.org/core/journals/behavioral -and-brain-sciences/article/abs/language-bioprogram- hypothesis/8E3812383ED990C3F0ECC874D9C73D9 7

###

If you enjoyed *The True History of Jude*, you can find
more abouts my books at my website.
Please consider leaving a review at Goodreads.
www.stuartcampbellauthor.com

You can leave a comment about *The True History of Jude*
at my website by scanning the QR code below:

Stuart Campbell

www.ingramcontent.com/pod-product-compliance
Lightning Source LLC
Chambersburg PA
CBHW020330120726
47904CB00002B/357